WE CRY TO THEE

Stephen Constance

Tim Saunders Publications

TS

Tim Saunders Publications

Cover design: Tim Saunders Publications

Baal we cry to thee,
Baal we cry to thee,
Hear and answer!
Hear and answer!

FELIX MENDELSSOHN - FROM HIS ORATORIO ELIJAH

CONTENTS

INTRODUCTION

A relatively peaceful, pastorale scenario in the village of Waterton is soon affected by the possibility that there are darker forces at work.

Set mainly in a post-war elementary school attended by pupils of all ages, the novel contains the fascinating dialects of two neighbouring counties and the unconscious humour of the forthright country children. The Horse and Jockey is a traditional hostelry where you would be served with a hunk of cheese and half a loaf of homemade bread; not an outrageously priced ploughman's lunch and the village bobby would not baulk at giving juvenile offenders a clip round the ear.

Commenced in 1973 and quickly abandoned due to the pressures of the author's main occupation, the handwritten, unfinished manuscript lay at the bottom of a rubbish filled cardboard box. It came to light in 2015 when its contents were emptied with the intention for them to be sorted and subsequently jettisoned. But after re-appraisal, the novel was soon completed and the suspense filled, horrific dénouement surely makes the decision to resurrect it worthwhile.

Stephen Constance

AUTHOR COMMENT

There are those who read this who may consider that the ending is scarcely plausible, but since evil rears its ugly head in many guises, I would say that the events that occur in the dénouement are distinctly possible. Man hides behind a perilous veneer of civilisation and still has the capacity to shock with periodic bouts of barbarity. The reason I am not a humanist is a result of the acts of mankind. Neither do I ascribe to the doctrines of religious bigotry, though I fervently hope that the human race is just a barely significant part of the plenteous universes and that there is truly an awesome and omnipotent being behind it all. Strangely, I would like to acknowledge the great composer Felix Mendelssohn; who may or may not be able to accept my thanks posthumously. His oratorio 'Elijah' has the chorus 'Baal we cry to thee' and hearing and performing in this gave me sudden inspiration.

ONE

Conspicuous in his leather zip–up jacket, Spencer looked down the long sloping green of the lush meadow and cast his eyes on the Victorian elementary school, which stood at the bottom of it.

A clock on the nearby church tower struck nine times and with no significance whatsoever, nine buxom Friesian cows bestirred themselves from a session of indulgent cud-chewing and ambled towards him. Spencer was not sure of Friesians. He had been brought up near a farm with gentle, sleepy Herefords, which could almost be patted and cosseted like pets and was well aware that Friesians were not always amiable. Giving a last wave to his father, who stood in the churchyard, he hastily turned and ran down the meadow through the clutching grass until he reached the stile at the bottom. With two jumps he was over it and into the lane, which ran before the school. He could hear the steady hum of voices from the yard and paused to contemplate the big black motor parked outside. The car displayed one broken window patched up with cardboard, was square in shape, had long running boards, two big headlights and a bulbous hand horn, which Spencer was sorely tempted to press. But before he could make any decision over this daring impertinence, two scruffy young tyros emerged from nowhere to do the job for him; leaving him to face the presence of a tall, dark, moustachioed stranger, who hurriedly appeared from a side door.

To his surprise and relief, the newcomer gave him a pleasant and re-assuring smile. The eyes were sparkling and the demeanour friendly.

"Ah, you must be the new lad." A north country accent. "Well, we'll forgive you this time. I know it's a temptation, but don't let it happen again."

Ushered inside by a careful hand on shoulder, the new boy stepped into a large, rambling hall, cluttered with ink-stained desks. Awestruck, he walked up to a solid oak bureau at the top of it, where his mentor, whom he had deduced was the headmaster, rifled in the drawers of the cumbersome piece to emerge with a battered, well-thumbed register.

"That's it; you'll be, in form three. Down the other end."

Spencer realised that there were two classes in this hall, divided by a partition in the middle. It was now open but could presumably be closed during lesson time. This enabled both classes to concentrate without hindrance from next door, but also meant that the headmaster was never very far away, and that bad behaviour was rare and seldom worthy of severe punishment. An ancient stove which, due to its antiquity, might have graced the inside of a historical museum, stood or rather leant against one side of the hall. Where there were not high, sashed windows, the walls were hidden by shelves of books; with a step ladder placed nearby allowing small persons easy, but precarious access to the upper volumes.

Without a glimmer of acknowledgement, a somewhat older and dishevelled young lady brushed past Spencer and clung to the threadbare bell rope, which disappeared into the eaves above. She pulled vigorously and the bell sounded forth; summoning a deluge of scruffy, small humanity to invade the place from all directions. A small knot of teachers gathered round the headmaster's desk and one bespectacled member sat in readiness at the piano. The headmaster held up a hand for silence and addressed his captive audience.

"This morning we welcome a new boy to our school, and I want you to treat him as one of yourselves. His name is..."

Spencer felt eyes upon him from everywhere. He underwent being jostled by near neighbours and appraised from behind. It was an almost insufferable ordeal for someone of his shy disposition and he was glad when after the announcement of the opening hymn, the piano struck up, and he was able to lose his discomfort in a lusty, but not always tuneful rendition of *Onward Christian Soldiers*. A short reading by a youngish female teacher followed and then, without further ado, the sprightly headmaster began to interpret an epic biblical tale in a manner both unusual and vastly entertaining. In the space of barely ten minutes, he jumped up on his large mahogany desk to be Daniel; growled down on all fours to impersonate the vanquished beasts of Daniel's triumph; somehow transformed himself into Shadrac, Meshac and Abendigo and stood tall and imperious as King Darius. He appeared to revel in the brouhaha of it all and his interpretation was a colourful, enthusiastic enactment that not only amused, but largely impressed the rustic country children.

Then they all sang *God be in my head* and assembly was over. The smaller ones tramped out to their classrooms, the partition was closed, and Mr Jones trooped out with his class to the hut over School Lane at the bottom of church meadow. Spencer found himself in the hands of a Mr Allen; a young, serious and blatantly keen assistant teacher. Mr Allen sat him next to a boy called Martin Lewis, a son of the soil who was inky, unaware of the smell which emanated from his person and had a wide gap in his front teeth. He waited until the teacher was otherwise occupied and challenging the nervous newcomer in the typically forthright and uncomplicated fashion that he and his ingenuous peers were want to employ, said without preamble, "Where d'y' come from, then?

Ant sin you before? Can y' play conkers?"

"Ross," replied Spencer, "an'-an' I can play conkers." He dipped his pen in the inkwell, which appeared to be the only habitable spot in a sea of desk top graffiti and looking at the neat problems on the blackboard, tried to do a sum. But the carvings and gracious ink memorials to a generation of village children captured his attention. 'Henry loves Janet,' said one. 'Wado is a heavily deleted...,' proclaimed another. He could just make out noughts and crosses and some questionable drawings; including the faded outlines of some girl which the precocious artist, probably consumed with pubescent lust, at some time or another may or may not have explored.

Martin Lewis was still talking. "D'y' like football? I'm bloody good at football. D'y' like it? It ent much good you comin' 'ere t' school if y' don't!"

"Y-yes, though I haven't played much."

A rubber sailed through the air and landed heavily on Martin Lewis's left ear.

"That's enough, Lewis. Leave the lad alone and get on with your work!"

Thinking it wise to do so, the garrulous Martin Lewis heeded the remonstrating teacher and left unmolested. Spencer managed to solve another of the simple blackboard sums. But he soon felt a searing pain in his backbone and swivelling round, confronted a shock haired, blue-eyed antagonist with a red shirt and limp tie who'd been assailing him with the sharp end of a broken ruler.

"What d'you do that for?" he whispered. The reply was menacing and unequivocal.

"We don't like Rossites comin' 'ere. I 'eard about you from my uncle. 'ee lives near you!"

A concerned turncoat, Martin Lewis intervened. "You touch 'im an' I'll 'it you, y' bloody bully!"

Mr Allen peered over the top of his low-lying glasses. "Come out here, Lewis. I warned you once. Right, now stand there until I say!"

Rough justice, but the beleaguered teacher had learned that it did not pay to waste time getting to the bottom of things. When required, most of the children could lie like troopers and didn't seem to resent it if he chose the wrong culprit. It all seemed to even out in the end and Martin Lewis was certainly not what Bob Allen's Mum used to call a 'paragon of virtue'.

Now exposed to the open grins and silent taunts of his classmates, Lewis lounged uncomfortably against the wall; his only solace being to grimace savagely at all and sundry; with an attempt at studied indifference when his erstwhile opponent - with the advantage of relative safety - sporadically stuck up two fingers in derision. All this had to be accomplished whilst Bob Allen, immersed in concentration and inclined towards tearing his hair out; was otherwise engaged in trying to decipher the hopeless mess most of the class had made of yesterday's English lesson.

Allowed some respite, Spencer finished his sums quite quickly and began to look round the classroom. He noted that a demarcation line meant that those made of 'slugs and snails and puppy dog tails' sat on one side and that the other half was occupied by those alien creatures who were supposed to be all 'sugar and spice'. Of the latter variety there were fat ones, thin ones, some wearing heavy rimmed glasses; pigtailed ones and one surreptitiously sucking a sweet behind an opened desk lid. Of the former, few wore ties, nearly all were heavily ink stained, and some had their backsides out of their short trousers. They all varied in cleanliness; not always dictated by their family circumstances and more likely to be caused by the activities they had been engaged in before arriving at school.

On Bob Allen's desk and scattered about in various jam jars, stood various posies of wildflowers, brought with no thought of currying favour for a teacher, who was both strict and well-liked. A huge green apple enhanced this ad hoc floral display and Spencer idly speculated whether the teacher would remove his false teeth before partaking of it or if he would throw caution to the wind and opt to leave them in. He was sure Mr Allen had false teeth and reasoned that no-one nearing thirty, a great age, could still have their own, let alone ones of such whiteness.

From where he was sitting, Spencer could not see out of the high windows, so he took to monitoring the big plain clock on the wall, which pronounced the time from a vantage point on the oak panelling behind Mr Allen's head. It was five minutes before playtime, a break he was dreading. All the new faces, countless questions and this boy behind spoiling for a fight. Agonisingly, the hands on the clock stuttered on. Four minutes to go and Martin Lewis was now feverishly crossing his legs and holding his frontal regions. He put up an anxious hand and after a full and lengthy minute, Mr Allen noticed and sitting back in his chair said irritably, "Yes, Lewis?"

"Please sir, I want a pee!"

Bob Allen managed to look both angry and amused.

"The correct expression, Lewis, is 'please may I leave the room?'"

"P-please may I leave the room?" replied Lewis desperately, his whole anatomy quivering in anticipation at the relief that permission to do so would bring.

"Yes, you may but..."

The bell rang.

"Ah, wait a minute. Girls first, file out slowly. Now boys, quiet there! Not you Lewis! Right, now go and do what you have to and come back here when you've finished. Ah, Spencer, can you spare a minute? Let's see how you're doing."

All understanding, Bob Allen looked at the boy's work, noting his nervousness and smiling encouragingly. He seemed well satisfied.

"Very good, you've been well taught."

He went on talking to Spencer until a vastly relieved Martin Lewis returned to the classroom. The teacher turned to the newcomer and addressed him with mock severity. "Right, Mr Lewis, I want you to take Spencer here into the yard and look after him. You are responsible, d'you understand? I want no trouble. And if you must talk to him in your inimitable way, do it in the playground and not in class! Go on then, off you go!"

Mr Allen waited for them to leave and then went through the partition door for a cup of tea and a little educational gossip. In these Spartan days following the war, the school had not yet succeeded in having a staff room installed and usually, the school secretary, who inhabited a pocket handkerchief of a cubby hole near the cloakrooms, made the tea in the kitchen and brought it into the headmaster's domain on a tray.

"How's the new lad?" enquired Mr Jeremy, the headmaster.

"Oh, quiet enough. Reasonably bright. I sent him off with one of our premier rapscallions, the redoubtable Martin Lewis; though I don't know if that was a very judicious thing to do!"

"One lump or two?" The amicable female infant teacher poured out the tea. They all stood in various poses near to the currently unlit stove with Mrs Trout, the second form teacher, an attractive woman of about thirty-two, sitting atop a convenient desk, dangling her long lisle clad appendages tantalisingly into mid-air. The headmaster was still engaged in talking to Bob Allen, whose mind was half on the cup of tea he was trying to avoid slopping and half on Mrs Trout's legs.

"Nice, isn't it," muttered the head, very observant and fully aware that a thesis on the merits and disadvantages of the British Empire didn't appear to be appealing to Bob Allen at the moment.

"Uh-yes, I mean, what's that you're saying?"

"Nothing of sufficient interest it would seem and take a tip from me boy; eye the menu, but don't sample the goods!"

Alarmed that the head's bold advice should be overheard, Bob Allen did 'eye the menu' and was re-assured to find that the lady in question was now in deep conversation with Miss Barnes, the infant teacher. He excused himself and 'girding his loins' made ready to join the turmoil, which would undoubtedly be breaking out in the playground.

"My turn today," he said, "better go and have

a look what's brewing. It's a wonder it's not raining and, in any case, it's not much use leaving it to you-know-who. If I know anything about it, she's probably having a drag in the dubs!" He walked hastily across the hall, down the passageway and out into the boys' playground.

The noise hit him hard, and he was ruefully conscious that, added to his usual three cups of pre-breakfast coffee, the tea had done little to eradicate the lethargy caused by last night's feckless imbibing in the local public house.

From one end of the barely adequate yard to the other, a frenetic, foul and fierce game of soccer was in progress. The object was to propel the much-maligned tennis ball against the jagged wooden fence at one end or to hammer it through the open wooden gates at the other. The second option meant risking life and limb if you happened to be the goalie, for to retrieve the ball you had to venture into the lane and although a vehicle of any sort seldom passed, it was still a hazardous business.

At the beginning of break Arnold's team were playing Woody's and those not skilful or pushy enough to be picked at the start for one of these twenty-seven a-side battalions, took the part of whichever side was winning. Or alternatively, if they had powerful enemies in the losing team; changed allegiance and allied themselves to these onetime dastardly foes by indulging in unrestrained obsequiousness. The game could hardly be recognised as the same *beautiful* one that such contemporary mortals like Stanley Matthews or Tom Finney played. When you had the ball, which by now bore no resemblance to its Wimbledon counterparts, you eschewed such diversionary tactics as passing it to another member of your side and providing you survived a series of horrendous tackles; were in a position to take a pot shot at which ever 'goal' happened to be closest. This achieved, you usually knocked over or thumped several opponents and concluded by hammering the ball past a stationary and terrified goalkeeper. However, if you were not so fortunate as to possess the subtle guile and flailing arms of a Woody or an Arnold, you could have your aspirations cruelly terminated without ceremony and would almost certainly be left for dead on the battlefield.

Just as the reluctant Mr Allen entered this seething arena, there was a slight cessation, and the bewildered teacher was surrounded by a forest of raised hands. Strident accompanying voices chanted, "Please sir! Please sir!"; and this imploring supplication usually meant that something quite serious had occurred.

A tall, gangling thick-lipped youngster, the mighty Arnold spoke up. "Please sir, I didn't mean it. 'ee just got 'is thing in the way!"

Nearby and close to tears, a small, pimply youth called Reggie bent double over the play bars, whilst a group of giggling girls gathered close to the dividing line of the two playgrounds, hoping to witness something sexually interesting. Concerned, Mr Allen walked over to Reggie, who belying his obvious discomfort, suddenly stood erect and with great fortitude, informed the teacher that Arnold had blatantly accosted a particularly delicate part of his anatomy or, as he rustically put it, "kicked me in the balls, sir!"

Mr Allen ushered the two antagonists inside and fetched Mrs Gubbins, a decidedly portly assistant, in order that she might take charge whilst he sorted out the trouble. Inciting howls of protest, the corpulent lady promptly confiscated the abused tennis ball; sat down under the boys' shed and took out her knitting. Such being the size of her abdominal regions, it was difficult to determine if the lady was knitting for an addition to her own brood, or whether this latest industry on her part was for some other cause or even for a friend who was to 'farrow down' shortly. The little girls, who were well aware that the human species did not emerge from beneath gooseberry bushes, were always speculating about the subject. Most thought that the much derided lady was just 'plain fat', but you could never be sure, especially as tiny Ellen Smith who lived in the semi-detached next door had often heard Mr and Mrs Gubbins-as she put it " 'avin a go" through the bedroom wall.

The unaware subject of this discussion ploughed on with her pearl and plain. She took little notice of the girls or the revived game of soccer, played with a rubber ball extorted from a very small boy, which in the absence of Arnold culminated in a victory for Woody's team by fifty-seven goals to thirty-one. At one point - and left to his own devices through Martin Lewis's desire to join the fray - Spencer had hesitated and with some reservations, followed his new friend's example. Not lacking in enthusiasm, Lewis quickly immersed himself in the frenetic combat and emitting a raucous "pass it to me Derry or Willie or Graeme" whenever the ball got within twenty feet, caused no-one to doubt that he intended to participate with gusto. Sadly, Lewis was not a great success and though daunted by his newness, Spencer thought he could do better and when play came near him, was not slow to take his chance. Acquiring the ball with a deft tackle on the halfway line, he dodged one lunging opponent after another and after a long and 'dazzling' run, lobbed the ball neatly over the fence.

"I'll fetch it," yelled Woody, duly impressed, and disappeared through a convenient hole into the orchard which the fence was supposed to protect. He emerged a little later with the ball and a smirk on his face. Just then, Mrs Gubbins blew a whistle signalling the end of playtime and they all formed lines, before marching back into school.

Woody and his friend Dudley were in the top class together and there was a time when Mr Jeremy was called to the phone, enabling the two of them to have a furtive conflab about what caused Woody to exit the orchard with a smile on his face. But several other boys pricked up their ears amidst the inevitable cacophony when a teacher leaves a class unattended and basking in the kudos it gave him, Woody told all.

"It wuz one of them things, you know." And embarrassed by this revelation, Woody's face reddened to the hue of mulberries.

"One of them?" queried Dudley, not knowing, but pretending and conveying the shattering information to his nearest neighbour. Eventually it reached the girls who, one by one and with no idea why, could not prevent themselves from becoming the same shade as Woody.

Mr Jeremy re-entered, and the noise subsided. The bell sounded for dinner and with mounting excitement, those who were not on first sitting crawled through the hole in the fence to view the now notorious object. But there was nothing to be seen except Theresa, the orchard owner's goat, dolefully chewing away in the corner by the water tank and thwarted; the juvenile invaders departed the scene nursing a distinct air of disappointment.

As the instigator of this tall story, Woody

was called a liar by his best friend and a fight started, around which a full circle gathered, all shouting for his or her favourite. Woody and Dudley were the best of friends normally, but like all young lads, could switch their loyalties violently when offended. As they stood poised, waiting warily for the other to make the first move, both boys displayed unadulterated belligerence towards one another. It was the sort of animosity, which might in later life blossom into a willingness to wield a bayonet or cause smoke to curl from a barrel after the deadly bullet preceding it had lodged itself into the brain or breast of some similarly hell-bent antagonist. Only the adult version would often have no means of fathoming which person this action eliminated and this, of course, was acceptable; because in war 'Thou shalt not kill' became 'Thou shalt do no murder': a distortion of the biblical commandment propagated by the church to try and justify the excesses of the British Empire.

Woody stabbed at Dudley and the children howled. A fight was something to relish and as it progressed, the crowd round the two adversaries increased. Dudley countered, catching his erstwhile friend a hard blow in the face and a rivulet of blood poured from Woody's damaged mouth. He looked as white as the 'toilet walls' and retaliated in a flurry of fists and unbridled fury.

His timing just right, Dudley stepped back from this barrage, brought back his left elbow and landed a deadly uppercut on his opponent's chin. Woody staggered and as he fell, hit his head and lay still. Dudley burst into tears and Julie, a girl with some sense and a liking for Woody, went to fetch 'sir.'

The head and Mr Allen rushed out and carried Woody into the secretary's small room where the medical box was kept and a large bump on his head was attended to by a very concerned Mrs Trout. Showing the resilience of youth, he soon revived and though assuring those present that he was all right, it was decided to ring the local doctor whose surgery was in the village, and who agreed to come and see Woody when he'd finished his rounds. A visibly palpitating Dudley was told to go and sit in class and wait for Mr Jones, who would come to deal with him and Mr Jeremy re-emerged into the playground. He blew his whistle and in an unusual spate of ire; made them all get into lines; proceeded to give them a lecture on the evils of fighting and told them what would happen to anyone else who dared to engage in this dangerous pastime.

Shaken by this savage encounter, Spencer and Lewis retired to a quiet spot in the playground. They resolved to embark upon a gentle game of marbles until it came time for them to have dinner. Lewis explained the mysteries of 'bombers' to Spencer and this initiation into the ancient art was furthered during the afternoon break when a boy called John Taylor joined them. He boasted a selection of some forty marbles, which he somehow managed to carry around in his none too capacious and long-suffering trouser pockets.

Spencer immediately took a liking to John Taylor and after school had ended without further mishaps occurring, they walked with Lewis up the meadow to the parish church. Lewis lived way up towards the woods and arriving at the bottom of the churchyard pitch, bid his friends farewell and made his solitary way home. Walking down the lane, the two remaining boys soon came to Taylor's neat little terraced house and stood outside, avidly talking to one another. With great enthusiasm, Taylor talked of birds and flowers and things in which Spencer thought boys weren't supposed to be interested. He thought boys were meant to be tough, but he found his new friend very sensitive and was pleased to have found another offbeat character like himself, already a strong devotee of classical music and jazz.

"An' there 'ee was," Taylor was saying, "sittin' there, large as life. I've never sin one before or since."

Just this minute, Spencer wasn't interested in the peculiar habits of certain rare nocturnal owls and stolidly interrupting, he asked Taylor a question far removed from any matter of avian concern.

"What d'you reckon Woody saw in the orchard then, Taylor?"

John Taylor grinned, flushed and looking behind to ensure that no-one was eavesdropping, said, "Oh, well, one of them, you know. Only I chucked it in the dustbin when I went to the dubs just before dinner. I sneaked into the orchard when you'd all gone in and when the others came out. They didn't see me cos I was quick!"

Spencer did not quite believe this, but caught the bus back to Ross-on-Wye in a contented frame of mind, glad to have left the posh private preparatory school his parents couldn't afford and resolved to do his best at Waterton Elementary.

TWO

The Ward sisters kept that universal bastion of local gossip, high prices and postal services, the Village Stores.

This particular June morning, Miss Emily Ward, junior partner in the business, clad in long skirt and wearing her bun neatly tied with black ribbon; swept the front steps as assiduously as she had done every morning for the past twenty years. It did not matter a jot that the broom she was plying had only the remnants of a few bristles left beneath its paintless head. This was the implement she had been using all those bygone years and would continue to wield until it gave out; on snow in winter; mud in spring; hay from agricultural clients' size twelve boots in summer and fallen tints from the overhanging beech trees in autumn. A sprightly figure of fifty-seven, Emily Ward had been the belle of the parish in the days prior to the Great War until Kitchener-like some precursor of Orwell's 'Big Brother'- had taken her Johnny Wilson for the Kaiser to make into cannon fodder. The futile escapade of the Somme had also claimed half a dozen other eligible young men from the village and despite a spell away in the glamorous arena of that Queen of the Cotswolds, Cheltenham; Emily had returned to assist her elder sister with the running of 'commerce' and to secretly mourn her lost hero.

The mellifluous bell in the church clock struck the half hour and round the corner in a battered Armstrong Siddeley came Bob Allen; hat askew, grinning and screeching to a halt outside the shop.

"Morning, Emily."

He bounced jauntily out of the vehicle and deliberately greeted her with her Christian name; fully aware and cheekily disregarding the fact that she disliked this familiar form of address.

"Good morning, Mr. Allen." Emily flushed, picked up her broom and preceded him through the shop door. She washed her hands carefully in an enamel sink and proceeded to dry them slowly on a spotless towel, knowing full well that he was impatient to be served.

"Twenty 'Woods' please, Emily."

"Certainly, Mr Allen and how's that cough of yours?"

As if maliciously prompted, Bob Allen began to cough violently and adding fuel to the fire, opened his recently purchased packet, extracted an unfiltered cigarette and lit up.

"That won't improve matters you know."

The schoolteacher smiled. "Neither will a number of things, I suppose, Emily. I'm afraid a fag and a pint or two keeps me just about sane. It's not an easy task having to deal with all those little so-and-sos over in 'bedlam' every day."

He quickly changed the subject.

"By the way, how are you getting on with Mr Steinbeck?"

Emily raised her eyebrows. Bob Allen had lent her *Grapes of Wrath* a week ago and whilst she had little time for the schoolteacher's undesirable habits, she had a healthy respect for his considerable intellect.

"I have to say that it's unlike anything I've read before but, none the less, I am enjoying it, thank you."

The schoolteacher and the shopkeeper were about to embark upon a discussion concerning the merits and flaws of John Steinbeck, when into the shop bounded Woody and Dudley; now the best of friends again and hell bent on a couple of gobstoppers before school started. They were taken aback at seeing 'sir', but to save them an agonising decision; the schoolmaster promptly said goodbye to Miss Ward, gave the boys a curt nod and left the shop. He jumped down the steps, slumped into the car, fired the engine and with a limp wave of farewell, roared off round the bend towards Gloucester.

Left to their own devices, Woody and Dudley spent some time in deliberation. It was difficult to know how to spend sixpence and get value for money. But after about five minutes thwarting the impatience of two other customers, they left the premises with four large gobstoppers and two sherbet suckers. Walking up the lane towards the church and pushing their bicycles, they caught up with Spencer and John Taylor who, being smaller and therefore lower in the school hierarchy obediently fell behind as they ambled through the churchyard. As an advanced reader, Spencer had recently enjoyed *The Three Musketeers* and happily envisaged himself as the swashbuckling D'Artagnan. He was not sure which of his friends should be assigned the roles of Athos and Aramis, but mischievously had no doubts that the slightly tubby Martin Lewis would make a good Porthos. He did not dare reveal this fantasy to his rustic companions, but resolved that if ever a film were to be made of Dumas's masterpiece, he would try and persuade them to come with him to see it. They would then be able to make wooden swords and attack the Cardinal - probably the unaware Dudley - and his men in the playground. It would make a great change from playing football and as they ran and cycled down the meadow through the long grass, he even took to wondering which of the girls could play Lady de Winter. Not that it was important, but he supposed he'd have to include one as the evil aristocratic lady, 'cos she was in the story' and you had to get things right.

Upon reaching the stile at the bottom, they all paused. It was not time to go in and it wouldn't do to appear too keen. Mr Jeremy would always find them something to do and being naturally inclined towards youthful indolence, they decided to stay put until they were summoned by the school bell.

Dudley, the master pugilist and Cardinal designate, had arrived before them and having taken his bike to the ramshackle bike shed by the boys' toilets, sat astride the stile. He leant forward, imposing himself in the slightly aggressive way boys are wont to adopt when trying to gain the ascendancy. He had a habit of doing this when he considered that what he had to say was of earth-shattering importance. It appeared that a unique revelation was about to be made and before launching forth, he paused to take a deep breath. Disappointingly, his first words were something of a letdown.

"I 'eard my mam talkin' t' Ma Gubbins last night. They didn't know I was listenin'."

"So what," interjected the injudicious Woody. "Old Ma Gubbins is always chopsin' and my dad says if 'er aint chopsin' 'er be..."

"Shut up, rat face," riposted Dudley, "'an' try listenin' t' what I've got to say for once!" Having established control, he continued without further interruption. "You know we've sin Mr Allen slope off with Miss Fishy in the dinner 'our. Well, old mother Gubbins was tellin' my mam that she saw 'em in Gloucester together last Saturday. Swears she did. They wuz sittin' in a milk bar she went into an' they didn't notice 'er, cos 'er wuz sat in a dark corner."

"Could a' bin somebody else," rejoined the

indomitable Woody, not having learned his lesson and not in any way possessed of a timid disposition.

"And pigs might bloody fly!" countered big-eyed Dudley, thinking this a very profound answer.

"Anyway," said the dogged Woody. "I bet y' won't go up, y' clever bugger an' ask Miss Fishy what's she doin' this dinner 'our. Go on, I dares y'!" He poked his tongue out and only the sound of the school bell prevented another unarmed combat, which would have likely caused a further 'slaughtering of the innocent'...

An attractive figure on an attractive morning, Margaret Trout came to the end of her brief walk from the bus stop at the bottom of the lane and entered the school building. How she had ever managed to catch the bus at all was an unsolved mystery. She had long since abandoned a normal relationship with her hapless husband; but still felt it her duty to take care of him. He had returned from Burma with a strange glint in his eyes; hungry for her, but incapable; the violated victim of some particularly foul Japanese tampering. She had tried to be reconciled to the situation, telling herself that here was a man who had sacrificed his masculinity in the cause of his country; a poor creature deserving of all the comforts she could find for him. But it was useless. Always hot blooded, she had found it difficult to impose a rule of chastity whilst he was away and found it even harder to preserve loyalty when he returned with nothing to offer. There were no children, but he could be worse than a child. At times he would weep, as if recalling some abhorrent memory dotted with the ghosts of little yellow men in grey uniforms; and on other occasions he would run her silly in the night for glasses of water or a writing pad in which he wrote scarcely lucid accounts of his horrendous wartime experiences. And sometimes he would wake up in a cold sweat; unrecognising and in a high, menacing falsetto, call her 'a filthy yellow bastard' whilst flaying the pillow in an uncontrollable tantrum. It was becoming more than she could stand. She would have to leave him or have him committed to the county asylum in Hereford; neither option serving to leaven the guilt she would feel at the prospect, and she endlessly agonised in an attempt to find an acceptable alternative.

Mingling with the children, scurrying along the corridor to get to their classes for registration, she encountered Bob Allen and gave him a tremulous smile.

"Hello Margaret," he said simply and went on to his classroom in the divided hall.

THREE

Bob Allen eyed himself in a disarmingly truthful mirror. Although he still cavorted round the football pitch most weekends in the winter, there was no denying that his candle burning at both ends this summer was having an effect. Slight lines were already marring his forehead, the eyes had faint purple blotches going off at a tangent and contained traces of red which after a particularly heavy night out reflected alarmingly back at him on this otherwise glorious July day. Was it possible, murmur it quietly, that he was becoming dissipated? Him, the formerly immaculate Bob Allen, once slim, handsome and much sought after? Now, slavishly devoted to eight pints a night and forty woodbines a day? He had to admit, it was more than possible. In fact, it was highly probable, and it was high time he did something to address the problem for Margaret's sake; though how long the hole in the corner situation could go on between them, he was at a loss to fathom. Poor woman, with a husband mentally deranged and a lover who was too fond of the pop, she was most decidedly stuck between a rock and a hard place!

He sat on his bed looking aimlessly out of the window at Clement's Grove, a quiet side street in the backwater of Ross-on-Wye; a small market town with the famous shimmering river running through it. And here he was, at the age of twenty-seven, a single teacher, sweating his precious life out, trying to hammer some semblance of knowledge into dense and mostly disinterested junior yokels. Not that some of them weren't bright. They were, but for every bright one, you seemed to acquire about fifteen 'thickos'. It was probably a lot to do with the in-breeding hereabouts. Everybody was nearly everybody else's cousin varyingly removed and the process of re-production tended to stop just short of incest. Waterton was a hangover of a pre-war elementary school and Bob Allen had an arduous task in trying to teach practically everything to a wide age range of nine- to twelve-year-olds. Each year and with a lot of hard coaching, a couple of his charges reached the exalted heights of Ross Grammar School, but as it was not planned to open a secondary modern school in the town for some four years, nearly all his pupils stayed on to receive what attention they could from having arbitrarily to remain at the village elementary.

The teacher was abruptly aroused from his cogitations by a thunderous knock at the front door. Both stout and deaf when it suited her, but on this occasion consumed with feminine curiosity, his landlady hastened to open up and effusively greeted the unexpected visitor, who turned out to be the local parish priest. Bob Allen recognised the exaggerated tones of Reverend

Michael Cannington, Rector and Rural Dean of Ross and Archenfield; a particularly unctuous and smarmy version of the species. Church on Sunday, afternoon tea from Monday to Friday, croquet on Saturday when it wasn't wet and a predilection for sherry at any time.

"Please to come in, Reverend, an' what can I be doin' for you?" Suitably subservient, Mrs Adderley ushered the clergyman in, at the same time inviting him to hang his hat and coat on the mounted deer head which did duty as a clothes receptacle in the hall.

"Actually, it was young Mr Allen I wanted to see, if you don't mind. Is he in?"

Upstairs and made suddenly wary, the sought-after schoolteacher groaned inwardly. He could hear Mrs A, servile and anxious to please; now shepherding the priest into the hallowed front room.

"Mr Allen!"

Not for the first time, the schoolteacher thought Mrs Adderley would have made a good sergeant major.

"Just a minute, Mrs A!" Grabbing his trousers and a gravy stained tie, yet rejoicing in his scruffy condition-which he knew his undesired visitor would eye with distaste - he forced himself to saunter slowly down the stairs into the front room.

"Good morning, Bob," said Reverand Cannington with what Bob considered excessive ebullience for a Saturday morning after the Friday night before. The Rector liked people to think him 'quite a lad' and the sort of cleric who goes down well in the pub, though his appearances in alehouses were rare and perhaps restricted to the festive season. He was usually accompanied at that time by a collecting box, with which money for church funds could be extorted from generous, but usually well inebriated customers.

Bob Allen tried hard to generate a measure of amicability towards the man, which he did not feel.

"Mornin', Mr Cannington, what can I do for you?"

"Nothing too arduous, I hope. I'm just wondering if you would be able to do a little job for me on Friday nights."

If he had been suspicious of the bland clergyman's motives in coming to seek him out before, these doubts were now confirmed. A proposal concerning the formation of some kind of holy youth club came from the cleric, but in replying, Bob Allen placed very definite cards on the table.

"You know my views on your church, Mr Cannington. Nevertheless, if I can assist you in any way without implicating myself in the religious side of things, I might be prepared to do so."

"Well now, that's fine." The pseudo

avuncular clergyman clasped his hands together and beamed; unmoving eyes negating the warmth of his smile. There was a slight pause whilst he collected his thoughts and Bob Allen waited patiently, though longing to escape to the kitchen where a couple of tablets would probably assuage his thumping headache. Eventually the rector launched forth.

"The point is, I am trying to start a sort of youth group on Friday evenings and in considering the type of person who would be suitable to assist me in this project, I came to the conclusion that you might be the very man."

Patronising bastard thought the suffering schoolteacher. A ruse to get me embroiled in the church. Funny, it was how one of the most rampant socialists in history had so many true-blue followers. He recalled how one morning when he'd been taking assembly, he tried to tell the children about the Christian Knights of Malta and their pleasant habit of firing live prisoners from the mouths of canon across the blue waters of the balmy Mediterranean. Had the youngsters been of sixth form material he would have probably chosen Cardinal Mazarin's mistresses or the lively eighteenth century sessions played in Bath Pump Rooms for livings, but the head had returned from a dental appointment and the subject had hastily to be jettisoned.

"I'm sorry, I don't think so, Mr Cannington," he said. "I am, of course, very interested in the welfare of young people. In case it has escaped your notice; I spend five days a week concerned with it and other educational things. Maybe you should find someone of your own faith to help. In any case, there is a council run youth club in the town, which I am told is perfectly satisfactory."

Like some beheaded fish on Mr Wilkes's the fishmonger's cold white slab, the clergyman's face went ashen and provoked a feeling of animosity, which he was not supposed to display towards a fellow human being. But he hated a rebuff. Even if people were not members of his flock, he could usually persuade them to do things for the church by imposing feelings of guilt, or simply by calculated charm. Intellectuals sometimes baffled him; particularly if the intellectual in question was not on his side. Steeped in the imposition of a thorough theological grounding, he had almost lost sight of his original Christian verve. All the unacceptable corners had been knocked off at college. He knew how to preach a brilliant sermon, how to raise money for this and that and how not to offend the rich, bonnet bedecked wives of the wealthy who mostly made up his congregation. All of which often added up to a creeping amnesia where the original message and sacrifice of Jesus Christ was concerned. Seeing that Bob Allen was not to be swayed, he turned to go. Gone was the Christian name familiarity and his voice became icily formal.

"I can see that there is nothing to be gained by discussing this further, Mr Allen. A pity. I had hoped you would have taken a different attitude, but there it is, I'm afraid." He wasted no more time, strode briskly into the hall, retrieved his coat and briefly stood nervously fingering his wide-brimmed hat. "Well, I'll bid you good day and I'll doubtless see you again sometime."

Bob Allen saw him off the premises, closed the door and turned to go back upstairs.

"Is the rector gone?" shouted Mrs Adderley from the kitchen.

"Yes, and he sent you his love, Mrs A!"

The startled landlady came out into the hall. "Go on with you, Mr Allen," she cooed, "and would you be wanting lunch yet?"

The thought of food revolted Bob Allen. Liquid refreshment called and he hesitated before replying. "Uh - I think I'll give it a miss if you don't mind, Mrs A. Got to go out just now."

"Please yourself, Mr Allen. In a huff, Mrs Adderley walked back into the kitchen. It was almost a cardinal sin to miss a meal in this household, but just now he could not stomach it. He went back upstairs to finish a belated visit to the lavatory; dressed and prepared to essay forth in order to partake of 'the hair of the dog' that had grievously gnawed his insides the previous evening. Another Woodbine disintegrated into flames and Bob Allen began to think of Margaret. It was a bloody pity. A pity for them both. That poor sod of hers; promised a 'home fit for heroes', the wrecked occupier of a crumby two-bedroomed council house. Not able to earn a bob or two or satisfy a wife. He, Bob Allen, schoolteacher and drunkard, was lucky. Bloody lucky. Teaching, even teaching thickos, occasionally gave him some sense of fulfilment and drink partially immersed his nocturnal solitude. And then there was Margaret: even if it was only for the odd hour in the back of his battered old convertible. Wouldn't the educational overlords in Hereford frown if they knew! He sensed that Mr Jeremy knew. It had first happened in early June and thence kept on happening. She had got hold of him like nothing else, not even Woodbines or his onetime love affair with Irish whiskey. Okay, there was nothing like a soft, preferably feather-filled mattress, but the back seat of a car or a ripening summer hayfield had a lot to recommend it.

He glanced at his wristwatch. Twelve noon. Time to replenish old stock. Putting on his faded sports coat, he once more dismounted the creaking stairs and bracing himself for whatever portended, emerged into the nascent afternoon.

FOUR

School re-assembled the second week in September. To lessen the blow after a mostly balmy vacation, a number of pupils called upon the gracious Ward sisters for the purpose of gratifying their vulnerable and often decaying teeth. Amongst them was Spencer, now aged nine- and-a-half and no longer a newcomer. He had hopped off the bus from Ross and in a spirit - for a small boy - of surprising generosity, procured two gobstoppers; one for himself and one to give to John Taylor en route. He knocked vigorously at the cottage door, but no reply was forthcoming and as he knew that Taylor's mum left early to work for the local doctor's wife, he assumed that Taylor had already departed for school. He set off up the lane, but the only person he met by the church was the indomitable Martin Lewis.

"'ave you sin Taylor?" During his short time at the school, Spencer's accent had quickly conformed.

Martin Lewis seemed surprised. "'ant you 'eard?"

"'eard what?"

"'ee's ill. 'is mam told mine. 'ee went into 'ostipal yesterday.

Spencer tried to look shocked. "Was it tonsils or somethink? I 'ad mine out last year."

It took a while for the limited grey matter within Lewis to respond. "No, from what 'is mam told mine, it wuz more serious 'n that."

The concerned Spencer persisted. "Well, what was it then?"

"I dunno, but 'is mam said somethink about 'im bein' para-para, oh - I dunno, 'is leg had gone all stiff and that. What did 'er call it? Would it be 'polo' or somethink?"

Spencer didn't really know what 'polo' meant; he thought it was something to do with horses and hoped that whatever Taylor was suffering from could easily be treated and that he'd soon be recovered and back at school. Lewis concurred and sobered by the distressing news; the two boys walked briskly on in comparative silence.

After the first hymn in assembly, the headmaster briefly and quietly informed them of John Taylor's illness. He looked grave and anxious, said that the boy was very ill and included a special prayer, which brought home to them the seriousness of it all. Spencer, who was probably more anxious than most, could even hear Lewis, who normally mumbled incoherently, adding a plaintive 'Amen' on the end of this particularly moving supplication. Casting his eyes around, he could observe those soft girls with handkerchiefs clasped tight and was struck by the serious aspect of the usually ribald Woody, a diminished figure with a look of something akin to fear on his pinched features.

Assembly dismissed and after maths - a recitation of tables, which the whole class attempted to achieve in unison - Bob Allen announced that for English they were all to write a letter to John Taylor in hospital, so that when he recovered he could read them all and this would hopefully help his convalescence. The entire school, including the infants, were to write and he suggested they kept the letters cheerful; included news of what they did in the holidays and above all, wrote clearly with correct spelling.

And all that could be heard throughout this small country school on a blustery autumn morning was the faint scratching of nibs on paper, an occasional cough and the progress of teachers' feet as they paraded up and down the rows of desks; correcting and encouraging willing hands.

In the infants' room the concentration was perhaps more noticeable than anywhere else. Miss Barnes had to write notes for the very small ones and even put a name at the bottom for those who had just started that day, who were confused and yet sensed something of importance was happening and did not want to be left out. Little Jennifer Smart, aged five-and-a half, painted Taylor a picture of Mr Jeremy, which she thought he'd like and Douglas Wood, normally a vile younger sibling of Woody actually managed to write his signature that very morning, after a term of trying.

During break, children stood around aimlessly. They didn't appear to have the heart to indulge in normal activities like football or 'fag cards'; a strange game where cards were collected from parents' cigarette packets and somehow won and lost by throwing them against the brick wall, which divided the playgrounds. The girls were playing a desultory game of tag and even the sight of Dawn Martin's blue knickers failed to arouse Woody's baser instincts as she stumbled and fell over near the cloakrooms.

Mrs Trout helped the slightly distressed girl to her feet and having established that the child remained in one piece, resumed her conversation with Mr Jones.

"It's touch and go," Mr Jones was saying. "Only fifty-fifty, so they say."

Mrs Trout sighed. "A bright boy, that one. Unusual interests, the head was saying. Apparently, he called the other day. Taylor has a huge collection of butterflies and moths; all mounted in glass cases. And having talked to the lad quite often, I reckon he knows more about flora and fauna than all of us! He's a proper creature of the earth. We saw him walking alone..."

Here she clammed up, realising that on this occasion she'd been with Bob and the boy had walked by without observing them.

Fortunately, Mr Jones's attention had wandered elsewhere. He was absent-mindedly looking at a group of boys who were engrossed in some sort of juvenile banter in the corner of the playground.

Arnold was holding forth to the others. "'ee'll be alright. 'ee aint as soft as 'ee looks."

"I aint too sure," said a dubious Martin Lewis, "not by the way 'is mam was chopsin' to mine."

Dudley looked worried. "D'you think 'e'll die? And d'y' think 'ee'll go t'eavan? D'y' think all that crap they tells us about in RI is true?"

Arnold gave scant credence to this pessimistic outlook. "Don't be so bloody daft, Dud. 'ee aint gonna die! It's the conker season soon an' 'ee's good at conkers. 'ee had a thirty-three-er last year. Mind I think 'ee pickled it!" He said this with a conviction he possibly did not feel and then the ice cream van came. Those lucky enough to have pocket money avidly queued to buy and those without contented themselves by putting a small amount of sand into the petrol tank of the vehicle when its owner, a Mrs Baglioni, wasn't looking. As a result of this perfidy, the headmaster had to be fetched and the irate owner of the non-starting ice-cream van pacified. Not at all sure that his charges were guilty, Mr Jeremy nevertheless phoned a garage and resolved to deal with the matter later.

Flustered and with the thought of lost

coppers through delay her principal concern, the beleaguered lady ice-cream vendor terrorised a lone and impassive mechanic until he pronounced with that gleefully and irrevocably doom-laden voice with which all motor repairers are endowed; declaring, "er'd 'ave to go into the garige" and with the head's co-operation, promptly rang for a breakdown truck.

This resolved, the staff had to entertain Mrs Baglioni to school dinner; a prime old Italian dish of watery cabbage, potatoes the Potato Board didn't want, lumpy swede and a sweet of suet pudding and lumpy custard. Contrary to what might have been expected from the good lady when confronted with this culinary delight, it only served to make her reminisce about halcyon times in Italy. She rhapsodised about the art of making authentic spaghetti and gladly reminisced about her long-lost days of selling ice cream to bambinos and bystanders in the noble city of Sorrento. All this was accompanied by much Latin gesticulating and made a welcome relief from the topic of the hour.

Bemused and with underwhelming enthusiasm, Bob Allen sat trying to digest the contents of his plate. He was fascinated, not by the imposing lady's oratory, but rather by the fact that her crowning glory seemed to be held together by a multi-coloured selection of simple elastic bands. This odd way of constricting her hair was also further enhanced by a large wart, which being situated in the vicinity of her nasal regions, must surely have impaired her sense of smell. Moving downwards, the eyes encountered faded and battered imitation beads, a soiled amply filled twin set and a long check skirt in what could be termed mixed shades of green. This weird assemblage concluded in questionably grandiose style with a pair of grey - possibly formerly white - ankle socks and two odd plimsoles needing instant resuscitation. Bob Allen wondered what special surprises would await Mr Baglioni when that obviously purblind gentleman took to excavating beneath this eclectic and highly original mode of dress; but decided it was too ghastly to contemplate and concentrated on trying to consume the overcooked swede without being sick.

During the afternoon and never slow to miss an opportunity, Mr Jeremy persuaded his dinner guest to convey memories of her childhood in Italy to the assembled school; complete with maps and another talent for singing favourite Sardinian airs in a rich, sonorous, unrestrained baritone. Unfortunately, this latter accomplishment only excited gales of laughter and with break not far away, the head had to intercede and interpret various rustic questions, which he invited the boisterous audience to submit in their heavy local dialect to the largely uncomprehending lady. And all this served to lessen the apprehension over John Taylor.

In this small country school, despite differences and petty squabbles, a definite esprit de corps existed and though it was perfectly acceptable to fight and experiment with the girls, it remained a caring and close-knit little microcosm of a world. Faced with anything unusual, such as this potentially devastating illness, the children presented a united front and even those girls who previously professed to not liking the sensitive, non-macho John Taylor and would not have gone within a yard of him, suddenly melted and with uninhibited endearments, scrawled large kisses at the bottom of their letters.

Not long after break the abused ice cream van returned and pacified with promises of re-imbursement, the vociferous Mrs Baglioni bid everyone a theatrical farewell and promised that if she ever returned it would be with a bolted, double-padlocked and wholly irremovable petrol cap. In the meantime, she hoped that Mr Jeremy would apprehend the culprits; flog them, hang draw and quarter them and otherwise chastise them until they pleaded for mercy. This the amused head agreed to do, but later - with tongue-in-cheek - reneged. He later commented to Bob Allen that it was not something he intended to carry out because it did not include de-capitation or hanging and was not likely to gain parental approval, or ultimately enhance his prospects for advancement even with the liberally inclined local education authority!

At half past three school ended for the day and at four Mr Jeremy departed with a large cardboard box full of envelopes, all addressed in a variety of hands; some of them so unrecognisable that he'd had to spend half-an-hour repeating them underneath in block capitals. Lumbering down the lane, the pre-war Model T Ford turned left on to the main road, meandered round the dangerous bends in the village proper and pulled up at the shop, where Mr Jeremy purchased a packet of Players. You could not visit the emporium of the gracious Ward sisters without exchanging some gossip and a few pleasantries and this being accomplished, he drove a little way up Church Lane with the intention of visiting Mrs Taylor. She had just returned from the hospital and evidently there had been some improvement that day. Taylor could now move a toe and though still in isolation, was showing surprising fortitude. The doctors were impressed and pleased by his progress and there was no question of capitulation on his part.

After a cup of Mrs Taylor's unsurpassed tea, Mr Jeremy sat back in his vehicle and made for Ross-on-Wye post office. The wood which spread its way along the hill from Waterton to the town was just beginning to lose the full green opulence of summer. Soon the children would be scuffing their way to school through carpets of leaves fallen from the deciduous trees and doing so until Mr Brain, the roadman, gradually got round to removing most of them with his ancient wheelbarrow. Over and above it all, the sun began to lose itself in the solid grey clouds and as he reached Ross, the head had to bring his unreliable windscreen wipers into action. He parked and removed his laden box from the car, carrying it into the post office. An amicable assistant agreed to stamp the contents and having done so, requested the princely sum of two pounds twelve and four pence, which the customer duly handed over. His business concluded, he entered the internal telephone kiosk and rang his wife to know if she required him to pick up anything from town. He then lit another cigarette, left the post office, crossed the road and entered the popular meeting place known as Don's Milk Bar. The proprietor himself greeted the popular headmaster and after providing him with a black coffee, agreed to display a poster advertising the proposed formation of an archaeological society in the district. After a short chat with Don and his wife about the 'steamy and licentious metropolis' that was not Ross-on-Wye, he sat down with some relief at a wickerwork table to consume his now cooling cup of coffee.

At another table and trying hard to be inconspicuous, sat an embarrassed Spencer, who had arrived to meet his behind-schedule mother and was now attempting to wait; feeling utterly at sea and not knowing how to react to his superior's mighty presence.

"Hello Spencer." The brown eyes twinkled in their customary fashion.

"Hello zir," grunted Spencer, hapless and unable to cope with the situation.

But Mr Jeremy was a master at putting children at their ease.

"You know Taylor pretty well, don't you, Spencer?"

"Yes, zir."

"Did you see much of him during the holidays?"

"No, zir. We were on' 'oliday in Tenby the last two weeks an' I never got out t' Waterton much before that. 'ee was alright when 'ee came t' see me one day at 'ome."

Encouraged to talk, the boy wistfully went on to describe rambles in the woods, bonfires they had lit in Taylor's garden and even, when he forgot who he was addressing, tales of epic marble competitions between Taylor, himself, Lewis and little Reggie Morris, whose small stature did not prevent him decisively winning most of these fiercely fought contests.

The headmaster stood up, smiled, picked up his empty coffee cup and returned it to the counter. After a little more polite banter with the proprietors, he went back over to Spencer and patted him on the shoulder.

"You'll be glad to know son that your friend is just a little better. Is your mum meeting you?"

A solemn nod of assent from the youngster was all the response he received, and he continued, "Goodbye, Spencer and we'll see you tomorrow."

The cumbersome car took off from the post office and somewhat enlivened, Spencer greeted his just arrived mother with, "Mum, John's getting better."

Perhaps an overly optimistic statement, but an encouraging one. Not having had the advantage of attending school that day, Spencer's mum did not know of the child's grave illness and on being informed, consoled her offspring as much as she thought necessary and promptly changed the subject.

"Did I give you a clean pair of socks this morning?"

"Yes, Mum."

The universal maternal frown appeared, accompanied by a disbelieving look of disapproval.

"Doesn't smell like it," she said and seating herself, vigorously stirred her sugar-laden tea. "Think you'll have to go in the bath tonight, young man!"

FIVE

Mr Brain the roadman pushed his wheelbarrow over to a verge where he had in one small pile, Church Lane's accumulated detritus. Mr Brain had six children, a cloth cap, a pipe and probably the most amiable disposition in the entire parish of Waterton.

Unconcerned that his actions might be hazardous, he lit his pipe, set fire to the rubbish in the ditch and sitting on his ancient donkey jacket, proceeded to make light of his bread and dripping sandwiches. Reaching to the haversack that hung on his bicycle, he pulled out a flask containing tea and began to eat, drink and smoke in strict rotation; though the latter 'discipline' was slower in that pipes need constant drawing and if not afforded that attention, need re-lighting at frequent intervals.

It had been a fine, abundant summer; he'd not had unpleasant conditions in which to work, and the warmth of the sun-soaked mid-year months had merged into a splendid September, with sharp, heavy frosts giving way to brilliant sunshine. After dawn, if you happened to be in the upper reaches of the parish,you could look down into the mists wafting through the valleys below and imagine yourself solitary and disembodied; vaguely non-human and wishing not to return in order to partake in the uncertainty of it all. Non-indigenous birds were procrastinating; perhaps wondering whether they really needed to migrate to distant lands and on their way home, the children of the village still dallied in the afternoon light, released from indoctrination and glad that all but the most deprived of them would be filling their insatiable bellies for the third time that day.

When only halfway through his ritual repast, Mr Brain became distracted enough to notice the local doctor's seventeen-year-old daughter, Janet Langford, rattling noisily towards him and looking highly precarious on a small two-wheeled vehicle known, appropriately for its size, as a Corgi. She stuttered to a halt, parked the machine and came bouncing over to the startled roadman. She wore unbecoming trousers, a large mud-spattered sweater, hadn't succeeded in disguising the fact that she was really a brunette and completed this tasteless ensemble with a pair of decidedly masculine walking boots. She had somehow contracted a bad dose of chicken pox towards the end of the summer holidays and though recovered; to make sure, would not be allowed back to her posh boarding school in Oxford for a week or so.

Mr Brain positively disapproved of women wearing trousers. It was a new fad and one, in his archaic way, which he found utterly repugnant. His dear wife had always been clad in skirts and dresses, never trousers, and this undoubtedly made procreation easier; an assertion proven by the fact that she had succeeded in giving birth to six healthy offspring and still did not look anywhere near her age.

Despite his mild animosity towards the girl, the roadman did not let it cloud his judgement or natural courtesy and touching his cap he removed his pipe and greeted her with, "Mornin' Miss Janet."

"Hello, Mr Brain." The young girl spoke in decidedly horsey tones, inclining towards condescension and if you chose to disregard her assorted garb, there could be no denying that she was mostly a feminine version of her father and therefore, engagingly attractive. "Have you seen Mother about this morning?"

Mr Brain ponderously removed his cap and scratched his balding pate before reluctantly replying; parting his lips to reveal a full set of yellowing, but still firm teeth. Living right on the cusp where the forest met Waterton, he had acquired the strong accent of the woodlands and though aware that he might not be understood, made no effort to translate the dialect into anything resembling Queen's English.

"'er did come up theese waiy this mornin' with thaiy dogs an' Oi yunt sin 'er come back down, zo Oi daime 'er's still zum waiy up thair with thick uns."

Which being simply interpreted meant that

Mrs Langford had passed by in the morning and to the roadman's certain knowledge, not yet deigned to return.

"Oh, thank you and how are your wife and all the small ones?" Janet Langford emitted a nervous laugh at the end of each sentence, as if trying to make up for an extreme lack of conviction in her speech.

The worldly-wise roadman ruminated at length before replying. He thought of his eldest, five-feet-nine, with a healthy girth and expensive appetite. "'er be well enough, Miss, an' Roger be leavin' school at Christmas."

Not knowing how to respond, the girl became even more disconcerted and made her excuses. "Fancy, well, uh, I must be going. Cheerio and thanks for the information."

She re-mounted her curious machine and shot off up the lane on a quest to find her mother. As she disappeared in a cloud of noxious fumes, the roadman idly wondered if her hind quarters were actually fouling the ground and if so, whether or not the display of blue sparks being emitted came solely from the humming internal combustion engine beneath her. He resumed his interrupted meal, re-lit his pipe and in the true peasant amicability of his forebears, decided that the maniacal pursuits of the parish's gentlefolk were not his affair and he'd remain subservient; just observing their strange antics and keeping his own counsel.

Maude Langford, who had been gently exercising her Great Danes and herself further up towards the wood, found her comparative peace shattered by the rattling spectacle of her fond daughter careering round a corner and screeching to a precarious halt within six inches of the party. The gargantuan canines set up an almighty howling and it was all that 'Mother' could do to restrain them.

"For God's sake, turn the bloody engine off." Always inclined to be on a short fuse, Maude was irate.

"Sorry, Mummy." Janet complied and sat there, knees unnaturally bent, to await the usual torrent of verbiage that accompanied such confrontations between mother and daughter.

Mud spattered and harassed by her disturbed charges, the doctor's wife duly admonished her errant offspring and issued autocratic instructions. "And if you like to go back and tell Daddy that, despite your efforts to ruin my constitutional, I shall be back in half-an-hour. And for God's sake, push that damn machine a good way down the lane before you start the bloody thing! And don't you ever rev it up near Hamish and Hetty again!"

Disregarding the last of these maternal commands, Janet revved the 'damn thing' up once more and amid a lot of mud and renewed howling, was gone.

Dr Langford sat in his surgery supposedly dealing with his last patient, who was actually Mrs Taylor, John Taylor's mother and the Langfords' daily help.

"You'll be glad to know he can come home in about a fortnight. This does not mean things will be straightforward. It will need a lot of co-operation between yourself, John and myself. And on another matter, I'm sure we can manage without you during the recovery period; you'll get your money as usual, and I don't want you to feel you have to come back until John is fit and well again? Will that suit you?"

Mrs Taylor beamed pleasurable relief. She knew it was unlikely that her boy would ever be fully active again but had her own stoic ideas on the subject. Rising to go, she thanked the doctor profusely and bidding him good day, went home to put the kettle on.

His work completed, Dr Langford ambled out through the surgery doors. He could plainly hear Janet stuttering up the front drive on that extraordinary machine, her latest plaything. Why she could not take a serious interest in boys or something, he could not comprehend and thought seventeen a late age to still have the desires of a child. With slight relief, he realised she would be finished at that damned expensive school at the end of the academic year, and he supposed the lure of university might beckon, though he hoped she would just leave and get a job.

Over lunch, a peculiar potage concocted by Janet herself, talk naturally turned towards village affairs. Helping herself with scarcely concealed disgust, to a larger proportion than she meant to take, Maude Langford reviewed the table and possessed of her usual unprotesting audience, launched into her customary mealtime monologue. She rarely had competition in these family gatherings, for Dr Langford ate with one hand and was engrossed in *The Times* with the other and Janet's healthy appetite meant that from that source came only single syllable answers. This allowed endless scope for Maude's speculations and subtle vilifications and although these defamations of character were not of an obvious nature, they had that peculiar English gentlewoman's ability to tear all and sundry to pieces in a polite, yet devious manner. The imperious Maude Langford could in less charitable moments, be described as a flagrant example of 'royalty' thirty-seven times removed and were it possible to prove that such a fragile relationship existed, then the doctor's wife without doubt would have willingly attached herself to that small army of hangers on who, like noble parasites, suckled off the glory of the monarchy.

Being the daughter of a Knight of the Bath, she considered she had cause to resent that marriage to a simple GP had lowered her lofty status in life and found it hard, though a big fish in a small pool, to be content with opening fetes, attending rural district council meetings and being the endless president of Waterton WI. She had an almost indecent love of dogs which, despite Mrs Taylor's efforts to 'polish' them away, constantly tainted the household with their dubious odour and considered all well brought up young ladies should cultivate horse riding as a substitute for lying beneath and responding to the base desires of brutish and oversexed young men.

"Did you have a good walk, dear?" Dr Langford made a rare appearance from behind the folds of the British establishment's newspaper.

The lady eyed him with near contempt. "Those damn dogs take me for a walk!"

A succession of poodles had given way to the current trend in Great Danes, primarily because Mrs Coningby-Wilson at the Dower House had recently taken to breeding Alsatians and Maude Langford could not allow anyone to possess a larger version of the canine species than her. A folly which her facetious husband condemned as an inclination towards unconscious 'masochism'.

"But an odd thing happened when I went through the churchyard. I met that silly woman who used to work for that organist fella. What was his name? Gallaher or Gardner or something? Well, you know, the poor man died. I forget when. Frightful musician he was, but still, very faithful. Anyway, there was this Fryer woman cleaning up his resting place with carbolic soap and a large bucketful of water. The silly creature had tears in her eyes and when I asked her what she thought she was doing, she said she always came to his graveside once a year to 'clean 'im up.' I told her I thought the church people might take a dim view of it, but she still went on scrubbing and murmuring to herself in that low, guttural tone she has."

Unusually talkative, the doctor intervened. "Ah, yes. We tried various treatments for her some years back. Didn't do much good. She's harmless enough. I see her wandering around the village some times. Her husband's a nice fellow. Works for William Johnson up at The Green."

Content that he had contributed more than enough to the conversation, he immersed himself once more and waited for Maude's verbal barrage to re-commence. But his words had seemed to silence his spouse for a moment and only re-awakened dormant memories in Janet, who had once stumbled upon Mike Fryer when walking along a path, which ran along the bottom of the wood. Adjacent to this path, a broad arable field swept upwards to a tall uncut hedge and through it Janet had seen the stocky figure of Mike tilling symmetrical furrows in the corn stubble with a plough drawn by an old, battered Fordson tractor. It had been during a similar autumn a couple of years ago; far from 'white horses' and the open sea. Parasitical seagulls swirled behind the plough and this flagrant encroachment on their territory was resented by the local birdlife, who were tagging along making vain attempts to sample the juicy 'goodies' that were being unearthed. Suddenly the swarthy ploughman halted his progress and thinking himself unobserved, dismounted from his 'steed' and performed a natural function right in the middle of the field.

The first thought of the doctor's daughter was to run, but she stood transfixed and whenever time and the sometimes ceaseless chastising of her overbearing mother allowed, took to stalking the big man in the hope that a repeat performance would be forthcoming. Unbeknown to her parents, she had made the acquaintance of a similar manly symbol a little while later and only the fear of becoming 'preggers' had limited an enjoyable, but risky pastime.

Janet couldn't recall Mike Fryer's wife, but she thought the poor man must have been a saint to stick by such a wan creature when he could be the provender of such obvious attractions.

Mother was talking again. "And I don't know what's going to happen over that schoolteacher. As if everyone is not aware of what's going on. I saw the young floosy at the governor's meeting on Wednesday. What Mr Jeremy is thinking of, I don't know. Letting it drag on and ignoring it. One or the other should be removed or both. It must be having a frightful effect on the school."

Janet began to collect up the dishes and Dr Langford lit his elegant pipe. He comforted himself with the fact that he had his work, his intelligent person's newspaper and his 'Gold Block.' How he came to be saddled with Maude was, he reflected wryly, sometimes beyond his comprehension. Daily encountering various assorted afflictions, he had never wished any of them upon a single soul, but he could not help thinking that the verbal sense could have been denied his espoused without harming her or the often-cowed victims of that pink appendage within her mouth. He mumbled some sort of a reply through the stem of his pipe, causing wreaths of smoke to amble upwards; further besmirching the ceiling, where it dubiously enhanced the patch of brown caused by the fact that he always sat in the same place.

"Have you thought what we're going to do when Janet goes back to college? You know Mrs T won't be back for a while, of course?"

Not at all cognisant and hardly sympathetic with her daily's problems, Maude terminated another outburst of unreasonableness with a raft of trivialities.

And not content with that, she paused and

added a coda. "Are you sure she won't be able to come some of the time, dear? It's such a wretched nuisance."

"Quite sure."

"Couldn't one of the neighbours help out, d'you think. It's all so wretchedly inconvenient."

Dr Langford decided to be firm. "My dear, that boy has just had a serious illness and will not be fully recovered for some considerable time, if at all. I hardly think your housework should take priority under any circumstances. Mrs Taylor will have a tremendous task. I must ask you to be reasonable for once. If you like, I will try and get someone else for a while, though it would not hurt for you to have a look round as well. For example, what about Harry Green's wife? She doesn't seem occupied at the moment."

Faced with this scarcely veiled reprimand, his wife became curt. "I'm certainly not having that woman in the house!"

"Why ever not?"

"She worked for the Coningby-Wilsons last year!"

The beleaguered doctor lost patience. "What the hell has working for old Mrs C-W got to do with it?"

Thoroughly roused, his wife stamped her foot. "Don't shout, Henry! Do you know why Sarah Green left the Coningby-Wilsons?"

Dr Langford fumed. "It was never proved. They've got so much hanging around down there. I doubt if they knew if whatever was supposed to have gone missing was there in the first place! And what if she did take ten bob, it wouldn't make much difference to those two mean old skinflints!"

"Henry, I don't intend to be lectured by you. If that's all you can suggest, I'll find my own replacement. Please calm down!"

Janet, who had been listening avidly and loving a potential row, suddenly broke into the contest. "How about Mildred Fryer?"

"What?! That simpleton? Please don't you start, dear." Maude went slightly pink round the jowls, a flushed state not disguised by her extensive make-up.

Sensing an opening, her husband smiled. "Now, that's an idea. Mildred may be tuppence short of a shilling, but she's a willing worker. Kept old Garner's place spotless." He turned to his daughter. "Damn good idea that, Janet."

A tall woman, Maude Langford stood up, hardly able to constrain herself. "Well, if you two think I'm going to put up with that frightful creature, you're very much mistaken."

"Don't be silly, Mummy, I'm sure Mike Fryer would like it." At the thought of him, Janet too, turned the shade of a damask rose, but still continued to stand up to her mother. "They tell me he's been trying to find something to occupy her since old Mr Garner died; you as good as admitted she needed something to keep her out of mischief. Who knows, she might even scrub the front doorstep for you."

Affronted and stubborn to the last, Maude Langford tossed her head, shoved her chair angrily under the table and with a "we'll see about that", strode from the room in high dudgeon.

SIX

The days were wearisome for Peter Trout. With Margaret at school, he sat beside his uncomprehended radio on an endless November afternoon seeing pictures in the fire and sometimes these became faces; yellow faces with motionless staring eyes. In a fruitless attempt to avenge himself on these unsought visions, he would periodically heat a poker and with it, penetrate a log in the fire. This afforded him great satisfaction, was his only means of vengeance and in his mind's wanderings the scorched piece of wood metamorphisized into the sallow face of his one-time oppressor. He imagined it writhing in agony as he had writhed and he wondered how it would react to a whip being wielded over its back; plied viciously across a torso already emaciated by the enervating effort of digging an endless road.

The clock on the mantel sounded four o'clock and this meant that Margaret would soon be home. Feeling his way out of a trough of bitterness, he walked into the kitchen and put the kettle on. Margaret was a lovely woman; she surely wouldn't be long, then everything would be alright. Before it all happened, they would never have slept apart, but it was better this way. Better for both of them. A succulent apple is no good to a man if he has no teeth to partake of it and such was Peter Trout's near emasculated condition, there was never a chance that a normal relationship between the couple would ever resume. The front door opened and shut and here she was.

"Hello." Margaret Trout walked in, a gabardine mac slung round her shoulders and a glint of despair in her eyes. She yawned and sat down at the kitchen table.

Brought back to something approaching sanity, her husband was all concern. "Have a good day?"

"So-so." She never looked him in the eyes these days. She could not bring herself to do so. "Lilian Marshall wet herself, Johnnie Wood found out that two and two amount to four and the youngest Brain was sick. Quite eventful really. And what about you? Have you done anything more to that mat the nurse told you to try and make?"

About three months previously the district nurse had advised Margaret that it was essential that her husband found more to do with his time. She suggested as a therapeutic exercise, a little rug making and Peter had started off with unusual enthusiasm until he once again lapsed into lethargy. He still did a small amount every day, but the first week's furious progress had been eclipsed by about half-an-inch per twenty-four hours and this only to humour Margaret and the district nurse, a woman of surprisingly scant understanding of mental health and not the most competent person to deal with the poor man's condition.

"A little," he said.

"Hmm, well anyway, isn't it your crib night? Is Mike coming for you as usual?" She knew that reproofs were not in order and would only serve to exacerbate his mental strife. One of the things which had not deserted Peter's shattered psyche was the inherent ability to play an honest game of crib. Every Wednesday, Mike Fryer would arrive in a friend's Austin Seven and carry Peter off to the Horse and Jockey in Waterton where, once ensconced, the war victim would find his concentration fully occupied by the matter in hand. Tonight was a friendly against one of Ross-on-Wye's many alehouses and knowing some of the opposition fairly well, he didn't wish to miss it. He replied in the affirmative and whilst his wife remained in the kitchen to prepare tea, he returned to the sitting room, hunched back over the fire and resumed his activity with the poker.

They ate tea in comparative silence and after he had assisted with the washing up and scarcely understood Dick Barton on the radio, he sat down to await his chauffeur.

Mike Fryer duly arrived and after refusing a cup of tea, which Margaret always offered, drove Peter off to the pub in the shaky machine he always managed to procure for the occasion.

As with most English public houses of the

period, beer supplied by a local brewery, was plentiful, tasted malty and good and could (and usually was) accompanied in the public bar by a combinative effect of Woodbines, Players, Gold Flake and Golden Virginia; mingling with a strong smell of St Bruno or Condor pipe tobacco. If a more nourishing and less damaging alternative to this working man's 'valhalla' was required, then yellow local cider drawn from the wood, drunk in consort with a massive great hunk of bread and cheese, often filled the bill. Only one variety of crisps could be purchased and if lucky, you could be blessed with the acquisition of anything up to four screwed-up blue packets of salt; dropped inside by an erroneous, but generous machine.

And somewhere in England at that time there must have been a mould explicitly designed to produce the prototype English landlord, for Phil Arnold was the personification of just such a man.

He was red-cheeked with a liberal paunch, had the necessary attitude in that he was never too obsequious or overbearing and managed to be just deferential enough to satisfy his varied and sometimes contrary clientele. His placid wife, who never worked less than fourteen hours a day, matched his cheerful demeanour and yet would quickly change her stance when half-an-hour had been surreptitiously added on to legal opening hours by her businesslike husband.

Then it was she with a “come on, ent you got no ‘omes t’ go to” who cleared the bars. Phil and Elsie were a popular couple, for the beverages they sold, the company they attracted and the grievances they tolerated. If a man was ‘in his cups’ and revealed anything too indiscreetly to the landlord, then Phil would make sure it went no further so that, when back in the land of sobriety, the imbiber would not have to suffer for his indiscretion.

All in all and given his unsettled mind, Peter Trout enjoyed his Wednesday nights at the Jockey or when away matches meant visiting other hostelries. The pub was a good place to try and forget and amnesia was one thing from which he did not normally suffer. They were playing the ‘Crown’, Ross, tonight; an avid party of crib exponents who had consented to come out to Waterton for a friendly, fresh from their triumph over a first division side the previous week. After pint swopping and general fraternising, the two sides took to the tables and apart from the occasional murmurings which accompanied alcoholic replenishment, silence reigned. A smoke haze filled the room and matchsticks advanced steadily round peg boards. Peter Trout partnered Mike Fryer and from the onset they struck a winning streak. Before his privations in Burma, Peter had been a whist player of some note, representing the county and some of the concentration required for that card game was still evident on the board. During a break between games his partner took hold of their two pint mugs and placed them heavily down on the bar; as was the custom to attract attention when the charismatic landlord was heavily engaged 'chopsin'' to someone in the lounge.

"Hold yer 'osses then, young Michael. Shan't be a sec!" Phil Arnold came round the semi-circle from the lounge and expansive as ever, loudly harangued his customer. "Now then, you cheeky young bugger. What's yer poison? Same again?"

"Two pints please, Phil, y' fat ol' bugger. One with a dash and one without, that's if you've finished talkin' to yer fancy woman!"

Mine host carefully pulled two pints with the aid of the brightly polished brass beer pump and all the while traded insults with the big farm labourer, who obviously relished the repartee and gave as good as he got. This rustic banter was all part of the scene. No one took offence and indeed, politeness would have been viewed with something bordering on suspicion. But there were one or two awkward customers and one of these was now causing Phil Arnold concern.

"Got ol' Charlie," he muttered under his breath. "Damn nuisance 'ee is. I'll 'ave t' be tellin' 'im shortly. Three nights runnin' 'ee's bin as tight an' full as the water tank on tank meada. It don' do much fur custom in the snug."

Shrugging, Mike Fryer paid for the precious

liquid and said, "I'd chuck un out! T'ent no good puttin' up wi' that silly ol' bugger beggin' drinks off all and bloody sundry!" Unlike the discreet landlord, Mike failed to keep his voice down and this had disastrous consequences. For a few moments later, the bar door swung open to reveal the subject of his hasty character assassination, the red faced, dishevelled figure of Charlie Watkins. He stood there for a minute, swaying on a walking stick; a prematurely ageing character, the victim of bad diet and an insatiable proclivity for the drink.

"Wuz you talkin' about me, Mick Fryer?" He somehow staggered over to the crib table, full of aggressive intent, his eyes glazed, but determined to corner his critic.

Phil Arnold thought it about time to intervene. Lifting up the flap, which gave him access into the bar, he hurried over to the belligerent Charlie and took hold of his arm. The drunk promptly shook it off and pointed his walking stick - a rudimentary shaped blackthorn - at his chosen adversary.

"Ah-Ah'm surprised at you, Mick Fryer. Suggestin' I wuz a cadger! If I wuz twenty year younger, I'd knock yer bloody block off!"

This riled the crib teams and amid cries of 'go 'ome, y' drunken ol' bastard' and 'Chuck 'n out, Phil!', the landlord tried to propel Charlie towards the door. But stronger than he looked, Charlie suddenly changed tactics. He turned his attention towards Mike Fryer's partner and with his deadly revelation, opened up an abyss for the beleaguered Peter Trout.

"An' I sees you got Pete wi' yer. Well, well. Now then. Poor ol' Pete. You'll never guess who I saw his missus with in Glo'ster last wik!"

Furious and anxious to protect his friend from further suffering, Mike rose from his seat, but was unable to stop Charlie from continuing.

"'er wuz with that thare schoolmaster. W'a's 'iz name? 'ee comes in 'ere. Allen, tha's right. Bob Allen. P-poor ol' Pete. Never mind, you goin' t' 'ave a pint wi' old Charlie, then? An' ow about bloody old Mike? No offence, my ol' mate, n-no offence. C'mon Phil, gi's another, jus' one more, jus'......" And here the drunken old man keeled over and landed flat on his face.

Thus disrupted, the crib temporarily ceased and four stout members of the two teams combined to carry the semi-conscious Charlie into the back kitchen for the long suffering but benevolent landlord's wife to provide ice cubes and black coffee.

The furore over, Mike Fryer resumed his seat. He fervently hoped his companion had not taken in the drunk's unfortunate disclosure. Their two opponents resumed playing, but when it came to Peter Trout's turn, he just sat transfixed; oblivious to what was going on about him and cowered, almost like a hurt animal.

"Your turn, Pete."

A flicker of response, followed by some tired detached ramblings constituted the reply. "I can't do it, I tell you. This road, where is it going? It's too hot. Please, I can't dig any more. Some water, please, Simo, I must have water...... What are you doing here, Margaret? What you doing here?" At this uttering of his unfaithful wife's name, a semblance of sanity returned. "What's that? Oh yes; take me home, please, Mike."

Drained of all colour, the stricken war victim arose and made for the door. The bar went quiet and with a word of apology to his opponents, Mike Fryer followed his partner outside.

The limp figure of Peter Trout leant against the high brick faced car park wall. Tears coursed freely down his ashen face and his distressed state was made worse to behold by the occasional emission of an odd, almost childlike laugh.

Big Mike Fryer placed a gentle hand on his stricken friend's arm; concern emanating from this lusty, work hardened, yet compassionate being.

Anxious to help, Phil Arnold came out and between them; they guided Peter Trout to the parked Austin Seven. The landlord was worried.

"Shall I ring Doctor Langford?" It never occurred to anyone in Waterton that the good doctor was not on call twenty-four hours a day. He was too highly regarded by the villagers and those in the parishes, which he also covered and given a choice of being attended to by the doctor or going to hospital, he 'won' over the medical institution every time.

"Please tell 'im I'll bring 'im round."

"Right." A man of quick decisions, Phil Arnold took himself off to the telephone.

Mike Fryer started the engine and glanced anxiously at his passenger, who became agitated again. "Oh Maggie, Maggie, not you. Not bloody you! I'll kill the bastard! The filthy yellow bastard! Where are you going? You can't go. Please don't go. I don't want you to go. That's silly of you. I'll put the kettle on. Look at the marks, Doctor. Dirty great bloody marks. Whipped me they did, Doctor and what am I doing in a Yank hospital, Doctor?"

The monologue went hysterically on and Mike coaxed the poor little car to attempt a speed beyond its pre-war capabilities. They soon came to the Langford's entrance and shot up the long driveway, scattering the gravel and skidding to a halt before the imposing front door.

After a quick inspection, Dr Langford administered a sedative and despite Mike Fryer's slight dissent, decided the patient should go home to his wife. The farmworker had given a brief explanation of the scenario in the pub and expressed his doubts over this course of action, but the doctor could not see any other solution and they set off, with Peter Trout transferred to Dr Langford's Rover and Mike following in the much maligned, but gallant Austin Seven.

The council house wasn't in a very salubrious part of Ross and upon arrival they rang the bell and received no response. The sedative was now kicking in and whilst Mike held the patient upright, the doctor rummaged through his pockets and with fortune favouring him, found a key. They opened the door and not without difficulty, virtually carried Peter Trout into the hall and up the stairs to the bedroom; switching on the shade less light and revealing a bed, which had not been made. Mike Fryer left the doctor to keep a tenuous hold and quickly rectifying the bed, helped him to lay the patient upon it.

"Can you stay with him?"

Knowing the big man experienced similar troubles within his own domestic set-up, Dr Langford felt confident he could rely on Fryer.

"Yes, Doctor. As you knows, Mam lives at 'ome. She'll be alright with George. If you wouldn't mind callin' back round at The Green to let 'er know what's happenin?"

"Right, I'll do that and I think I'd better try and find Margaret. I don't imagine you know where she is?" As he asked it, the doctor knew it might be a rhetorical question and after a feigned cough, Mike Fryer reluctantly answered.

"Well, I told you what 'appened in the pub, Doctor. I's no good pretendin'. I think th' 'ole village knows what's bin goin' on. I don't say uz 'er's bin out with 'im t'night, but I shouldn't wonder if 'er 'as."

The doctor sighed and sat down on a rickety bedside chair. "I had actually known of all this. A pity, but very difficult circumstances. And you're quite sure you have no idea where Margaret is?"

Mike Fryer shrugged. "Sorry, Doctor."

"Well, he should be alright now and I'll call the Ross surgery in the morning. Strictly speaking he's not my patient and I'll make sure they send someone round. It maybe that he'll have to go to Wainshill though, God help me, and I'd never send anyone in there unless I really had to!"

Wainshill was the county's mental hospital and not a place for which the enlightened General Practitioner had a lot of time. Once condemned to the place, you seldom escaped and Dr Langford was of the opinion that, if at all possible, it was better to keep people in a normal home environment. With Peter Trout now slumbering peacefully, he clambered back down the carpet less stairs and bidding Mike Fryer goodnight, was soon heard driving off in the purring Rover...

Left alone, Mike Fryer rummaged in the kitchen cabinet for some tea and set the filled kettle on the Aga. He had known the Trouts for some years now and been attracted to them originally through a sense of kindred spirit, caused by his own wife's affliction. Mildred, a slip of a girl, had borne him a son at the age of twenty and George had turned out to be a fractious child.

Mildred's subsequent ailment had been labelled post-natal depression, but finding marks on the child, the visiting midwife had found it to be a little graver. The reluctant mother often neglected to feed the child and its worried father often came home to find the baby unchanged and left to further defecate at will. This had not been allowed to go on and baby George was fostered until the age of two when, after his mother had received treatment, he was allowed to return home. After a period of initial anxiety, Mildred Fryer – with some assistance from her widowed mother-in-law who came to live with them – began to bestow upon George all the loving care, which most mothers lavish on their offspring, but never recovered from the unfortunate dim-wittedness that caused the local populace to brand her 'tuppence short of a shilling'.

To add to this, she became frigid, as if fearing that any sexual activity whatsoever would result in certain pregnancy and further treatment had been to no avail, leaving her frustrated husband with a problem that was difficult to assuage. Now forty, he had experienced a hardworking, but peaceful war on the land in attempting to keep Britons from starving and though he had toyed with the idea of joining the conflict, common sense had prevailed and tolerance of his frustration was made easier by daily contact with the sounds and smells of the earth.

Faced with the prospect of permanent celibacy, he had managed the situation in a far easier fashion than his fellow sufferer, Margaret Trout. Tempted, he had contemplated her obvious attractions, as had many others, but with surprising restraint and despite his lusty yearnings, shunned the idea of cuckolding the ravaged Peter Trout.

Margaret had once given him the chance during Peter's wartime absence; an opportunity which would have been snatched by frailer men and though surprised, she had respected his decision and upon her husband's return he had become a caring and useful friend to both of them. War, he thought, was a fine thing for the flag wavers left behind and the businessmen only too glad to take advantage of colleagues' absence to make a quick buck. But it was foul and hellish for those being shot to pieces and the women left wondering.

An hour later, Margaret Trout arrived and in an awkward, almost apologetic manner he told her about Charlie Watkins and she did not deny that she'd been with Bob Allen and seemed relieved that everything was now out in the open. She thanked him profusely for his help and mumbling something about it being nothing, he breathed a sigh of relief and took his leave.

Left alone, Margaret filled a hot water bottle

and climbing the stairs, put it in the bed in what used to be called the spare room. She returned to the kitchen, poured herself another cup of the now stewed tea and was in time to hear the sonorous wall clock strike eleven. Ten minutes later, she fell asleep at the table and by the time she went to bed it was three in the morning and the hot water bottle was cold.

Calling the next morning, Dr Coldwell from the Ross surgery did not hang about. He'd heard Peter Trout haranguing his wife before he'd even entered the house and he wasted no time in calling an ambulance.

The ambulance took the poor unfortunate man away to Hereford and he had to endure a short course of treatment before, under heavy medication, he was allowed home. Strangely, Margaret had pressed for this and scarcely recognising his wayward spouse, the disturbed man had remained docile and reasonably quiescent about most things.

Until, of course, one drab November Tuesday some weeks later, when Margaret had returned from school to find her husband in the workshop, a smile on his face. He'd always been clever with his hands and what he'd done had not caused him any great problems. He remained smiling as she fainted; his feet swinging eighteen inches from the ground and before passing out, she just had time to glimpse the child's skipping rope, taut from the rafters to his neck.

SEVEN

Carols were part of the Christmas Concert and the optimistically named School Choir was to perform some of the old favourites under the guidance of Mr Jones. Part of assembly was devoted to choir practice.

Spencer, who had been given, of all things, a battered old saxophone for a recent birthday, had offered to add his questionable accompaniment to this musical feast, but with infinite tact, the sagacious deputy head had declined this generous offer and agreed that the boy would be allowed to blow his inimical rendering of *On the sunny side of the street* later on in the programme.

Also present at this morning's assembly, the Reverand Michael Cannington had come along to talk about God and going to church.He was now droning on his ineffectual and boring way to a captive, but utterly disinterested audience. Unlike the exciting and vivid RI lessons given by the head, his address contained a lot of lengthy words and in a desperate attempt to get on the same wavelength, a tendency to lapse into talking down to the children. All present were glad when his arid tones ceased and dismayed when Mr Jeremy asked if they would like to ask any questions. An embarrassed, tongue-tied silence ensued and it was some time before a small hand lifted hesitatingly and a nervous voice said, “If Jesus wuz born in a stable, zir, did Joseph ‘ave t’ muck it out before they moved in? My Dad ‘az t’ muck out Johnson’s cowshed ev’ry night and mornin’ after milkin’.”

Laughter broke out and nonplussed, the clergyman tried to look unflustered whilst Mr Jeremy - trying to hide his own mirth - helped out by answering the question for him.

This being done to George Fryer’s satisfaction, a small girl with flaxen hair and irresistible blue eyes, put up her hand. “Please sir, what’s a virgin birth?”

Embarrassed as a beetroot, the flummoxed rural Dean went all round his hat to explain about the Angel Gabriel and visitations from angels, whilst Arnold whispered to Woody his own version at the back of the room from his vantage point as a non-singer in the school choir. Arnold’s cynically garbled account of our Lady’s possible dilemma in finding herself ‘up the spout’ without the involvement of a male appendage or artificial insemination, concluded with the blasphemous assertion that as the holy girl was not married, she might well have found herself assigned to a home for single girls who obliged boys too freely!

A withering look from Bob Allen, who was well placed to overhear the ‘Arnold Gospel’ and later knew not how he’d managed to contain his laughter during the telling of it, stopped this epic tale and after a few more feeble questions involving more lengthy answers, a verbally vanquished Reverand Cannington bid everyone an unctuous and God-filled day and departed for somewhere less synonymous with a lion's den!

Choir practice concluded with *O Come All Ye Faithful* and this being terminated in only two keys, with the growling adolescent boys pre-eminent, the entire school trouped outside for morning break. It was a cold, bleak inclement day, with the wind coming from the north and thick, threatening clouds above. To the delight of the children and the horror of Bob Allen, who was on playground duty, it began to snow and the infants had to be ushered back inside. Here they ruined the teacher's tea session with undiluted noise and in order to prevent mayhem, Miss Barnes had to hastily hand out the colouring-in books.

Outside, Martin Lewis stood beneath the protective corrugated roof of the boy's bike shed talking to Reggie of the pimples and a rather precocious girl called Marion, who shouldn't have been there. Perhaps more nubile than she should have been at her age, Marion was relating her alleged experiences with that renowned lady killer, Dudley, in a barn the previous weekend. The two younger boys were agog at this shocking revelation and determined that, given the chance, they would like to make a similar experiment. Marion, whose mouth was undoubtedly bigger than her claims, seemed highly disconcerted at this suggestion and skipped off to join her friends in the girls' cloakroom next door; feeling safer, but wishing what she'd said was true.

When confronted with the two small interested parties a little later, Dudley had hotly denied everything, declaring that Marion was too 'chopsy' and that her whole story was a pack of lies. Girls were just soppy and he wasn't interested, a statement which inferred that, unlike the nubile Marion, he was backward for his age. Upon finishing this unbelieved explanation, he returned to the nightmarish soccer match taking place in what had now become a blinding snowstorm and sliding into a solo run, fell heavily over Arnold's left boot, which just happened to be planted between him and the improvised goal at the time. Fruitless cries of 'Penalty!' were ignored by the perpetrator of the foul and since he was bigger than anyone else, a goal kick was taken, hoofed down the length of the playground and in the absence of the opposing goalie, who was engaged in a snowball fight, the ball hit that part of the fence which had been whitewashed over to serve as 'the goalposts'.

Not impressed by this prime example of juvenile perfidy and worried lest there could be injury, Bob Allen decided to call a halt to the treacherous pastime and blowing his whistle early, sent them all into their respective classrooms. He followed his own charges into Class Three and started the older ones on a text book, the last in a series on Roman Britain, whilst the younger ones were set to finish the maths they'd made such a pig's feast of the previous day. Christmas was not far off and although he made his talk on the abandonment of Britain by the Roman legions as interesting as possible, he could sense that the children were only really concerned with the glitter and acquisitiveness of the coming festive season. He wondered how some of the parents, poor and having to deal with constant financial problems almost daily, would cope with the extra demands made on their often derisory incomes. But they usually managed and the start of the new year term nearly always brought to school proud little girls with new dolls, boys with startling cap guns and surprisingly, some of the more fortunate ones with such expensive items as train sets and new bicycles.

As the older ones settled down to see what they could write about the Romans, the schoolmaster lit a cigarette and began to patrol up and down the rows to offer help to the young mathematicians. Oddly enough, following the dreadfully upsetting internment of Peter, Margaret Trout had gone off to 'Gaul' to stay with relatives on her mother's side and Bob was not at all sure she would return to Waterton for the start of the new term. His relationship with her had become enigmatically strained. They had almost deliberately avoided one another at times and strangely, now that the main encumbrance had been removed, the affair now seemed less honest than it had before the appalling suicide. Bob Allen was experiencing a period of darkness on a par with that which must have engulfed Britain after the Romans left. And a heavy heart was no aid to teaching. He would be relieved when this term and Christmas was over and did not look forward to surviving it without Margaret.

Dinnertime arrived and Bob Allen decided to drive his now hooded Armstrong Siddeley down to the village shop. The snow had settled, necessitating caution, but the main road with its fair amount of traffic was almost clear and after cautiously negotiating the bends, he soon stood stamping his feet outside the village stores; for it would never do to enter this domain without eradicating all traces of snow and mud from one's boots.

Neat as ever and spotting his imminent arrival through the broad shop window, Miss Emily stood waiting. Unlike Phil Arnold at the pub, she did not pre-empt her customers' requirements. One day, Bob resolved to commit sacrilege by letting Phil open a packet of Woodbines and then asking for a packet of Sobranie. The stout landlord was just the same with the beer. Super-efficient, he would know every toper's poison practically before the client had thought about leaving his warm hearthside. Upon sensing a mere whiff of a patron's pending arrival, the big man would have his drink on the bar and his 'smokes' opened and ready. It must be something to do with telepathy, the schoolteacher thought flippantly and was obviously something, which only rotund landlords and mystic felines had in common. The shop bell sounded, heralding his entry and alerting the proprietor, who was currently engaged in operating the bacon slicer.

"Twenty woods, please Emily."

"Thank you, Mr Allen. Is there anything else today?"

The attractive old maid frowned at his liberal usage of her Christian name and not for the first time, Bob thought what a stunner she must have been in her youth.

"No thanks." And then he remembered. "Oh - yes. Did you manage to get those bullseyes for me?"

"Yes, I quite forgot. They came in yesterday, as a matter of fact. How many would you like? I ordered a jar, so they should last quite a while."

The schoolteacher gave the decision some thought. "Ooh - I should think half-a-pound will be enough to be going on with, thanks."

Using an old fashioned scales with brass weights, Miss Ward carefully measured half a pound of Bob Allen's favourite childhood sweet and halfway through, bestowed upon him a demure smile. “And does this new eating habit mean I shall be selling less of those cigarettes you seem to purchase at an alarming rate?”

“Possibly,” said the potentially reforming smoker. “Though as it isn’t the new year yet, I may be being a bit premature.” He had every intention of making hay while the sun shone and, of course, there would be no question that he would renounce it all with great ceremony on January the first and never let a Woodbine sully his lips and lungs again. The shopkeeper, whose views on smoking were well ahead of accepted opinion, was not aware that her customer’s sole reason for giving up the weed was financial. He thought the idea that fags were a health hazard was a load of b****cks, but he had to cut down on something and giving up seemed the sensible thing to do.

Back to the role of being the shopkeeper who was aware that the customer was always right, Emily Ward handed over the sweets and sighed. “Well, I hope it’s better than this year. An awful lot seems to have happened in the village in the last twelve months. There’s poor John Taylor’s illness and that other ghastly business…” She realised her mistake and hastily tried to cover up by re-arranging the periodicals on the counter.

Ostensibly unperturbed, Bob Allen changed the subject. He ignited one of the objects he well-meaningly, but half-heartedly intended to supersede with bullseyes and enquired after the health of Miss Ward's older sister, the ageing Miss Lucy. When her health permitted, Miss Lucy would take a turn in the shop, but the decade between her and her sister made her steadily less mobile and of late, arthritis allied to failing eyesight had more or less reduced her role to cook and housekeeper.

"She's well enough really, but she's not as sprightly as she was." Here a brief moment of anxiety showed on Emily Ward's face and sensing a sympathetic audience in Bob Allen she went on, "only I do wish she'd leave this other business alone." The boot now seemed to be on the other foot and Bob tried to show empathy.

"And what business would that be, Emily?"

"Oh, this wretched spiritualism. Every Friday evening a friend picks her up and they go into Ross for some sort of meeting. She claims to have received messages from people dead and gone. I don't know much about it, she says it's pretty harmless, but I'm not sure and I wish she would give it up."

Bob Allen heard her out and then said, "As a matter of fact, I did see her the other night. Does she go with William Johnson's wife, you know, from The Green? I thought I saw young Lizzie Johnson helping your sister into a car in Ross, at about a quarter to eight?"

A picture of disapproval, Emily Ward answered the question. "Yes, that's right. You know young Mrs Johnson, then?"

"She helped with several school jumble sales. Pleasant enough in a way, but she soon got tired of it. I understand she's been involved in most village things at one time or another, but she soon loses interest. You say this spiritualism's her latest hobby?" Bob Allen measured his words with care. He was aware of Lizzie Johnson's reputation and had once experienced her feminine wiles. He had been invited up to The Green for coffee and had he still possessed his long gone virginity, could have quite easily lost it. She left him in no doubt over her intentions, but he hadn't fancied it; primarily because she was suspected of being the biggest whore in the district and also because he respected her husband too much. The couple were constantly at loggerheads and if rumour could be believed, one of the reasons for their unhappy union was that they were unable to have children. Neither of them would submit to a medical examination and for this reason, they blamed each other for the situation. But now Miss Ward was answering and inwardly castigating himself; Bob decided that, like his small charges, he must learn to pay attention!

"Yes, and what is more, she wants me to go. She says - she says that I could probably contact old friends..." Here the deprived spinster cast her eyes down and thinking that she had displayed too much of her emotions, went back to fiddling with the magazines on the counter.

Bob Allen looked up sharply. After all those years, constancy. A rare thing. He wondered if she still kept things like her engagement ring and the letters from her 'Tommy' at the front. Here was a woman with incredible fortitude. A woman who, given a chance, would have remained faithful forever. A direct contrast to Lizzie Johnson and her promiscuity. A woman, who had been beautiful, didn't realise it and in all probability, had never consciously set out to hurt a man.

He didn't know what to say, but recovering, gave Emily Ward a bright smile and made as if to leave. "I don't suppose it'll hurt," he said, "now if you'll excuse me, I really will have to go before the little so-and-sos start running riot."

"I wonder," murmured the shopkeeper wearily, as the door shut behind him and the Armstrong Siddeley roared off in the direction of Gloucester. She began re-stacking an untidy pile of detergent packets at the back of the shop, but did not get very far before the doorbell sounded again and in walked Lizzie Johnson.

"Mornin', Emily." Cometh the hour, cometh the woman? And Miss Ward had no option but to disguise her enmity and serve her.

EIGHT

Displaying an inscrutability which would not have disgraced the legendary Chinaman, Mr Brain the roadman continued clearing the pavement in School Lane and tried to ignore the 'droves' of chattering mums who, like slaves released from the galley, had left their kitchen sinks in order to attend the school concert. This unmissable event in the village calendar provided a chance to witness their various offspring in a variety of roles and often produced highly original entertainment; much of it unrehearsed and as a result, unwittingly humorous.

Several cars had gingerly traversed the now treacherous lane and out of one of them stepped the almost childlike figure of Lizzie Johnson. This caused the roadman to pause in his snow shovelling, to place a foot on the blade of his spade and to adopt an attitude normally more in keeping with a less conscientious breed of British workmen.

"Afternoon, Mr Brain." Despite the slippery conditions, Lizzie bounded across the lane, bent on foisting her unwanted company on the startled roadman. "Keeps you fit, this weather, doesn't it?"

For what must have been a full minute, he contemplated her, then, as a prelude to saying something quite portentous, coughed and resumed his labours.

"I don' do it fur me 'ealth, Mrs Johnson." A simple statement, made with considerable gravitas and a modicum of contempt.

"Could I have a go? Great fun, clearing snow!" Lizzie made to grasp the sacred shovel and the outraged roadman recoiled with horror. This attempt upon his statutory and territorial rights was unthinkable.

"I be zorry, Mrs Johnson, but this bist my szovel an' my job. I daime you wouldn't like me t' come up The Green an' zort out your kitchen fur y'!"

The aspirant snow remover shrugged and laughed derisively; an unconvincing, low pitched effort. She spread her arms wide. "Huh, as a matter of fact, you'd be very welcome. Needs someone other than a lazy madam like me to take over! Still haven't done last night's washing up. However, I must go. Nice to see you. Bye for now." She skipped into the school just as the gaggle of women, nearly all recognisable as the mothers of the entertainers they had come to see, drew level and out of courtesy, Mr Brain had to touch his cap and mumble almost incoherent salutations to 'Mrs Arnold', 'Mrs Marshall', 'Mrs Wood' and those others of his acquaintance that merited the greeting. They and those that followed, were soon amid the glitter and glamour of the school hall, decorated profusely and provided by a local builder with a makeshift stage. This shaky construction had a moth-eaten curtain draped before it and a sign above, which proclaimed to all a MERRY CHRISTMAS. The partition in the middle of the hall had been thrown back and somehow the entire school plus visitors had managed to defy the old adage about not putting a quart into a pint pot. The high Victorian window sills were filled with small forms dangling legs displaying grubby kneecaps and the main body of the auditorium consisted of gossiping mums, a few reluctant dads and a small knot of allegedly distinguished guests. Amongst these were Maude Langford; that creaking representative of the local aristocracy, Mrs Coningby-Wilson and the notorious alcoholic and unofficial 'Lord of the Manor,' Sir Arthur Wilton. The latter gentleman owned half the parish, imbibed too freely and owed his position entirely to feudal ancestry and the careful and not always honest manipulations of discreditable relatives engaged in dubious practices in the City.

After a short welcome from Mr Jeremy, the first item was a carol led by the school choir - a euphemistic term for a polyglot chorus of older pupils, some of whom could sing and the rest coerced to make up the numbers. This took some time to be activated, due to the fact that Mr Jones at the piano had mislaid his spectacles. He could not function without them and after a frantic search and inherent intuition engendered by a decade or two of experience, found them on top of the music stool, ready to be sat upon. He had no time to seek out the culprit and somewhat flustered, launched into a flamboyant 'ark the 'erald' with one or two naturals creeping into the uncomfortable sharp laden key signature.

There followed a nativity play by the infants and after some difficulty in revealing the scene on stage through the stubbornness of the curtains to part, the audience were treated to the sweet sight of Louise Marshall, aged five, nursing a big china doll with the choir trying to murmur 'We will rock you' in the background. Various 'oohs' and 'aahs' greeted this touching scene and after carefully adjusting her headdress and robe - a heavily disguised sheet - Louise laid baby Jesus none too gently in the manger and standing stock still, sang the second verse all on her own. This further affected the maternal instincts in the audience; handkerchiefs were applied to corners of brimming eyes and at its conclusion the sturdy figure of Joseph made his grand entrance. In a strong accent, which could best be described as 'erefordshire Gallilean, he shouted in strained and high pitched tones, "'ow are you today, Mary?"

Mary replied demurely and undaunted. Joseph announced that there were 'three shep'erds come t' call on baby Jesus' and 'should he let 'un in?"

Mary gracefully assented and a trio of infantile sheep minders carrying walking sticks cleverly disguised as crooks, tramped over the boards and one by one, peered into the manger.

"What a lovely child," asserted the first shepherd.

"'ee iz beautiful," confirmed the second.

"'iz 'ee truly the Son of God?" questioned the third, backing away behind the others; evidently relieved to have successfully carried off such a demanding role.

"Yes 'ee iz," replied the Virgin, as if intending to quash all mankind's doubts about the matter, and encouraged by Mr Jones's more relaxed introduction, everyone was invited to sing *While Shepherds Watched.* This carol concluded, the Three Shepherds tumbled off to sparse applause and after four abortive attempts; the recalcitrant curtains were made to meet in the middle by sheer brute force. After much coughing and whispering, they opened again to reveal the happy couple sitting together and somewhere offstage – actually out in the corridor - could be heard a trio of hesitant croaking voices proclaiming that despite heavy, localised accents, they were from afar and undeniably of Oriental lineage. These disembodied voices soon materialised into three strutting kings, attired in rejected eiderdown material - ensconced precariously upon their untidy locks - with crowns devised of cardboard and decorated with gold paint. During this dramatic entrance, one of these illustrious personages tripped over his predecessor's train and fell; revealing his off-white underpants and spoiling the effect created by his coal dust engrained physiognomy. As the laughter caused by this incident subsided and the poor unfortunate hastily recovered, the first king greeted the parents of Jesus in squeaky, but magisterial tones.

"We bring you gifts," he pronounced, "of gold, frank-frankincense and-and-myrrh." And having enunciated this with very careful diction, he became distressed and harangued his second-in-command in a sibilant whisper. "We ant got the presents, 'enry. Go off an' get 'em!"

Startled, the second king jumped off the stage and fumbled about underneath for the missing gifts, which took some time to locate. Meanwhile, all the actors stood about awkwardly, until number two monarch - alias young Henry Wood - found what he was looking for and breathlessly returned to join them.

"'ere iz my gift of gold," said the first king, handing over a brown parcel and "'ere is my gift of frankincense," added the restored Henry Wood, showing great aplomb and equanimity.

"An' 'ere-an' 'ere iz..." but poor Melchior, who was having a sad time of it one way or another, found that his parcel had not been secured properly and had to content himself with handing over the utilitarian contents; two pieces of wood left over from the stage construction.

With a rousing rendition of *We three Kings*, the scene ended without further incident and a 'Chorus of Angels' - all painstakingly and lovingly dressed by their proud mothers - arrived to take over and were shortly joined by a motley selection of animals; all come to pay homage to Jesus. By now well in his stride, Mr Jones played the introduction to *O Come all Ye Faithful* and the entire company, plus choir and audience set up a jubilant, if slightly out-of-tune noise, which rounded off the not exactly flawless, but sterling performance. Tumultuous applause followed and after several lengthy curtain calls, everyone waited expectantly for the next act.

Encumbered with an instrument almost the size of himself, a terrified Spencer was introduced and though positively green about the gills, rendered a gallant performance on the tenor saxophone of *The Ash Grove*, complete with attempted embellishments and an accompaniment provided by Mr Jones at the piano. This varied anything between half a bar and two in difference, according to whether Spencer's attempts to cope with the difficulties involved, meant slowing the tempo in places or making another attempt at bits he got wrong. By some miracle, the two instrumentalists managed to finish together and amid clamouring for more from the audience, Spencer launched into his unique version of *On the Sunnyside of the Street*, which meant having two 'goes' at the high note in the middle whilst all thoughts of time and rhythm were totally disregarded. During this 'number', Mr Jones so far forgot himself to revive memories of his NAFFI canteen days with a stomping second chorus and those that appreciated this display of jazzy pianistics were not slow to clap and tap their feet in time. Amused by his normally staid colleague's performance, Bob Allen thought it might be an idea to exploit Jonesey's latent talents in the pub at the weekend and wondered if the sober deputy head would acquiesce. Bob resolved that there would be no harm in asking and awoke from his musings just in time to applaud an exhausted Spencer, who bowed very formally and fled the scene.

Members of Form Three then gratified Bob Allen by giving a creditable 'Christmas Recitation' and were followed by Martin Lewis who, unknown to his tutors, looked fast on the way to becoming a conjuror of some ability. Unfortunately, he accompanied his tricks with some homespun anecdotes, some of which were in dubious taste and Mr Jeremy had to hastily intervene by saying, "Thank you, Martin," before going on to introduce the next performers.

This was a display of country dancing by a mixed company who, hampered by the limitations of the stage, got in the sort of hopeless tangle, which would have caused the illustrious Sir Roger de Coverly to turn over in his grave. Disentanglement of the dancers was eventually achieved and the stage set for a play by senior pupils. Based on a well-known Dickens story, it provided a vehicle for some very inept and apathetic acting; the highlight and most exciting bit happening when the lights failed and the already beleaguered Bob Cratchet, unconsciously making a desperate attempt to instil some drama into the performance, fell off the boards on to the piano. This caused startling reverberations, but aware that virtually anything can happen in teaching, the alert Mr Jones caught the lad and making sure of his well-being, set him back on stage; where he once more had to encounter the not very intimidating wrath of a feeble Ebenezer Scrooge. Compared to the fare provided at the beginning by the infants, it was poor and perhaps typified the general attitude of the performers, quite a number of whom were to leave at the end of the academic year.

The concert concluded with a prayer and the lights - now in full glow again - and another hearty bout of carol singing by all present. Mr Jeremy finished by thanking all the 'hard-working staff and performers' and Sir Arthur Wilton, who had hopefully managed to subdue his alcoholic propensities for the evening, mounted the stage to deliver the prizes. Despite his weakness, he spoke with the accustomed ease that is usually the way of the 'privileged few' and pre-warned as to what would happen if they misbehaved during his speech. The children complied, creating a rare interlude when not one, but several pins could be heard falling about the place.

"It gives me great pleasure, boys and gals, to be with you this afternoon, especially after such a splendid show." His oration went on with that deeply ingrained 'gift of the gab' beloved of the British aristocracy and he finally distributed the prizes, with a special one going to John Taylor, whose appearance on crutches was the signal for heart-warming applause. He had made a tremendous effort to be present on this very last day of term and sympathetic acclaim was further shown when he received the very latest book on flora and fauna from Sir Arthur, who graciously left the stage to present it.

Redoubtably having the last crotchet, Mr Jones struck up the national anthem and this being sung in desultory fashion, Mr Jeremy stood by the entrance bidding goodbye to everyone and Bob Allen, exhausted by the term's events and glad it was all over, assisted in controlling the deluge of humanity who struggled to get out.

Some hours later, having helped to put things away with the rest of the staff and all the usual willing parents who stopped to assist, Bob Allen set out for Ross. He was soon warming himself in front of his landlady's kitchen stove and partaking of a cup of tea the like of which he considered no-one else on the planet, except her cousin Mrs Taylor, could make. The lady herself sat at her scrubbed kitchen table, knitting and sporadically going over to the stove to inspect a stew, which tantalised Bob Allen's nostrils and permeated the entire household.

"What time would you be goin' 'ome, Mr Allen?"

"Soon after breakfast tomorrow. I don't think the roads are too bad."

"I 'opes not. You don't want t' take no risks!"

"Don't worry, Mrs Adderly, I shan't."

Reminded of something, the landlady put down her knitting and waddled over to the big Welsh dresser, which took up much of the room in the small kitchen.

"I nearly forgot. This come for you this mornin'." She handed over a small envelope with a French stamp franked 'Le Havre,' and though affected by a sudden frisson of excitement, Bob did not want to read the contents in front of her and placed it in the inside pocket of his jacket.

"Don' you want to read it?" The personification of inquisitive landladies, Mrs Adderly expressed disappointment.

"No, it'll do after tea. No hurry."

"Well, you might as well sit down. It's about ready." She ladled a generous portion of the steaming concoction on to a plate and despite his preoccupation; her paying guest could not resist the aroma, which was equally matched by the taste. After sago pudding and a coffee, he hurried upstairs with the envelope and lit a Woodbine, which had not been supplanted by a bullseye. In his haste to read the contents, he tore at it haphazardly and cursed when he discovered he had damaged a small, but artistic Christmas card. He fumbled in opening it and devoured the words in almost the same fashion that he had devoured Mrs Adderly's sumptuous stew.

Then the day went black. Margaret would not be coming home. With an excellent command of French, she had landed a job as an English teacher in a Le Havre school. She was sorry, very sorry, but that was the way it was. For the moment, this was the only way she could cope with things and hoped he would accept it. She wished him a merry Christmas and... He did not read the rest of it. He slowly crumpled it up in his fist and consigned it to the waste paper basket; resolving when Mrs Adderly was out of the way, to burn it in the kitchen Rayburn.

The distraught schoolmaster drank a bottle of Irish and smoked twenty cigarettes in two hours. Destroyed, he then dragged himself into bed. In the morning he would drive home to spend an agonising Christmas with his family in Shropshire and dear God, he thought, I'd let the rest of the world have Jesus if I could only have Margaret.

NINE

Lizzie Johnson walked up the church steps amid the gentry with their Sunday best and their exaggerated accents. The Sunday ceremony again, she thought. Sometimes she wondered if this contradiction, this enigmatic behaviour, stemmed through an obsession with the supernatural. The bells thundered forth and the morning, a fresh March forenoon, clad itself in a maddingly type of cheerful holiness as the large saloons purred to a halt and disgorged their smartly attired passengers. Fate decreed that if you didn't come to Waterton Church in a Bentley or a new Rover, you walked. This morning, she supposed, there would be the usual preamble with Easter in mind. The newly-installed vicar was a young man, an unusually urbane and man-of-the world type, endowed with blond hair and a fine figure.

The bells hove to in that lingering, almost reluctant manner they had and the five minute tolling, interrupted by coughs and whispering from the children, preceded the choir's entrance. A hymn was announced and Lizzie joined in with the rest; a pious bleating, a strictly controlled and very English raising of voices to the Lord. Lizzie Johnson knelt and during the spot reserved for quiet private prayer, attempted to banish the visions of last night's experiences, which impeded dangerously and provokingly. Was it possible that even here she could not be free of this alien element; the very antithesis of all this sacred building allegedly stood for?

"And now to God the Father..." The sermon was over, the last hymn sung, before Lizzie Johnson noticed the doctor's daughter and they walked side by side into the porch. It must have been half-term for the girl to be home and Lizzie answered positive and negative, hoping she was getting them in the right order. She thought the teenager looked peaky and had put on weight and wondered if being in the sixth form meant you were able to shun games; not a desirable thing for any young person, let alone a doctor's child. Out of the corner of her eye she noticed the young clergyman stood at the lych-gate bidding farewell to his recently acquired flock. She exchanged pleasantries with the doctor, who came out with his aloof wife to collect their irritating daughter and after their departure, felt free to approach the priest.

"And how are you enjoying Waterton?" she asked, noting his eager expression and speculating about his age.

"I'm enjoying it, thank you, Mrs Johnson," he replied. "Though," he resumed quietly, "it needs a bit of reformation."

Lizzie flushed and sensed an opportunity. "How about coming up to the farm for a coffee?"

"Perhaps another time. I'm sorry and thank

you, but the Coningby-Wilsons have invited me to dinner. I don't really want to go, but after that sermon, I suppose I have to appease the gentry!"

Not having assimilated a word of the meek being able to inherit the earth, she noted his beguiling smile and said, "you preach very well, but it means I can't go to sleep any more!"

He was not a flaccid hand shaker and there was warmth about him. She would have liked to linger, but realising that those behind her might want a word, she returned his smile and made her way to her car. Without his knowledge, she studied him for a while and fumbled around in her handbag for her car keys. A base instinct told her she would eventually seduce him. A clerical notch was not something she had managed so far and with her record in such matters, she didn't think it would pose too many problems. She clambered into her car and acknowledging various waves as she drove down the lane to the main road, turned right and sped erratically through the bends and along the flat until, half way along, took a left turn up the road to The Green.

There, before the large kitchen range, sat her large, brooding husband, with his large calloused hands and his large, odorous sheepdog, Katie.

"Am I to get any dinner?" He'd been out tending the stock all morning and didn't think it too much to ask. Lizzie was not an advocate of regular mealtimes and where food was concerned, did not treat Sunday like any other day. She sighed, but supposed she would have to comply.

"What would you like?" Her voice descended about a fifth and contained more than a hint of asperity.

"What I'd like and what I can get you to cook are two entirely different things." He said this in tones long suffering and resigned.

"I'll do you some cauliflower cheese."

"On a Sunday?"

"You know I hate cooking."

"And you know I don't actually enjoy being up half the night late lambing, milking cattle early in the morning and sitting on a tractor with the wind cutting me to the bloody marrow, but I bloody well do it! We've got two hundred head of sheep on this farm, as well as the milkers and it seems we're breeding all these lambs for someone else to eat. It'd been pleasant to have a lamb chop on the table for a change!"

Lizzie Johnson shrugged, the very embodiment of uncaring.

"You had meat the other day."

He laughed derisively. "Sorry, I must have forgotten. Cold ham takes a lot of cooking."

She remained obdurate. "Well, do you want me to do cauliflower cheese or not? You can please yourself. I'm going out this afternoon, so don't be too long making up your mind.

"When are you not going out?" He said this

with scorn and a little resignation.

She gave him a penetrating stare and stood defiant, hands on hips. “We agreed. You go your way, I go mine.” She began the limited preparations necessary for the controversial meal, set it upon the cooker and as if looking for some means to vent her frustrations at having to deal with this man, suggested it was about time he gave Katie and himself a bath, preferably in the same water. She averred that one of the cattle troughs would be suitable, as she did not want her white bathing place besmirched by the grime from his and the innocent canine’s body.

William Johnson ignored her petulance, lit a cigarette and as if wishing to assuage any hurt sustained by his loving companion, gently fondled Katie by the ears.

“By the way,” he said, “I think I’ve let the cottage, should it interest you.”

This did elicit mild interest from her. “Who to?”

“Pleasant young couple. At least, I thought they were. Came up this morning. Saw the advert. He’s some sort of designer or architect. He did say. Works in Ross. Attractive girl, the wife. Looks like she’s got Red Indian blood in her. Says she’ll come and help in the house if you want her too.”

“Good, then perhaps she’ll cook the odd meal...”

A deep bellied chuckle erupted from William.

"With a baby and a husband to look after? Pigs might fly. I think she was meaning housework." And sarcastically he went on, "I should be grateful, because some of the cobwebs in this place have been here since Elizabethan days."

He resumed his introspective posture and ignoring his facetiousness, Lizzie half-heartedly busied herself with the meal, throwing the cutlery on the table and snatching a brief look at the Sunday paper. The front doorbell rang and Lizzie impatiently ran through the rambling farmhouse to see whether the intrusion should prove interesting.

"Oh, it's you. I've told you before to come round the back. I don't particularly like having to tear through the house to deal with your trivialities. What d'you want, anyway?"

These encounters with the hapless Mildred Fryer could take aeons and not possessed of much sympathy, Lizzie tried to hurry things along.

"Sorry, Mrs Johnson. I's a nice day, ent it? I can't be stoppin' long. I've got Mike's dinner in the oven and then there's the grave t' see to this afternoon. I's a long time since I'ave took flowers. 'ee was so good t' me, Mr Garner wuz. I wouldn't like 'im t' think 'ee wuz forgotten. No, indeed not, that'd be terrible. I wuz only zayin' to Mrs Langford the other day; you know, the doctor's wife-I does fur 'er a bit when Mrs Taylor can't - I wuz only sayin'..."

"What do you want, Mildred?" Consumed with impatience, Lizzie spoke coldly and sharply.

"I'm sorry; Mrs Johnson, but I found this in the yard. You must 'u dropped it. Yes, that's what you must 'u done. Anyway, I did promise 'im I'd gow. D'you think 'ee'd like some daffies? Mike thinks 'ee would. 'ee give me 'alf-a-crown, said Mr Garner 'ud like 'alf-a-crown's worth of daffies on 'iz grave. 'ere it iz, Mrs Johnson." Mildred handed over a small white shoe box, which she drew out of a shopping basket and Lizzie tried to look grateful. She felt overwhelmingly relieved, but could not think where she had mislaid it. Then she remembered. She'd got out of the car last night and in order to lock it, put the shoebox nearby and promptly walked into the farmhouse without it. Her mouth went dry as she touched the box and minute beads of sweat disfigured her forehead. Gratitude was not a thing the farmer's wife normally displayed in abundance, but she did offer the poor woman perfunctory thanks, shut the door and left her to go away, gibbering to herself as she departed.

Mounting the oak staircase at the end of the hallway, Lizzie scuttled along the creaking floorboards to her bedroom and exhaling with relief, opened a drawer and put the shoebox within. She undressed and stood naked before the full length mirror. My body, she thought, at least it had been her body before William Johnson had taken it, coolly shunned it and cast it aside for his many successors to partake of it. There was just a glimmering of protuberance around the lower regions and her quim had the odd grey hair, but her small breasts were still firm and her forehead showed little signs of what could be termed the ravages of sexual promiscuity and advancing years. Otherwise unspoilt, she reflected, though not infrequently abused. She exited the bedroom, crossing to the bathroom to shower and having done so, returned to dress, touched up her make-up and went downstairs.

"Had you forgotten something?"

"Oh, shit, the dinner!"

"It's alright. I rescued it. I don't understand you."

Famous words of incomprehension which will probably be said by mankind about womankind until the end of time.

The big farmer sat down and with visible distaste, began to eat wholly unappetising cauliflower cheese. The animals almost ate more lavishly than he did and on several occasions he'd had recourse to go down to the pub, where the jovial Mrs Phil was just beginning to venture into catering for a few of the locals.

"I don't need you to understand me." A brusque and hurtful reply, full of bitterness and disinterest.

"For God's sake. You're still my wife!"

"In name only. It's a pity I can't afford to do

anything about it."

William remained silent. Lizzie and not Katie, he thought, should be called a bitch.

The Donaldsons had settled in. He went to work on the bus at eight-thirty every morning and she usually set about the cottage before going over to the farmhouse for a couple of hours. Pamela Donaldson found the farmer's wife a pleasant enough person and yet there was a strange almost childish air about the woman. Almost as if she concealed a supreme misery beneath a shield of immature jocularity. This uneasy demeanour showed its ugly face in unguarded moments. Lizzie Johnson could be derisory and short-tempered without apparent cause and Pamela at first attributed this to the obviously strained relationship between the wife and husband. But as time progressed, she suspected something more. For some indefinable and illogical reason, she began to actively dislike entering the farmhouse with baby Sarah, upon whom Lizzie lavished great attention and generosity and she conveyed this uneasiness to her cavalier husband upon his return from work one day.

"I think you're just imagining things," he opined in his sometimes too dismissive manner.

Pamela was not impressed. "I don't know. I can't make it out. You never know where you are with her. She's so mer-merc-what's that word you use sometimes?"

He came to her rescue. "'Mercurial' and I wouldn't try understanding the woman. You know what they tell me about her down the pub?"

Pamela's large nut-brown eyes gleamed and she pushed her hair back, exposing her fine Indian profile and her high cheekbones.

There was a hint of mischief in her voice and she said, "so what do they tell you Mr Clever Cloggs?"

Her husband took a swig of Weston's cider and chuckled. "Just that she's the local charity."

"Really?"

"It's pretty certain."

Pamela feigned indignance. "Well, if that's so, I'm not letting you anywhere near her!"

Tom Donaldson forsook his cider, jumped up from his chair and encircled his young wife round the waist.

"One man's meat is another man's poison and what need have I of other wenches with a gorgeous creature like you around?" He slapped her bottom and she simulated a protest in a feeble, but wholly unconvincing manner.

"Do stop it, Tom," she said half-heartedly and sincerely hoped he wouldn't. And the springs on the bedstead needed oiling.

TEN

Free for the holidays, Arnold and Woody walked boldly along the track, which swathed its sinuous way through the spring wood. On either side, whimberry bushes sprouted with promise and the pale green mantle of awakening trees complimented the fast moving clouds above. If you cared to climb one of the sturdy, mature silver birches, you had before you, the best of two counties: to the east the orchards and Forest of Gloucester and to the west, the undulating beauty of the border country, with the imposing Welsh mountains towering behind. In this delicious middle world, boys could play, unfettered by urban restrictions; their only immediate horizon a job as a farmhand or some other rural pursuit, which would hopefully keep them in their natural environment from birth to death. That this would change with improved educational facilities and the advent of light industry had not occurred to them and as through every age, childhood was a thing to be held on to for as long as possible.

A scud of unreliable April caused the pair to take temporary refuge under an isolated yew and with that constitution of the junior male, which enables him to be impervious to all weathers; they sat on a damp low-lying branch reviewing the situation.

"Wunt be much," observed Woody. High up a grey squirrel flitted through the branches and Arnold let fly at it with his lethal homemade catapult; missing the small creature by several feet, as he had fully intended to do.

For want of something to occupy himself, Woody began to whittle a stick, which he had acquired from the willow tree that overhung the stream near his house. Unfortunately, it was still sap-laden and frustratingly his efforts ended in fracture. In disgust, he threw it aside and resolved to wait for the summer when the tree would be dried out and sufficiently mellowed for him to make a strong, homespun longbow and a host of arrows. Woody's forebears were probably largely instrumental in turning the torrid Battle of Agincourt for Henry V and some of this spirit evidently manifested itself in the small boy, for he had once been known to illicitly bring down an out-of-season pheasant from a distance of a hundred yards.

Restless and exploratory, Arnold wandered round the trunk of the big yew tree - in itself a curious thing to find in the middle of a deciduous wood - and came full circle. And as he did so, it stopped raining. "Hey, Woody", he said. "There's a track be'ind. I've never bin up it. Don' know where it goes."

"Course y' don't, y' daft bugger, if y' ent bin along it," affirmed his positive friend. "C'mon, let's 'ave a look."

"'ang on a minute." Arnold put two fingers to his mouth and whistled, alarmingly fortissimo. This signal was shortly followed by a desperate scuffling in the undergrowth and soon Mugsy, a mangy terrier, who had achieved the unlikely distinction of being co-owned by both the boys, made a breathless appearance. Woody appeared to think that the little dog needed some reassuring and patted his head with one hand while scratching his battle-scarred ears with the other.

"Never mind, Muggs, y' silly sod," he consoled. You'll never catch a bloody rabbit uz long uz you lives, so y' might uz well come along with us." Now complete with the accompanying mongrel, the two friends plunged into the unknown. How in all their ramblings they had come to miss this particular fox trail, they were at a loss to understand, particularly as only the other day Arnold had boasted of his prowess as the most knowledgeable woodsman in all Waterton. The trail grew darker as coniferous trees usurped the deciduous and pressed about them, blotting out the sky and after about a quarter of a mile of this slightly sinister progress, they suddenly emerged into what was obviously a small manmade clearing. Woody stopped dead in his tracks and Arnold, not expecting this sudden halt, bumped into him.

On the opposite side of this little arena

stood an odd stone construction with a curious framework constructed above it. Dead ashes littered the ground before it; the remains of some quite recently extinguished fire; and looking again at the framework, Arnold realised that the cross centred within it was more like the shape of the swastika, which he'd seen in some of his war comics. With the uncanny sense, which most animals are endowed, Mugsy began to whimper and the two boys stood rooted to the spot, unable to drag themselves away from the scene. Woody eventually plucked up enough courage to go and inspect the edifice and after this uneasy survey, announced with a nonchalance he did not feel, that "it's prob'ly somewhere where ol' 'appy comes t' eat." Why the local hobo, one 'Happy' should have recourse to come here to satisfy his hunger was a matter for considerable conjecture, but the scared Woody hoped this could be a sufficiently plausible explanation and one that would quell the awful forebodings that were assailing him.

Arnold, who had remained with the now quivering dog, was unconvinced.

"There ent no shelter for 'im t' kip in. I don' like it, Woods, I's givin' me the 'willies'. Muggs don' fancy it neither. C'mon, let's go."

Even though fearful and glad he was wearing his brown trousers, the incorrigible Woody was not satisfied. "What d'y' reckon it is then?"

"I dunno. But I don't like it. Feels all wrong t'

me. C'mon, let's bloody well go home!"

A man of decision, he set off back down the fox trail with Muggsy and although still curious, Woody was certainly not prepared to stay on his own, and taking a last look, he shuddered and followed his friend back the way they had come.

Reaching the yew tree, they both slumped on to the same branch and Arnold expressed relief at leaving the incomprehensible scene in the clearing.

But they were not alone.

"And where you two boys bin?" Stocky and aloof, Mike Fryer, cast two dark eyes on them; inciting quite groundless feelings of culpability.

Quite quick-witted when it suited him, Woody spoke up. "We went fur a bit of a walk, then we come back 'cos there wa'n't nothing along there."

"An' what was y' doin' before that?" Mike Fryer was persistent.

Woody was still dogged. "Just shelterin' under 'ere," he said.

"It stopped rainin' some time ago. What you bin doin' since then?"

It was Arnold who saved the situation by adding to the falsehoods. "We knows, but we bin climbin' an' all that, y' see, an' we didn't know what the time wuz." He knew the farmhand did not believe him, but Mike Fryer relented. "Y' better get on 'ome. Yer mams'll be wonderin' where y' bin. It's nearly teatime. Go on, bugger off 'ome and don' waste no time getting' there!"

Glad to escape from both a traumatic experience and big Mike's remonstrances, the boys hurried off and accompanied by the revived Muggsy, were soon in Church Lane and heading for home. Mike Fryer waited until they had disappeared, then rounded the solid yew tree and took the trail the boys had followed some fifteen minutes earlier.

On the way down from the wood, Woody and Arnold met Dudley.

"Hi y'," said Dudley. "I bin lookin' fur you two. Thought you'd be up 'ere."

With time an irrelevancy and all the strictures of coming home by teatime ignored, the three of them deposited themselves in various attitudes around a five-bar gate, talking and masticating on blades of grass. Reluctantly and a little nervously, with one eye over his shoulder, Woody told Dudley of recent events and Dudley did not know what to make of it.

"An' y' say Mr Fryer as'ed y' what you wuz doin'?"

"Yes, an 'ee weren't too 'appy about it, neither. I could see 'im didn't believe uz."

"What d'y' reckon it wuz?"

"I dunno. But I ent goin' near it again!" Always reluctant to display a lack of courage, Arnold made no bones about the matter. He would fight anyone or climb the most hazardous trees; even watch while his dad strangled a fowl for the pot, but this was something different, something unknown.

Woody changed the subject. They were overlooking the Coningby-Wilson's apple orchard and the blossom was beginning to flourish on the trees.

"Good bit o' scrumpin' there in a few months' time."

"More 'n a vew," asserted Dudley, who reckoned the apples wouldn't be ready until well into the autumn.

Arnold was scornful. "Can't see you two buggers comin'. You buggered off when I nearly got caught by ol' Wilson and 'is nasty great Alsatian last year! You were so bloody scared you run in the wood before I 'ad a chance t' get out o' the vield." Glad to forget his own recent discomfort, he vehemently condemned his two companions.

"I wasn't scared," retorted Woody. I didn't want Marion to get caught. 'er dad works fur ol' Wilson an' 'ee'd 'it 'er!"

"Bloody Marion!" commented Dudley, still smarting from the fact that at the time, the flirtatious Marion had preferred the company of Woody rather than him.

"You didn't say 'bloody Marian when you was behind the dubs with 'er the other day..."

"You're only bloody jealous," shouted Dudley,

"just 'cos 'er don't like you no more..."

Infuriated, Woody swung at Dudley who, expecting the onslaught, parried the blow and pushed his adversary on to the damp verge. A wrestling match ensued, with some brutal underhand blows exchanged and then as if resenting a fight taking place, which didn't include him, Arnold pulled Woody off and told the two opponents not to be 'bloody silly'. Feeling his grazed knee and other damage, Dudley stated that he would 'get' Woody and in a fit of umbrage and concealed relief - because he had unusually come off worse - took himself off down the lane, all the while hurling insults at Woody from a safe instance. When he finally disappeared, having delivered a parting burst of derisory comment, Woody leant back against the gate, feeling triumphant, but a little annoyed at not being allowed to score a notable victory. He had never beaten Dudley in the several encounters they'd had previously and expressed his disapproval of Arnold's intervention in no uncertain terms.

Arnold was contemptuous and unrepentant. "'er's only a girl. 'er ent worth fightin' over!" Even at the advanced age of fourteen his interest in the fairer sex did not match his obsession with football or any other sporting contest and he was much more interested in becoming a fearsome fast bowler than meddling with girls.

The conversation lapsed and keen to vent his ire on something, Woody hacked a barely discernible insult about Dudley with a penknife on the topmost bar of the gate, while Arnold made a periodic inspection of his pockets and finding nothing therein but a glutinous mess, decided it was time to go home.

"I'll race you to the church." Woody issued an invitation, which was readily accepted and the pair hammered down the muddy lane; the wind ruffling their hair and the visions of the day banished to the back of their minds.

Half-an-hour later, shoulders hunched against the driving rain, Mike Fryer free-wheeled the same way on a lady's bicycle. His face bore a look of grim determination as he swept from the lane and headed along the main highway. Negotiating the slight gradient of the bends towards Gloucester, he sped along the flat and took the turn for The Green. This had been his afternoon off, a reward for working all day the previous Saturday. On the following Sunday he'd taken the chance to indulge in his only hobby, that of 'ooding-or idly rambling through the woods to forget his troubles. It was then that he had stumbled across the strange stone edifice tucked away within the fir trees. In order to confirm that the discovery was not just a figment of his imagination, he had returned to the scene and after finding the two boys snooping around, made a further inspection.

For some unaccountable reason he'd found

that the ashes-strewn clearing had a magnetic effect upon him, at the same time filling him with a feeling of utter revulsion. He'd convinced himself that the strange 'altar' was intrinsically evil and had torn the delicate lattice work frame to pieces with his bare work-hardened hands and with a mighty heave, incorporating almost every muscle in his body, tumbled the roughly hewn stone base into a ditch, which ran along the back of the clearing.

Now arrived at The Green, he was startled to be summoned by a call from the back kitchen of the farmhouse. Lizzie Johnson came to the open door and Mike couldn't think why she should still be attired in a dressing gown at this time of the afternoon. He approached warily and waited for her to address him.

"Mike, I'm afraid something serious has happened. Would you come in please and I'll tell you about it."

The farmhand hesitated. He did not fancy the idea of entering his employer's wife's sanctuary with her dressed as she was. But Lizzie Johnson insisted. "Come on. Please. I'm getting wet. Don't worry over your boots."

Despite her imprecation to hurry him up, Mike wiped his boots carefully and with nagging misgivings, entered the 'vixen's den'. She gestured towards a chair and he sat astride it, nervously beating his fingers on the kitchen table.

"I'm afraid your wife's had an accident. We didn't know where to find you. She's been taken to Hereford General." Pausing, Lizzie appointed herself uncomfortably near him on another chair. Mike Fryer rose to his feet, his face the colour of putty. The words would not come, but he eventually managed to say, "w-what 'appened?"

"She was walking down School Lane and that old fool, Arthur Wilton can't have seen her or something. They're going to operate shortly. It must be done, Mike. They say she hasn't a chance otherwise. Pamela is looking after George and your mother went with the ambulance to the hospital. In your absence she had to sign the consent form."

He put his head in his hands and tried to control himself, to no avail. "The drunken old sod! They'll fix 'im this time. The ol' bastard shouldn't be drivin'! Oh God, don' let anythin' 'appen t' Mildred! Please don' let anythin' 'appen t' Mildred!"

Lizzie carelessly laid a hand on the big man's shoulder, an action that made him flinch.

"She'll be okay. I've got the kettle on. We'll have a coffee, and then I'll drive you over in the Landy." Lizzie was now purring obscenely, like some feline on heat and he began to suspect her motives. "It's only five now; no point in going yet. There's nothing you can do." She gave off an aroma of bath salts and expensive perfume and as she turned towards the stove, her untied dressing gown flopped open. Mike had read something in a cheap novel about 'milky white breasts'. Horrifically, it almost served to divert his thoughts. He felt a sensation, which he had managed to arrest for years mounting inside him and as Lizzie brought the coffee, she casually let the dressing gown fall apart right down to the floor.

"Interested," she said, giving him a treacherous smile. He looked at the female form before him. The female form, which he had not partaken of for what seemed a lifetime. Then he slowly arose and made for the door.

"But Mike..."

In the yard he came across Pamela Donaldson valiantly retrieving a scarcely dry selection of nappies from the washing line.

"George is okay here for as long as you like, Mike," she said anxiously. "How is it with you?"

Distraught, it took him some time to answer. "I dunno, but I'm goin' t' take the Landrover over to 'ereford. The keys is allus left in it and Will'am wunt mind."

"Okay, then. But I thought Lizzie was going to take you? She said she was."

He lit a cigarette and apologised for doing so.

"Doesn't bother me, but why isn't Lizzie taking you?"

"Huh. Don't ask and the less I have to do with that callous, filthy-minded bitch the better! I'll be off now and I'll ring the pub to let you know what's appenin'. I'm not ringing Lizzie, that's for certain. Thanks for lookin' after George. I take it Will'am did the milking 'fore 'ee went out?"

"Yes, he'd just finished when the news came." She felt desperately sorry for him and returned his farewell as he crossed the yard to the lean-to where the Landrover was kept.

ELEVEN

Recently appointed vicar of Waterton, the Reverend David Oliver was holding a confirmation class at the vicarage. Ninety per cent of what he was saying fell, not unlike the seed of the parable, on stony ground. His youthful audience gazed vacantly, largely uncomprehending, coughing and fidgeting; dumbstruck when questioned and only attending through the diligence of Mr Jeremy in impressing on them that they were in need of the Holy Spirit.

The phone rang, causing the clergyman to pause in his oration to pick up the receiver.

"Mr Oliver?" A deep female voice on the other end of the line.

"Speaking."

"This is Sister Martin from Hereford General Hospital. I wonder if you would mind conveying a message to Michael Fryer who, I believe, lives at The Green in your parish. I'm afraid we've been trying to contact the number he gave at the farm without success. We also tried Dr Langford, but his wife said he was out on calls and though she was prepared to go, it would probably be better coming from you."

"Is it bad news?"

"You knew there'd been an accident.."

"Yes, I was told in the village shop about an hour ago."

"Well, I'm afraid Mildred Fryer passed on at half-past-six. It was touch and go and I'm sure we can rely on you to convey the information to Mr Fryer, if you would, please."

"Of course. I'm sorry and I'll go up there immediately."

"Thank you Vicar and goodbye."

"Goodbye." David Oliver returned the receiver to the cradle and faced his young audience who, by now, were probably consumed with curiosity. He thought they would learn of this latest village tragedy soon enough through the unfailing bush telegraph and in a perverse way, quite looked forward to doing something altruistic for once.

"I'm afraid we'll have to cut it short tonight. I'm sorry, but something has cropped up. I've got to go out. I'll see you all at the same time next week."

The class trooped out. Their hurried and grateful exit accompanied by polite and relieved 'goodnight zirs', did not eradicate their resentment at having to miss an episode of 'Dick Barton, Special Agent' on the radio. This popular detective holding a far higher position in their youthful pantheon than the Holy Spirit, they did not see why they should acknowledge the existence of the unlikely wraith, whose part in the holy triumvirate they found utterly incomprehensible.

With a good private income and a personable manner, David Oliver had found it quite possible to serve both God and mammon. Not in a manner he thought would upset his parishioners, but rather inclining towards a situation, which enabled him to run a state-of-the-art motor, drink a regular amount of beer at home when no-one but himself or a few friends were present and to consume afternoon tea in households high and lowly without, he hoped, favouring any one class of the community. As yet, he had not managed matrimony, but was well served by his doting housekeeper, a Mrs Lyall, who had been recommended by a friend and who tended to his every need. All in all, it was a comfortable existence and should he more or less toe the line, he hoped it would, as the Good Book says, guarantee an extension into eternity. He was constantly trying to persuade his flock to concern themselves with this possibility, but most of the time felt that a losing battle was his. His present task was not a pleasant one, but he resolved to get it over quickly. Notice of death was always difficult to convey, especially in this case and despite the fact that he'd notched up quite a few through unfortunate accidents, he was still worried whether he could accomplish the task with sufficient tact and compassion.

Halfway up the lane, which led to The

Green, good fortune or the Holy Spirit conspired to make him meet the Landy with Mike Fryer in it, coming down. A brief exchange made the farmworker reverse into a gateway and the clergyman followed him back to his cottage near the farmhouse.

David Oliver delivered the grave news with as much sympathy as he could muster and Mike Fryer sat mutely staring at the pallid green sitting room wall which, in a prominent position, displayed a print of Constable's 'The Haywain'. An idyllic picture and not far removed from the present day scenario in Waterton. The normally phlegmatic countryman did not want to believe it. Then he said quietly, "could she be laid next to old Mr Garner? I know 'er'd like that."

Also quietly, the young Vicar replied in the affirmative and said that he'd discuss the arrangements later if that was what Mike wanted.

A knock at the door preceded the arrival of Pamela and Tom Donaldson with freckle-faced George. Pamela had seen Mike quickly return, had guessed what had happened and thought it best to bring the boy home. Father and son embraced and Pamela suggested she should go into the kitchen and make tea. They would of course go if Mike wanted them to, but though in obvious distress, with the distraught George clinging to him, he managed to approve of her first suggestion and she left the stricken pair, intent on making a strong brew. A few minutes later she returned with a tray and a glass of 'Tizer' for George and not long after, expressing his deepest sympathy once more, David Oliver gave them all his blessing and departed. He said he would call again on the morrow and after seeing him out, Tom Donaldson came back and asked Mike if they should also go or stay awhile.

Stunned, Mike Fryer eventually summoned up enough awareness. "I'd like y' t' stay awhile. Then I must get over t' 'ereford to see Mildred and pick up Mam who's still there. Poor Mam, 'er's 'ad it all t' do'."

There was a long silence and after pouring more tea, Pamela sat on the sofa and pulled the stricken George to her, encasing him in what she thought might be a consoling hug.

"It's my fault," his father said, "shouldn't 'ave done what I done this addernoon. It's all my fault."

Tom Donaldson answered this plaintive cry by putting an arm round him. Now was not the time to hide behind some sort of macho stoicism.

"Course it's not, Mike. Why should it be your fault?"

"Shoul 'ave bin 'ere. 'stead of careerin' round the 'ood adder things what 'ad nothin' t' do with me. Should 'ave bin 'ere lookin' after Mildred on me addernoon off. Astin' fur trouble, it was."

The Donaldsons had no notion as to

what Mike Fryer was alluding, but frantically searching something helpful to say, Pamela asked if Mike would like Tom to go with him to the hospital.

"No thanks, but if you'd just 'ave George 'til I get back."

The heartbroken boy protested that he wanted to go to the hospital with his dad and not possessing the will to refuse, Mike Fryer agreed to let him come. This was not a decision the Donaldsons really approved of, but were powerless to prevent. Do you allow a ten-year-old to see a corpse, even if it is that of his mother? Tom Donaldson thought not, but did not dare intervene.

A trouper, Gran Fryer took over all the funeral arrangements and unable to cope, Mike Fryer was glad that she did so. The end of the month of April brought heavy precipitation and Mildred Fryer was laid to rest in an unseasonably sultry thunderstorm. Her husband was riven with regrets for destroying something he had now come to believe had been a place for offering a paean of praise to the Devil. Had he not seen it with his own eyes, he would scarcely have imagined it credible, but the thought of what black litany might have been carried out before it, filled him with dread and made him physically tremble.

Mildred Fryer was buried in the spot she so frequently inhabited in life. Next to Mr Garner, her old organist friend. Wreaths came from nearly everyone in the village except Sir Arthur Wilton, who sat in his study on the tempestuous afternoon, contemplating the likelihood of being prosecuted. As there were no witnesses, it would be straightforward. Yet he knew he had killed Mildred Fryer and that he could be convicted of manslaughter, but by the time the local constable had arrived, he had sobered sufficiently to give a good simple explanation which PC Adam readily accepted. Sir Arthur was also a local magistrate and this may have influenced the police decision not to press charges. His story that Mildred had simply stepped in front of his car without looking was accepted and this was partially true, though had he not drunk four Scotches before the tragedy occurred, his reactions would not have been dulled and the accident might well have been averted.

On the large bureau, which stood in what had once been the grand hall of the stately manor house, stood a bottle of 'Johnny Walker's' and Sir Arthur picked up a glass from a cabinet and walked over to it. He unscrewed it and with a faltering hand, began to pour. He then walked over to the latticed windows of the wondrous Elizabethan mansion and making to partake of a dram, resisted the temptation and set the glass down on a windowsill. Returning across the vast room to where the bottle still stood, he picked it up, surveyed it briefly; and then flung it against the wall and the expensive striped Regency wallpaper. Glass splintered everywhere and the 'nectar' lovingly prepared from crystal clear Scottish burn water, dribbled plaintively down the green and white stripes. This accomplished, Arthur Wilton, Knight of the Bath, Magistrate, Vice-Chairman of Herefordshire County Council and near alcoholic, slumped heavily into a chair with tears - aping the course of the violently decanted whisky - running freely down his cheeks.

Now only hampered by a slight limp, John Taylor mounted the church steps with grit and sheer determination. In one hand he clasped a bunch of late daffodils. Where he had acquired these was a matter for conjecture, but he'd been talking to Mrs Fryer just the day before the accident and he wanted to pay tribute. A creature of habit, she had once more been busy in tidying up the old organist's resting place. He knew she liked daffodils and coming to the fresh earth mound beside Mr Garner's grave, he placed his offering amongst the many wreaths and stood back with head bowed.

A house martin flew into the sanctuary provided by the church eaves and quietly approaching, the boy looked up to see a newly-crafted nest, which he decided should on this occasion remain inviolate. Here would soon be hatched new life and for once, he decided with a bout of selflessness bordering on masochism, that his prized egg collection could well survive without any addition being made to it.

TWELVE

Doctor Langford whittled a few minutes out of his crowded schedule to purchase a wad of tobacco at the village shop.

"How's your sister?" he enquired of Miss Emily, having a few months previously treated Miss Lucy for depression.

"Much better, thank you. Particularly since you persuaded her to give up that wretched business."

The doctor grinned. "No more messages from the occult?"

"No thank goodness, Doctor." Miss Emily showed sudden consternation. "But I am being very remiss. What can I be getting for you?"

Slightly guiltily, the medical man requested two ounces of tobacco and as he did so, the doorbell gave off its uncertain scraping noise and Bob Allen walked in; instigating the commencement of a three-way conversation.

"Back to the Woodbines, then Bob?" Dr Langford's eyes displayed a smidgeon of amusement.

"'fraid so, Doctor."

"Won't help that cough, you know. Let alone anything else."

"People in glass houses," began Bob.

"Not so harmful," interrupted the doctor

quickly.

The schoolteacher smoothly and tactfully dealt with this minor impasse. “Nevertheless, old Walter Raleigh has a lot to answer for. It’s always been a source of wonder to me why the Irish race has turned out no fatter on average than most other nationalities. I suppose heavy smoking must offset the bad effects of stout and the ‘murphy.’

The doctor laughed. “I used to know a very obese Irishman. Although to my knowledge, he neither smoked, drank nor ate a lot, thus, I suppose hoisting me with my own petard!”

Prompted by all this talk of excessive habits, Miss Emily cautiously asked after the health of Sir Arthur Wilton.

Mindful of his professional conduct, Dr Langford was non-committal and realising she had maybe been a little indiscreet, Miss Ward resorted to her usual ploy when flustered by fiddling with the magazines on the counter.

After further exchanges of less controversial things in the village, Bob Allen and Dr Langford left together, continuing their light banter until the doctor had to excuse himself. Time pressed hard when you had a selection of bad backs, ‘flu, gout and sundry diseases to attend; all of which had to be appeased in a couple of hours. As it happened, things went well and after re-assuring a couple of bed-resting expectant mothers and making all his other calls with surprising and unusual rapidity, the doctor drove down the long gravel drive to the imposing Waterton Hall, avoiding the glorious peacock and his consorts and pulling up outside the front door.

A cousin, who owed her presence in the Wilton household through premature impecunity, opened the impressive iron-studded entrance and beckoned Dr Langford inside. The woman had a kind, but unimpressive face and the doctor imagined her existence as housekeeper to the irascible and drink-sodden old knight would not be an easy one. There had been a Lady Wilton who sadly died from the ravages of cancer and this circumstance had largely been responsible for causing Sir Arthur to hit the bottle. The doctor made his way to a small tastefully furnished drawing room full of eclectic antiques and being apparently sufficiently sober to perceive the GP straight away, the landowner motioned to an armchair opposite his own; both these relics of gracious living reflecting the glow of a log fire, oddly out of place on a mild spring afternoon.

"Good afternoon, Henry." Hands clasped under his chin, which gave him a wistful look, Sir Arthur addressed Henry Langford with accustomed familiarity. They were old friends and this was more of a social visit, given priority over any medical concerns which the doctor might have about Sir Arthur as a patient.

"Good afternoon, Arthur." Henry Langford dropped the title when with Sir Arthur in his own home, but always found it incumbent on him to use it when they had company; a courtesy he was sure his patient and friend appreciated.

On the glass-topped coffee table in front of the knight, an empty chess board had been placed and the pieces lay in haphazard fashion round and about it. This was something the doctor had not seen before and it gratified him to think that Sir Arthur might be taking an interest in something else other than the contents of a whisky bottle. "And how are you today?" he enquired.

"I'd feel a hell of a lot improved if I could find some damn personage in this parish who could give me a game of chess now and then." The reply was forthright and tentatively encouraging.

There was also a much-worn and opened book on the table and the doctor looked at it with astonishment. "Good Lord," he exclaimed. "It never occurred to me that you were THAT Sir Arthur Wilton. I practically learnt the game from that book, your book. How extraordinary."

The knight sighed and reflected bitterly. "Yes, British Champion and Grandmaster 34-35-36 and damn near British premier alcoholic 48-49-50 and who knows?"

"What stopped it all?" asked Dr Langford, regretting the question immediately after putting it.

"What d'you think, old man? I only inherited this place because elder brother Charles got snuffed out by the jerries in the war and then, of course, Jonquil passed away. Couldn't be bothered any more."

The doctor could hardly believe it. "But you've never mentioned it all the time - some five years - that I've known you. Why the sudden renewal of interest?"

The newly-revealed Grandmaster scratched the nape of his neck and resolved to go into Ross for a haircut. He didn't know whether this would stop his hair itching, but it was a possibility.

In two minds, Henry Langford hesitated, then pulled a tobacco pouch out of his jacket and, lighting up, added to the aroma of wood smoke that of 'Gold Block'. He knew that permission to indulge was not necessary and sensed a 'golden' opportunity.

"It's a pity you didn't tell me this before," he said, "I just had no idea."

Not slow to sense an opportunity himself, Sir Arthur started to put the white pawns in a neat line along the second row. A long dormant look came into his eyes. A challenge to combat.

"You admitted you played," he said rhetorically and leant forward over the board. "How well?"

Dr Langford puffed hard to keep his pipe going and put the black rooks on their extremities. Now that it came to it, he was just a bit worried about whether he could give the ex-champion a game.

"Nothing special," he said. "I played eighth board for Yorkshire a few times. "As you know, I come from up there." He'd been too long away from what someone had once called the 'English Texas', for he had no trace of an accent, though he still retained his membership of Yorkshire County Cricket Club and tried to see one or two of their matches per season.

Displaying long, elegant prominently veined fingers, his patient first placed his bishops, then his corner- sited rooks and finally moved his knights into position. His royal couple not having moved from their home squares, he turned the board round without letting either army waver and sat back in his chair. Satisfied, he then proceeded to fire a salvo of questions at his doctor.

"Am I your last port of call?"

"As a matter of fact, you are."

"What time d'you eat?"

"About seven."

"What about surgery?"

"Not tonight, Dr Thomas comes out from Ross to take it. This ensures I at least get one night off!"

Sir Arthur consulted his watch. "Well now, it's half- past-four and you can have white."

"May I just ring my wife? She'll wonder if I don't."

"Yes, old man. You know where it is in the hall? Help yourself."

Having assuaged his wife's startled disbelief, Henry Langford returned to the drawing room, placed his hand on the Queen's pawn and propelled it forward two squares.

Raising his eyebrows, his illustrious opponent did likewise. "A tight game," he muttered.

The doctor moved another pawn, the Queen's Bishop's, in support of the first one and Sir Arthur countered similarly. The opening proceeded conventionally and soon Black brought a knight into the fray. This caused the doctor to ponder his next move whilst re- filling his pipe and leaning forward over the board, he looked up and met Sir Arthur's bloodshot, but interested eyes. It was very unlikely that he could beat such an eminent opponent, but that perhaps was not really the object of this confrontation. He set his King's Bishop on its diagonal course across country and spoke to his adversary slowly and meaningfully.

"Now that knight of yours has come forward, I wouldn't like it to regress at all, Arthur."

Sir Arthur put his elbows on the sides of his chair, and his hands to his mouth, from where he exhaled heavily.

"That depends," he mumbled, almost incoherently.

THIRTEEN

Imperious and trying to impress herself upon her 'daily', Maude Langford stood awkwardly in the kitchen watching that person, a restored Mrs Taylor, ignoring these instructions whilst busy at the stove.

"Don' 'old with this fancy cookin'," interrupted the chef, "can't see what you're eatin'. Fred wouldn't eat it. 'ee likes plain cookin' 'ee does."

"My dear Mrs T," continued the exasperated lady of the house, "I'm pleased to say your husband won't be eating it. Now, if we could..."

But the indomitable Mrs Taylor grumbled on. "An' what's this soup, tomata?"

"That, Jessica, is prime game soup from M&S and I'd be pleased if you'd keep your remarks to yourself and just get on with things."

Not liking to be addressed by her Christian name, Mrs Taylor sniffed derisively and still voiced dissent, mingled with heavy sarcasm. "I didn't 'ave t' come an' cook yer fancy meal, Mrs Langford. Anybody'd think the Queen wuz comin'. If you're not satisfied.

"Of course, of course, you carry on, you carry on..."

Whilst exasperated beyond measure by Mrs Taylor's blunt attitude, Maude Langford was aware that her 'daily' was just about the best cook in the village and indispensable where dinner parties were concerned. She began counting on her long fingers, muttering a list of notables she'd invited. "There's the vicar, Mr Jeremy and Mrs, The Coningby-Wilsons, Percy Latham, Dr Shipley and Mrs... I think I'll just check the table." She used this as an excuse to leave the kitchen.

In the dining room, with dusk veiling the lush pastures before him, the doctor peered through the French windows. It was warmer for the time of year than it might have been and the pungent smell of late blossom, even at this late hour, percolated through the fanlight into his nostrils.

"You'll see them in, Henry, won't you?" Maude busied herself making last minute adjustments to the silver laden tableaux.

"Waasat?-Oh, yes-yes dear, of course." Startled, his reverie rudely destroyed, Dr Langford confronted his domineering spouse and hoped the possible onset of premature dementia would not prevent him providing the answers she required. "Uh-has the alcohol arrived? Does wassisname drink? You know, thingame? Hell, you know, the new man?"

His wife regarded him with overt contempt; hands on hips and not for the first time wondered why she had ever married him.

"If that incohesive mumbo-jumbo is an

enquiry concerning the Reverend David Oliver's drinking or tee-total propensities, then the answer is 'yes, he does'. Really Henry, for an allegedly educated man, your English sometimes leaves a lot to be desired. And since you ask, the drink is in the kitchen. Perhaps you'd care to go and fetch it. I'm sure everyone would like a sherry on arrival. I hope I can rely on you and don't disturb Mrs Taylor, who's in a very contrary mood."

Fifteen minutes later, the doorbell rang and Henry Langford - his attempts at controlling his wife's ceaseless upbraiding falling dismally short of his wife's daily help - gladly shuffled off in his decrepit old slippers to answer it. The guest was ushered into the sitting room, conspicuous by his lack of a formal dog collar and upon enquiry, confirmed that he was an avid approver of medium dry sherry. All smiles and expansiveness, Mr Jeremy and his wife were the next to arrive and with the numbers soon complete, they all retired to the dining room to tackle the soup which Mrs Taylor, stony visage showing scarcely concealed disapproval, chose to deliver hot and thankfully, highly edible.

"And how's the new archaeological society going, Mr Jeremy?"

Given his favourite subject to expand upon, the headmaster became even more extrovert than usual and had to be reminded that his soup was becoming cold. But undaunted, he concluded with the news that the Ross and District Archaeological Society, though only recently formed, was to do a major 'dig' on Waterton Hill.

"Whereabouts?" enquired one of the ancient Coningby-Wilsons; concerned that the wood they had known in ancestry for several hundred years should not be unduly 'vandalised'.

Made so through the exigencies of his occupation, Mr Jeremy was a master of re-assurance.

"There's a site recorded of an old Roman fort in that field below Morris' farm. I believe it's known locally as Nightingale Meadow. We have permission from Mr Morris and the British Archaeological Society has shown great interest."

Archibald Coningby-Wilson considered this explanation and thinking in his deafness that it would not be heard, broke wind. He then sat back contentedly and with the slight tremor he had in his gnarled hands, resumed his hazardous efforts to consume the remainder of his soup, which had now become more of a consommé. "Long as you don't chop down any trees," he remonstrated. "Those wretched Forestry fellas seem to be doin' their level best to wreck the place without any help as it is."

His flagrant indiscretion caused the lady of the house to pucker up her face. The revolting smell had just reached her. It had wafted under the table and collecting up the soup plates, she excused herself, marched imperiously into the kitchen and prevailed upon the indomitable Mrs Taylor to produce the main course. Here she found the temporary chef struggling to pull a large goose from the oven. The bird was laden with orange slices and to the perspiring Mrs Taylor; this was 'fancy' cooking. But her special roast potatoes garnished the steaming display, homemade stuffing oozed from the bird's hind quarters and various unusual vegetables were removed from the top shelf by the needlessly agitated Maude Langford.

"Just bring the goose in Mrs T, dear. I'll bring the veg's."

"Coulda' done with some proper boiled taters," bemoaned Mrs T.

Confronted by the succulent monster, Dr Langford lovingly contemplated indulging in the almost forgotten art of surgical practice. This had been an ambition of youth, never realised, but still latently displayed at Christmas, Easter or the infrequent dinner parties that Maude chose to foist on the questionably elite members of local society.

The party steadily munched its way through intermittent small talk, silence mainly prevailing; almost completely immersed in appreciation for Mrs Taylor's gastronomic prowess and savouring the meal to the full. The chef had managed to get her own way over the 'pudding' - of the simple rice variety with jam - and after cheese and biscuits, they all retired to the drawing room for coffee. At this juncture the frail Coningby-Wilsons excused themselves through fatiguing and premature old age and shuddered off in their equally decrepit old nineteen-thirty automobile to bed.

Percy Latham, owner of the local saw mills, confronted the new vicar with a largely toothless smile. He was what is known as a 'self-made-man' or - in the covert words of a cryptic and radical assistant schoolteacher known as Bob Allen had - 'trodden his way to the top by being a creeping and domineering bastard'.

"Funny old coot, don't you think, Vicar?" It was a false, cultivated nouveau riche accent; not a bad attempt, but nowhere near good enough to impress Maude Langford and others of her ilk.

David Oliver decided to be non-committal. Only having met Major Archibald Wilson once since arriving in the parish, he respected the old boy's knowledge and was not about to deride him to Percy Latham. On his only visit to the Dower House, the vicar had prodded the old gentleman into talking of his beloved trees and the clergyman had noted how his eyes lit up and the years fell away as he expanded upon the subject. His one great fear was that for purely commercial reasons, the pines would take over and to make way for them, his beloved beeches would be surreptitiously slaughtered.

Listening to his eloquent plea, David Oliver felt that Coningby-Wilson was a true lover of trees and that the mercenary Phillip Latham was merely a lover of money and trees; with the saw mill owner's first preference undeniably endangering the latter.

"I'm afraid I don't know him very well." A limp reply from the cleric and one which might be interpreted as typically 'Anglican' in its fence-sitting feebleness.

Anxious to expand upon his own subject further, Mr Jeremy eagerly interrupted.

"I can assure you that our members won't touch any trees," he said. "In fact, that was one of the first stipulations impressed upon us..." He chuntered interestingly on and whilst he did so, Dr Langford arose and deciding that the room had become stuffy, wandered over to the French windows and opened them. An almost spherical moon shone down, illuminating the lawn and the shrubs, which bordered the extensive garden.

This seemed to be a signal for the gradual departure of the remaining guests and satisfied that she'd chalked up another entertaining success, Maude Langford did not demur and bid them a gracious farewell as they left. For once, leaving her slightly inebriated husband to his own devices without comment, she returned to the kitchen and noted that Mrs Taylor had done all the washing up and departed. With her accustomed habit of deeming it not necessary to say adieu, she had gone and with honest good heartedness, left the place immaculate. Maude was not that unappreciative that she did not wish to reward the stout lady in some way and resolved that on the morrow she would make the effort to call round with her money and a small gift for the recovered John Taylor. She noted that the remnants of the goose had been covered with foil and was glad that when it had fully cooled, she would be able to put it into the refrigerator before that nefarious thief, Jasper the black-furred and black-hearted cat, was able to partake of it. All birds were fair game to the terrorising Jasper. Given the chance, the nefarious feline would eye this gargantuan example of the species as a gift from heaven and disregarding the wrath, which would be visited upon him by his irate mistress, would take his fill with impunity.

FOURTEEN

Mr Jeremy clambered wearily up the meadow and upon reaching the five-bar gate, paused for a short respite. He groped inside his sweat-ridden shirt pocket, pulled out a handkerchief and gratefully applied it to his forehead. Today the 'dig' had been tiring and as was customary, he'd left the site half-an-hour after everyone else. The enthusiasm generated by the discovery of several Roman coins some two weeks earlier had steadily waned and even the headmaster was beginning to doubt if anything else of note would emerge to justify their efforts. He turned to look back the way he had come. The gently sloping field was part of a farm closely surrounded by the woods and Church Lane - known up here by its vernacular title "ood lane' - started down by the main road, passed the church, entered the woods and ended in this cul-de-sac near Morris' outbuildings. During its journey it meandered up through the main wood, straightened out through a row of silver birches and continued past what had once been the imposing Waterton Castle. This ancient edifice was now just a solitary lump of rock; the rest of it having been filched for use in the building of Waterton Vicarage and one or two other imposing homesteads in the parish.

The wood was certainly opulent this year and beyond it, the forest proper loomed in the distance. There was the land of pig rustling and strong dialect; of coal mines and of deer; in itself a lifetime of historical study. In the foreground stood the hill known as Marpool Common - reputed home of fairies and other fanciful creatures and just to the left loomed the near mountain and geological misfit known as May Hill. On its summit May Hill had an allegedly magical number of trees, which many had tried to enumerate without success and the view from it was quite spectacular.

"Good addernoon, Mr Jeremy, zir." The headmaster started. This, of course, was just about the termination of the worthy Mr Brain's domain and it was obvious that the roadman intended to down tools in order to engage in a bout of conversation and - coming from him - probably accurate gossip.

"Oh, hallo Mr Brain. How are you?" The head had a lot of time for the roadman who, despite the restrictions of a meagre income, was managing to raise his large brood in a very satisfactory way. None of them were the brightest pebbles on the beach, but they were all polite and well-behaved and like their father, not frightened of hard work and this was something that could not be said about some of his charges, who almost daily had to be reprimanded and in extreme cases, given the cane.

The phlegmatic defyer of all the elements placed his spade against the gate and leant his person next to it. This meant that Mr Jeremy was confronted and therefore had to be resigned to an affable, but almost certainly long peroration from the roadman. That other indispensable item of the man's essential equipment - his filthy pipe - put in an appearance and he was soon alternately sucking and talking to the headmaster, who had to endure the wafting smoke head on. Mr Jeremy was one of the few people with whom the roadman could feel at home and this was probably because the headmaster; indifferent to the almost feudal creed of these parts, made it his business to be on everyone's wavelength.

"And what brings you up here, Mr Brain?"

The roadman shrugged. "Ol' Morris up th' varm. 'ee wanted thick culvert cleared out, afore winter comes. Zo I zaid I'd do it for un."

Mr Jeremy laughed. "We could do with your trusty spade down there. Some of them seem to flag a bit towards the end of the day."

Mr Brain contemplated this proposal and frowned. "I darezaiy," he said, "an' it'd do that young Mrs Johnson no 'arm to come up 'ere 'n 'elp either. Kip 'er outta mischief if anything could!"

Mr Jeremy tried to cough non-committally.

"Um - what makes you say that," he asked cautiously.

"I ent zayin', but I d' zee what I d' zee."

Mr Brain gave his tattered cap a sharp tug; pulling it even further down his forehead. This partially obscured his eyes, which half-twinkled through the smoke haze and revealed none of his inner thoughts. He too, in his simple way, was a practitioner of dissemblance and obfuscation and it was obvious he was going to take his time in elaborating on the misdemeanours of the wayward Lizzie Johnson. Knocking his pipe out, he eventually continued.

"I wuz clearin' up in Green Lane the other day."

Humming to himself, the wary headmaster wondered what dubious revelation might be in the offing. "That's interesting, but, I know for certain, not unusual. I've never known you being accused of neglecting any part of your neck-of-the-woods for any length of time."

The roadman scratched a brown ear and spat over the gate; impervious to what the headmaster might think of it.

"It weren't me job that wuz interestin' me at that 'ticular moment, Mr Jeremy. It wuz what wuz goin' on t'other zide of the 'edge. I ent sayin', but I saw what I did zee an' t'wasn't decent, like."

Not knowing what to say, Mr Jeremy kept quiet.

"'er's bin round prac'aly every other un in the village, but I never thought t' zee what I did zee then." Meandering on in this fashion for some time, Mr Brain never came to the point and seemed strangely reluctant to divulge what he had indeed seen taking place beyond the hedge in Green Lane. And with a lot of unanswered questions occupying his mind, Mr Jeremy excused himself, jumped into his faithful Model T Ford, fired it and trundled off down the lane; leaving the roadman to his verbal ramblings and his delayed ditch cleaning.

Passing the church entrance near the bottom, he stopped to talk to David Oliver, who was just emerging from the lych-gate. The conversation did not last long and as soon as the headmaster had disappeared, the young clergyman started to walk frenetically up towards the wood, arms behind his back and a distressed look encompassing his face. He reached the gate, which barred the way to the Coningby-Wilson's orchard and paused to cast his eyes down the falling, tree-dotted meadow whilst scanning the undulating countryside beyond. He was tempted to return to the church, but instead continued up through the now all-embracing trees to Whim berry Grove. Here he took the path to the isolated yew which of late, had sheltered both Mike Fryer and the two boys, Woody and Arnold. He did not loiter and soon came to the ominous clearing with its recently defiled altar. Here it was just as she'd described it, only someone had destroyed the woodwork and knocked the stone slab off the altar. Most of it lay shattered on the blackened ground where a fire had been.

The priest shuddered and pulled out the crucifix, which he always carried about his person; uttering a frantic supplication to the Lord he was not sure even existed. Nearly always cynical, even he had to admit that the place smelled of evil. He stood transfixed for what seemed a lifetime and the day suddenly changed. Amid gathering clouds, lightening cut through the air, the sky rumbled and a downpour of awesome proportions began. The bemused clergyman fled the satanic scene and heading out of the wood in a veritable frenzy, took ten minutes to reach the church; utterly saturated and consumed with a feeling not far removed from sheer terror.

Kneeling before the altar, David Oliver trembled; partly with cold, but mostly because of the conflicting thoughts that pervaded his mind. He concentrated on the benign Victorian scene of Christ distributing His body and His blood to His followers and wondered if he, David Oliver was still one of them. Did he really accept it any more? Was there any real connection between himself, a comfortable twentieth-century pretender and the rough, early evangelists of the church he purported to support? He glanced at the serene face again and lowered his eyelids. He knew the answer, but he had to live the pretence in order to continue his comfortable mode of living.

The church clock struck the half-hour and the savage storm abated. The Reverend David Oliver arose and went to the west door. A symbolic rainbow hung decorously over the village and where its mythical pot of gold should have been, stood the village pub. He pulled himself together and raised his eyebrows in a speculative manner. Not much of a difference, he thought. Where there might have been gold, there were golden hops and grinning wryly, he decided it might not be such a bad idea after all.

A few minutes later, he walked boldly into the public bar of the Horse and Jockey and ordered a pint of 'Alton Court', from the local brewery in Ross and much lamented when later lost to mankind by an inevitable takeover. Phil Arnold obliged and the clergyman knew that his not infrequent visits to the pub had - in that clear-cut manner of the working class villagers - established him as 'no different than the rest' or 'the same uz us' or even just 'a good 'un'. But it was strange how the mere sight of a dog collar in a public house inhibited the language and quite inexplicably, subdued the most ardent proletariat atheist.

He supped his pint slowly, passing the time of day with all and sundry; declined a further one from a well-meaning dart player and bidding the company farewell, made his way back to the vicarage.

His ever-vigilant housekeeper, Mrs Lyall, was

on the lookout for him and scolded him severely over his still sodden condition. She herded him upstairs where the water was hot and the bath luxurious. In the bathroom, an old radio stood plugged in on top of the medical cupboard. Whilst drying himself he switched it on and quickly back off again. A service from some cathedral, which allowed enigmatic feelings to arise within him. He finished drying, dressed and went downstairs. A watery sun still glinted through the sitting room window, but gradually began to sink into oblivion and the level of David Oliver's port decanter sank in unison with it. After a negative hour during which he consumed more than was good for him, the clergyman arose and informed Mrs Lyall that he had to go out again. The lady did not take pains to hide her obvious disapproval, but powerless to stop him, she stood watching through the window as he drove the big Wolseley down the lane past the now glowing Horse and Jockey. He turned towards Gloucester and negotiating the bends somewhat erratically, came to the flat and took Johnson's lane to The Green.

The door opened before he had time to ring the bell.

"Hello, David. Thought you'd come. Cup of coffee? Did you find it?"

The clergyman inhaled what smelt like the entire contents of Boots cosmetics counter and stepped inside.

"Thank you," he said tremulously, "and I did."

Lizzie Johnson led him through the warren of corridors to the kitchen. "Yes well, as you no doubt saw, someone must have discovered it; so we had to move."

FIFTEEN

Village cricket. Waterton were playing Malderwick, a picture book place of red sandstone situated in the apple growing district round the small Gloucestershire township of Newent. The accent of the fielding side had a decidedly different ring, and even to an outsider it was obvious that two counties were involved. This mellow scene was witnessed from a distance at the very summit of Waterton Wood by John Taylor and Spencer who, having youthful eyesight could make out from the tin plate scoreboard that the home side was 96-4, a pretty good score. Off to the left towards Leeside, they could just discern Mr Jeremy's loyal band of moles burrowing for signs of Roman remains near Morris's farmhouse and down below, traffic rumbled along the main road, impervious to the tense contest taking place on the village playing field. Several herds of cattle could be seen ambling in for the afternoon udder coaxing and over on May Hill, figures like ants were groping the steep incline; while a little further northwards, the slim spire of St Mary's withstood the nudging of occasional passing clouds and continued to soar heavenwards.

In other parts of the small gossip ridden community, various scenes were being enacted and had the two boys possessed a pair of powerful binoculars, they would have been well-equipped for a closer look at these activities.

Wearing an extremely battered and ill-fitting panama hat, Sir Arthur Wilton sat ensconced on his back veranda watching some young friends take advantage of his grass court in playing a less than enthusiastic and extremely inept game of tennis. His ageing gardener, Victor, did not approve of any part of his province being unproductive. An irascible old devil, he muttered oaths under his breath, went on tending his vegetable plot regardless and his animosity to those now occupying the tennis court was only assuaged by the thought that his kidney beans would be a little early this year. He wondered if he could persuade Sir Arthur to let him dig up the tennis court in the autumn, as for all the use it got, he might just as well use it to increase the mansion's productivity. Then the healthy young people could go off and do something useful like drinking or 'rogering' the girls.

In the village stores, Miss Emily Ward stood talking to the worthy Mrs Taylor about the cost of living; the second of these two nattering ladies pontificating at some length about the spiralling price of butter, which in her opinion was outrageously overpriced at one and six per pound. In reply, the shopkeeper nodded in her sagacious way, knowing that the customer was always right and that despite initial dissent, the customer nearly always paid in the long run.

And at Dr Langford's, Maude Langford was busily 'watering' and feeding the Great Danes and her husband had just escaped through the gates; heading for the tranquil atmosphere of the cricket field. His Yorkshire antecedents made him an avid follower of the game and he remained convinced that if more people chose to watch village cricket, less patients would be admitted to the cardiac clinics of hospitals. Cricket was balm for the troubled soul and if you compounded it with a passion for JS Bach and a daily drop of Guinness, the good man reckoned it could be a valid recipe for almost certain well-being and possible longevity.

Further along the main road, Mrs Gubbins nodded in the heat; her decrepit radio pouring out a repeat of the previous Sunday's 'Donald Peers Sings'. Surrounding her in the small cottage, tripping out and back into the place with irritating frequency, her offspring added to the cacophony of the wireless and the illustrious singer's 'Babbling Brook' rapidly became a 'Tower of Babel'. Woken up by this steady crescendo of noise, she applied two meaty hands to caressing various small backsides and apparently satisfied with her indiscriminate disciplinary methods, settled down to sleep again.

At the Horse and Jockey, Phil Arnold humped a few barrels around, perspiring with the heat, whilst his wife cut large hunks of bread and cheese, added homemade pickled onions of the sweetest taste imaginable and added to this gastronomic delight a good number of succulent tomatoes. The cricketers would be in later and although they would have availed themselves of an excellent tea, would soon devour this fare; particularly if the beer was up to scratch and Elsie could not remember a single day in all their long tenancy when this had not been the case.

In a thatched cottage near the pub, Mr Jones the deputy headmaster had visitors from the valleys. In his unassuming and deceptively subtle way he had suggested to the husband that the privet hedge was becoming overgrown and that well-applied shears would remedy the situation. As a result of this veiled hint, the willing guest found himself sweating under the armpits even while his sly teaching friend - now freed from the onerous task - quietly inspected his proliferating roses for marauding and potentially damaging insects.

Sitting on that stile, which ended the path below Church Meadow, developing fourteen-and-a-half year old Marion Howells consumed a lolly with great alacrity. She'd just been for an unsuccessful walk in the hope of seeing some boys and having found all their attentions subsumed by the cricket , she now contented herself with the aforementioned lolly and her weekly copy of *Girl's Crystal*; all other thoughts eradicated by the sterling deeds of the fourth form at St Margaret's'.

But by far the most voyeuristic scenario could be witnessed at The Green. There were only two witnesses, however, who were also the participants.

"Hell that was good." Sated, Lizzie Johnson lay back and looked quizzically at the man who had just pleasured her. "Did that bother you, David?"

"No, I enjoyed it," David Oliver lied. "Why should it bother me?" Oh God, he anguished, how is a man supposed to react when a woman reveals everything she's got? It had been the same in his student days. This was another facet of Christianity he did not understand. What was fornication? What did it matter when it provided relief as it surely did in the case of Lizzie, whose husband showed no interest? So why, God forgive him, shouldn't he take his fill? Alas, this would be another potential avenue for sermonising, lost. He would never be able to preach about carnal desire or adultery again. His God was, indeed, a cruel deity. Then he thought of those compassionate eyes pleading above the altar, and flinched. This was not the whole story and his misgivings increased. He had allowed himself to become ensnared by this wild, insatiable creature and the whole thing was heading he knew not where. Darkness even invaded his prayers and Lizzie was slowly sucking him in; pulling the very guts of his belief from him and weighing down his struggles for divine redemption with what seemed like a great black metaphorical stone.

The mentally tortured cleric arose and self-consciously began to dress. Here, a few hundred yards away from the farmhouse, they always met in the French barn at the bottom of the long meadow and he always had this constant fear that someone would happen upon them.

Lizzie smiled encouragingly at him. A pale face she had and the muscle contortion did not include any movement of the eyes.

"You'll come with us next time, David," she asked softly.

He struggled manfully with his trousers and tried not to show that the quandary almost consumed him. "A-well, I suppose so, but you'll have to give me directions..." What was he thinking of? The sheer madness of it had him momentarily in several minds.

Still unclothed, Lizzie tantalisingly put her arms around the cleric's neck and provokingly kissed him.

"You know Marling's Meadow on the right just before you enter the forest proper?"

"Yes."

"Well, walk across diagonally from the gate and there is a gap in the hedge on the far side. From there, walk along the path towards the cottages. Before you reach these cottages, notice the overhanging rocks on the right of the path. One of these rocks juts out more prominently than the others. Behind and above it there is another rough path, which leads to the caves. Carry on and make your way up through the conifer trees. Don't try and find a way through the rocks there, because you won't do it. Keep going and a bit higher up you'll find normal woodland and come to a clearing surrounded by broom. Beyond that there is another cave inside which we meet. Of course, I hope to see a lot of you before then and I'll go over it again with you."

Now fully dressed and resisting the effect her pressing quim was having on him, the Reverend David Oliver dragged himself away and took the short cut across the fields to the vicarage where Mrs Lyall had a salad waiting.

SIXTEEN

By the time Spencer and John Taylor reached the cricket, Waterton were 159 for 8, a good total for a village team. A corpulent and ageing Malderwick spin bowler came wearily in to bowl at Bob Allen and 'Sir,' who had been persuaded to join the club a few weeks back, was rapidly gaining touch and promoted for this game to No 5, had so far compiled an impressive 45 not out. At the other end and co-opted at the last minute in to the side at the tender age of fourteen-and-a-half, Arnold was valiantly defending his fortress well and every time he so much as made contact with the ball, a chorus of encouragement broke forth from all his schoolmates who were present to witness this early baptism.

Abandoning all caution, Bob Allen peremptorily despatched the ball over long off to the boundary and amid the applause Denis Smith signalled a declaration. And in a manner which seems solely to be emulated by the ponderous amblings of policemen on the beat; the two parched and sometimes maligned umpires headed steadily for the somewhat ramshackle building which was termed, euphemistically, 'The Pavilion'. The pavilion had a flap in front which opened upwards and it being such a balmy afternoon, most of the players forsook the inside; mingling with the spectators, drinking tea from enamel mugs and eating mega-sized scrambled egg sandwiches. These were provided by those worthy ladies Mrs Lewis, Mrs Marshall, Mrs Smith and one or two others; none of whom were the slightest interested in the noble game and probably thought a leg slip was a slightly naughty form of apparel.

A gaggle of small boys, aping a flock of encircling seagulls, displayed sudden interest in these good ladies and when the cricketing stalwarts had had their fill, consumed the leftovers with an alacrity similar to that of vultures picking the bones off corpses in the desert.

Near the entrance to the ground and next to the steadily decaying village hall, a familiar ice-cream van 'manned' by that redoubtable cementer of Anglo-Italian détente, Mrs Baglioni - evidently not a jot put out to be returning to the scene of last September's crime upon her person - was doing brisk business. Mrs Baglioni always did the rounds of the village cricket grounds on a Saturday afternoon and saw no reason why she should not return to the scene of her traumatic experience. Cannily and only noticeable to the discerning eye, she had attached a locking cap to her petrol tank and now felt impervious to any assaults from idle small boys or any other form of pestilential low-life.

The cricket resumed and two stolid

Malderwickian opening batsmen were weathering the left-handed fast bowling onslaught of the two Lewis brothers; one the father of Martin and the other a young uncle. Blessed with little success on the placid surface in his first couple of overs, Lewis senior made way for his younger sibling and grumbling at the indignity of it, retired to the outfield to indulge in a surreptitious cigarette. The two brothers' respective run-ups were not of the same ilk and whereas Lewis senior took short, modest steps to the wicket, whipped his arm over and caused the ball to leave his hand at surprising pace; Uncle Lewis had a vastly different approach. He was more one to strike terror into the minds of opposing batsmen by a uniquely vivid and intimidating ritual. Before each delivery, he would rub the ball vigorously on the off-white seat of his flannels, belligerently stomp off to a position close to deep long on - and after touching his toes in menacing fashion several times - come hurtling round in a wide semi-circular movement, gathering momentum as he reached the wicket. This frightening and lengthy process usually ended in one of three ways. Either the ball would fly perilously through the air beating both batsman and wicketkeeper, and result in four byes, or it would hit the batting crease and metamorphose into a deadly Yorker or - as was more likely - the expending of so much effort would end in a very slow ball parabolically landing five yards short; inviting the delighted recipient to slam it anywhere he chose. Uncle Lewis had been taken to Lord's a couple of years previously to see the great Australian team of 1948 and ever since had sought to emulate that illustrious thoroughbred of the fast bowler's union, Ray Lindwall. These rigorous and misguided attempts to ape his hero could only be used in short spells and this had soon become obvious to Waterton's captain and the long-suffering man only indulged the enigmatic 'quickie' for what he called the 'astonishment' effect. There were occasional times when Uncle Lewis managed to psychologically remove a batsman before even bowling to him, but this chance had long gone as a confident Malderwick No 2 despatched the fifth ball of a wayward over confidently for an imperious straight six, which sailed over the hedge beyond the boundary like a rocket.

Her trade diminished by the re-start, Mrs Baglioni had decided to move on to Ross, where the pickings at the town ground would probably be much larger. She climbed heavily from her vehicle and adjusted her elastic bands in the large driver's mirror. Climbing into the driving seat, she started the vehicle up and limped a few yards before coming to a halt. The owner of the now decidedly stationary ice cream van removed herself once more and a stream of ripe Italian invective rent the air, causing the Malderwick

No 1 batsman to mistime his stroke and nick to first slip. Appeals added to this hysterical demonstration of Latin discontent and during the advent of the new batsman, the fielding side rushed over to see what was wrong. Awakened from the bowels of his comfortable deckchair, Dr Langford got there first, assured them that he could pacify the good lady and proceeded to change the deflated tyre by exchanging it with the spare wheel. This displayed a practicality, which he normally kept hidden from his controlling wife, lest she cornered him into doing all manner of things he didn't want to do. Mrs Baglioni was full of profuse thanks and insisted on offering the medical 'mechanic' a large cornet, which he declined on medical grounds, the truth being that he didn't think it would suit his image.

Play had resumed without further incident and the ice-cream vendor was just making her exit through the gate, when the cavalierly inclined Malderwickian No 3, a pugnacious little man, took a mighty heave at an attempted Denis Smith googly. This soared upwards like some spherical skylark; lost momentum and lingered ominously before gravitational pull caused it to come lingeringly down to shatter the back window of the poor ex-patriot lady's fated ice-cream van. Now in School Lane, tyres burnt on the tarmac, the vehicle again came to an abrupt halt. Brandishing an implement used to purvey her product, Mrs Baglioni ran through the gate and with her skirts flying, tore into the middle of the pitch; her wart-ridden face now a deep shade of purple. The Malderwick batsman tried hard to be apologetic, but in the end was reduced to warding off the ice cream scoop attack with his sturdy willow, whilst Captain Denis Smith and his alarmed followers endeavoured to restrain and pacify the irate woman. After much argument and irreverent banter from the crowd, they managed to disengage the lady and promised re-imbursement from club funds. She was persuaded to take a consoling cup of tea in the pavilion.

The game continued and Mrs Baglioni, third time lucky, drove away muttering Italianate profanities under her breath and resolving never to visit the fateful parish of Waterton-under-the-Hill again.

SEVENTEEN

The Sunday following the eventful cricket match, Mike Fryer busied himself in the cowshed, mucking out between morning and evening milking. William Johnson had gone over to Cheltenham to see an ageing aunt and Mike had agreed to see to the animals. Several months had elapsed since Mildred's death. Several heavy, long, unenviable months. He frequently mulled the whole affair over and the more he ruminated, the more he came to the conclusion that there was some connection between his wife's demise and the actions he'd taken in knocking over that strange altar in the wood. He had hardly spoken to Lizzie Johnson since the night of the accident and took pains to avoid her whenever possible.

"Hello, Mike? Busy?" Tom Donaldson looked over the half door of the cowshed and made a derisory, but good natured sniff. "Pleasant task for a Sunday morning, I must say."

Mike Fryer grinned and leant on his shovel. "Gotta be done," he said.

"Fancy a cup of coffee?" Tom lit a cigarette, glad of the tobacco smell, which eliminated the strong odour generated by the cows and, grateful for the interruption, Mike cast aside his shovel.

"Cigarette?" Tom was a generous soul and admired the big farmworker for the courageous and uncomplaining way he carried his troubles on his broad shoulders.

"Thanks, but I'll adda take me boots off. S'long as yer wife don' mind me comin' in in me socks?"

Over coffee, the Donaldsons gently enquired about Mike's well-being, for although he only lived within 'spitting distance' of them, they didn't see much of him and still very active, his mother had taken it upon herself to see to things with great efficiency. On occasions the Donaldson's would have the Fryers to dinner, but Mike mostly depended on his 'Mam', who was a positive diamond. The son, George, upon whom the loss hung more heavily, had become quite introverted and as if to compensate for his maternal loss, spent most of the time with his grandmother.

Whilst they were convivially drinking, a wind which had made its unexpected appearance after yesterday's balmy ten-hour sunshine built up in intensity and drove fiercely against the kitchen windows. The Donaldson's cottage formed part of a square. It was adjacent to the farmhouse and opposite some buildings, which housed farm implements; the rectangle being completed by garages housing vehicles belonging to both the Johnsons. Pamela Donaldson loathed this wind, which seemed to occur at the oddest times. It sprung up suddenly and spewed through the only opening into the yard, cavorted round in a type of unseen whirlpool and then - as if it had been seeking an unknown exit - disappeared without trace; leaving others to pick up the scattered dustbin lids and rubbish spilt in its wake.

"Funny ol' wind we d' get up 'ere." Mike Fryer echoed Pamela's thoughts and from somewhere upstairs the baby began to whimper.

"Sorry Pam," said Mike, his voice full of contrition, "must be me loud chopsin'. 'ow old is the babby now?"

Pamela re-assured him. "It's not you Mike. It's her teeth. She's nine months now. Would you like to see her? I don't think you've done so for some time."

Glad of an excuse, Pamela mounted the stairs and soon proudly brought back down the ample bundle that was now Sarah Louise Donaldson, handing her to Mike. His knees went to jelly as the infant beamed and gurgled at him. He was invited to hold her and without a trace of self-consciousness, asked to wash his hands, lest he soiled the 'little un' with the undesirable flavour of his endeavours. He then sat and nursed Sarah for ten minutes fully, until a knock at the door allied to slight paternal jealousy in the eyes of Tom Donaldson, made him hand the large-eyed nymph over to her father and make to depart.

"No, you don't have to go, Mike. Have another fag. It may not be anybody for us." He motioned to the coffee table where a packet of twenty resided awaiting immolation and in his turn sat down; captivated by the soft brown eyes.

Pamela went to answer the door and after five minutes, returned with a worried expression on her face.

"That was Lizzie," she said. "Seemed quite elated. Apparently, William's been taken ill on the way to Cheltenham. He's in hospital. She's going over there now. Nothing we can do. She seemed extraordinarily and strangely excited about it. What a peculiar, callous woman!"

"Did she say what was wrong," enquired Tom.

"Oh, evidently some rare stomach complaint. Something only normally found in children. A twisted gut or something to do with the intestines. She's going to stay with his old aunt and she'll be back tomorrow."

"What's that box you've got in your hand?" Tom drew attention to a small oblong cardboard container; a shade smaller than those used for housing shoes.

"This?" His wife tried to explain Lizzie's random action in pressing this object upon her at what she considered a very inappropriate time. "It's some sort of doll, I think. Though I haven't opened it. Very nice of her, I suppose, though an odd thing to do just now, don't you think?" Pamela sat down and put the box to one side, but her husband was curious.

"Aren't you going to open it and let us see?"

Pamela shrugged. "For some reason I don't

want to and anyway look, the wind's dropped , the sun's out and I think Sarah should be outside, so if you'll excuse me, Mike..."

She took Sarah from Tom and the two men could soon see her arranging the protesting baby into the pram over the way by the outhouses. Their talk turned to farming and Mike commented about the fact that it was obviously assumed that he would hold the fort without much in the way of thanks coming his way and Tom, assenting, declared that where Lizzie was concerned, it was probably par for the course. In the middle of this discussion and with a sudden impulse, Tom reached for the cardboard box from where it had been discarded by Pamela on the old beaten-up kitchen sofa. He opened it up and was startled by the two beady eyes, which disconcertingly stared up at him from the sunken features of an ugly wax doll.

From outside, a sickening crash accompanied this revelation and after a few seconds, a white and visibly terrified Pamela Donaldson ran in, clutching the baby.

Jumping to their feet, they could see through the window that the far side chimney stack from the farmhouse had fallen and the main bulk of it was now resting within feet of Sarah's pram. The lethal whirlpool had returned to give a final flourish in a latent treacherous gust, before making its final exit.

EIGHTEEN

"A twisted gut, they reckons," said Mike Fryer; his voice like his gaze, projected upwards to the roof of the farmhouse where an intrepid Denis Smith - now recognisable as the undisputed overlord of Waterton's recently victorious cricket team - put the finishing touches to a new chimney piece.

"Think I'll come down now." Denis plodded surefootedly down the ladders from a precarious height, jumped the last three rungs and continued the conversation. "Well, ow's 'ee doin', then?"

Before responding, Mike took the opportunity to instigate a fag break. He lit both papers and replied, "not too good. Two minutes later 'n 'ee'd been dead."

"There wuz a lot o' talk about it in the pub las' night," said the builder. "They reckon 'ee wuz took bad 'alf way between Glo'ster 'n Chelt'nam. Is that right? 'ee wuz leanin' on some lady's dustbins?"

Mike Fryer nodded sagely. "Tha's right and wha's worryin' me is the farm. Looks as though 'ee'll 'ave t' sell up. Can't see 'im bein' fit to kip this lot goin', specially with 'er 'angin round 'iz neck. She's not bin once t' see 'ow I'm managin' - not that I wants 'er too; but if it wasn't fur George givin' me a 'and, bless 'im, I'd be right up the crick. As it is I'm workin' all 'ours as God's a mind to send! It'd be nice to come down the 'Jockey' once in a while, but I'm usually too bloody shagged by the end of the day!"

"That dog don't seem too 'appy about it all, either." Denis Smith drew attention to where the disconsolate canine lay, nose down in the sun.

"Ah, yes."

Mike Fryer walked over to Katie, fondling her ears and causing her to turn on to her back in anticipation of having the same treatment applied to her belly. Mike duly obliged and Denis came over to join them and after a while intimated that he must be off to do another small job for Sir Arthur at Waterton Hall.

"You'd better give him my love." Mike made a feeble attempt at facetiousness. "How is the old bugger, anyway?" Not awaiting an answer, he gave Katie one last pat and with an involuntary groan, stood upright. His back had started to trouble him recently and he hoped it would not lead to further problems in the future. It probably meant he was doing too much, but short of neglecting the animals, he did not see what he could do about it. "Anyway," he went on. "I don't s'pose Lizzie'll give you any thanks fur comin' so soon, unless, o' course, you'll take payment in kind?!"

The builder ignored this remark. "All a bit of a queer do," he said, with a countryman's classic propensity towards understatement and not prepared to prolong things further, he climbed ponderously into his battered ex-Post Office van - now sprayed an undesirable green colour - and attempted to start it. On the side, this relic of another pre-war age had what might be termed an eventual epitaph, which proclaimed that it was now surely ending its days as a venerable carrier for -

SMITH BROTHERS,
SCHOOL LANE.
WATERTON, NR. ROSS-ON-WYE.

Builders - Plumbers - Decorators
and Electrical Contractors.

Telephone - Waterton 208

After several perfunctory coughs, the ancient vehicle burst into hesitant revolutions and by virtue of the fact that the silencer had parted company from the exhaust system, thundered down Green Lane like a Sunderland bomber leaving the runway. Rattling bricks and sundry building materials added to this ear-splitting cacophony and with blue sparks complimenting this hideous soundtrack, the awakened Katie abandoned her siesta. She added still further to the noisy barrage by barking hysterically at the van's hind wheels and only a piercing whistle persuaded her to abandon the chase.

Mike Fryer removed his fingers and reflected that Katie was a peculiar dog inasmuch that she only chased the wheels of vehicles with which she was unfamiliar, never those belonging to friends or regular callers like the milk lorry, or the cars of friends and relatives with whom she was well-acquainted. To Mike's knowledge, most canines did not discriminate, but sheep dogs were endowed with superior intelligence and besides being a superb sheep gatherer, Katie could handle the cows with equal alacrity and it was seldom that a rabbit of less than exceptional swiftness managed to escape her clutches.

The sound of Smith Bros' van coming to the end of the lane, stopping abruptly and then crunching through the gears along the main road, was followed by a fainter rumbling. Pricking up her ears, Katie ran back to greet whatever was coming next. Perambulator wheels and unlubricated springs heralded a hot and dishevelled Pamela Donaldson, blouse sleeves rolled up, hair splayed haphazardly, charge asleep in the carriage and recently acquired dog padding and panting two yards in front as the vanguard of the little procession. The lady seemed quite irked about something and had upon her face an expression, which could feasibly be described as quite fearsome. Mike Fryer had not encountered this side of her before and wondered what to expect.

"Hallo, Mike. Who the hell was that bloody

cretin in that hideous green van? What a bloody row! I'm amazed Sarah's still asleep, but then I think she'd sleep through anything; even the cottage falling down." Here she put her hand to her mouth. "Oh dear, what have I said?" Consternation showed all over her young, sun-primed complexion.

It was a fascinating face, thought Mike Fryer. High cheekbones; very foreign looking. Didn't someone say her father had been an American? Possibly an American Indian. Anyway, she certainly had a different sort of beauty and one you certainly did not normally see around this neck of the woods. Come to think of it, there were a lot of attractive women in the Ross district with Waterton having its fair share, and he supposed he was now free to pursue one of them. Immersed in his own loss, he had failed to think of it before and though devoid of a normal marital relationship after the birth of George, he'd retained a strange fondness for the deranged girl who had been his wife and not in even one instance, strayed elsewhere. Nevertheless, a slight glimmering of hope for the future now possessed him and this perhaps indicated that the wound was beginning to heal. Realising he was perhaps being timorous; he emerged from his thoughts and answered Pamela Johnson, now decidedly more impatient than fearsome.

"Uh, that wuz Denis Smith. You know, 'ee's

the cricket skipper an 'ee's fixed the chimley."

"What d'you mean, cricket? Oh yes, I remember. I've seen him with all the other 'flanneled fools'. He came over and asked Tom to join. Luckily, Tom hasn't got time. Still, I suppose it's good of him to have come so soon. It would have given me the heebie-jeebies looking up at that blank space on the roof and thinking about what might have happened."

Pamela left the pram and its partially somnolent occupant outside the front door, carried in a mountain of goods just acquired from Emily Ward and quickly came back out to fetch the baby who, since the ghastly incident of the falling chimney, she barely let out of her sight. Half an hour later she brought out a cup of tea to Mike Fryer, who was now firmly ensconced with a serried row of cows in the milking parlour. It was not all that long ago since milking machines had become the saviours of dairy farmers and she could not imagine what it must have been like to milk this great lumbering row of bovines by hand.

"I won't ask you if you take milk," she said dryly and with all his machines in action, Mike paused to accept the beverage with considerable gratitude. It didn't matter where you were in the pantheon of society, a cup of tea constituted everyman's panacea.

"Tom says you're goin' up t'see Mr Johnson t'night. As 'er ladyship bin goin', d'you know?

'cos 'er ant been around 'ere much lately. An' thankyou fur feedin' the cats and Katie. I don' know 'oo 'er thinks does it an' they'd maybe starve if you didn't do it, cos I aint got the time."

"I wouldn't know where she is half the time, but apparently she's coming home from his aunt's tonight. She rang when I was doing my bit in the house this morning." And here she gave him a knowing look. "She told me she has to go out tomorrow night, though I don't know why."

The cowman removed the suckers from a gentle Guernsey called Martha, swilled them in a bucket and attached them to a bulging udder belonging to a less passive Friesian called Mary. These two had been originally 'Christened' by Lizzie during a period of warmth towards William, which also happened to parallel an enlightened period of religious fervour; a state soon extinguished and consigned to history by the enigmatic farmer's wife.

"You say these two are called Mary and Martha?"

"Tha's right."

"That'd please her new boyfriend if he knew and then again, it might not."

She took the empty cup from him and made for the cottage; leaving him slightly bemused and perhaps a bit slow to grasp the meaning of her last words.

NINETEEN

Replete from the consumption of a too ready supply of new potatoes, Woody sat nervously chewing a blade of grass, his legs dangling from what had once purported to be a five-bar gate. Sunken and minus one of its hinges, rot attacking the woodwork, it typified the state of the farm at the top of the hill. The property had about it an aura of ill-disguised inefficiency; illustrated by the deteriorating condition of the implements, neglected outbuildings and a general air of passive inertia conceivably engendered by its isolated position. Woody supposed that the owners, Mr and Mrs Morris, were getting old and that would perhaps explain a lot. They must at least be over forty and to him and his peers that was positively ancient.

By the side of the steadily decaying Georgian farmhouse, a small mobile caravan containing the goods, chattels and person of Charlie Watkins stood; evidence of the fact that the Morris's had plenty of heart, but very little business acumen. Just now, with a good deal of invective thrown in, someone was feeding the chickens and Woody was aware by the slurred tone of voice that it was probably Charlie. A dinner hour spent lingering in the Jockey, supplemented by an afternoon on homemade cider most likely explained why the drunken old toper was addressing them in their own language.

Charlie had never been the same since the hapless Peter Trout's suicide. When the full significance of his bibulously induced blunder had penetrated his limited perspicacity, he fully accepted the blame and this shouldering of culpability for something, which would have most likely happened sooner or later anyway, led him to indulge in frequent bouts of scrumpy drinking. Sadly, this and his obvious loneliness were probably contributory factors towards his subsequent descent into melancholia. Given the slightest chance, he would morbidly self-denigrate in the Jockey until closing time, unless a well-meaning punter managed to re-assure him or the pragmatic Phil Arnold told him bluntly to shut up. But neither cajoling nor empathy would erase Charlie's traumatic experience and perhaps in a paradoxical way, he now had an excuse for his alcoholic excesses. He had to forget and besides making his face take on an almost oriental pallor, the cider was helping to swamp his memory bank. He now had a dodgy cross to bear and he was prepared to make quite sure that the world at large knew about it.

The chickens went quiet and someone slammed a light door. Woody presumed Charlie had gone inside and down the lane the sonorous church clock struck the half hour. Half-past six. Woody had not come here on this non-paril summer evening to be alone. He wondered if she would come. It had been a whispered exchange by the cloakroom door. His nerve was going. He inclined to think, perhaps, that it might be better to go now, before she came. A blackbird alighted on a nearby elm, dominating the birdsong and lifting Woody's spirits. After all, wasn't what he intended to achieve as natural as birdsong?

"Hello, Woody." And there she was coming out of the woods on to the lane. It had not occurred to him that she'd come that way. There was a path from the main road all the way up through the bosky hill to the top and Mary had taken it as a short cut. Her hair splayed loosely about her shoulders, she wore a gingham dress, buckled sandals, and carried a wild rosebud, which she had purloined from the hedgerow. She climbed up beside Woody and adjusting her clothing, captivated him with her two shy blue eyes.

"Well there. I came."

Tongue-tied and visibly agitated, Woody could not reply and his feeling of uneasiness grew. He knew what girls were, for he'd made one or two forays in that direction during school breaks, but this was different. Here she was, a delightfully nubile young lady; arrived here alone at his sole behest. He decided to take the plunge.

"Le's go in the wood," said the callow boy; flushing and embarrassed to the point of clumsiness.

"Don' knows that I want to," said his amore anxiously, dangling her long legs and making to dismount from the gate.

Woody looked relieved. "I don't want t' do nothin' if you don' want to."

"'s not that. I don' really know how."

"Marion told me that y'..."

This inflamed her. "I ent Marion! I'm 'er cousin. But that don' make me like 'er!"

The girl flicked her hair in the reiterating way all young females are apt to do and the blackbird, seemingly unfazed by the young couple's close proximity or with an insight not hitherto credited to avian life form, resumed his lilting carousel.

"An' I don' think Marion does it, either. 'er's just got a big 'chops' on 'er."

Woody was a little emboldened. "I don' know much either, but you could let me 'ave.."

"No. You ent puttin' your 'and where you shouldn't, if tha's what you mean. Mam told me never to do nothin' like that." Mary was emphatic.

"Well, it 'oodn't 'urt just to 'ave a look would it?"

"No, you ent an 'if you kips on, I'm goin' 'ome."

Woody shrugged his shoulders, perplexed and frustrated. This girl had dared to come and meet him and here they had arrived at a full stop.

"Why did y' come then?"

"Well, I-I like you." This was an admission. The permanent pink country complexion changed to a deep crimson and Woody found himself looking at a delicate neck; a row of buttons and that long, lustrous, raven hair. He thought for a minute and then said "Mary?"

"What?"

"Can I - can I give you a kiss?" He was still looking at her back.

"If you wants to."

"Would y' mind?"

"Course not."

Woody slid his hand along and touched her small, stubby fingers. A Woolworth's plastic ring adorned one of them.

"Let's get off the bloody gate, then."

Standing amongst the corn and the too prevalent poppies; serenaded by a heavenly blackbird and aware of the contented clucking from old Charlie's chicken coop, Woody had never experienced anything so delightfully mellifluous.

"An' what be you two doin'?"

Disarmed, Woody jumped skywards and the suddenness of his reaction sent his girl backwards, resulting in a heap of poppies, wheat and revealed navy blue. A cunning smile distorting his features, Charlie Watkins leant heavily on the gate. As Phil Arnold's wife had once stated, 'im were at the back of the queue when looks wuz give out' and currently it didn't look if things would ever improve where he was concerned; more likely they would only get worse.

Frightened by the old man's sudden appearance, Woody still had the nous to help Mary to her feet and bravely answered his accuser. "We weren't doin' nothin', Mr Watkins. 'onest, cross me 'eart 'n' 'ope t' die, we wasn't."

"No we weren't," backed up Mary, adjusting her dress and composed beyond her years.

Charlie had a habit of working a protruding tongue back and forth through a row of disintegrating front teeth before speaking. These malfunctioning molars, like homesteads, were now wholly detached. They had long ceased to be terraced, were not even semi-detached and those that had managed to withstand the ravages of Charlie's sugar-laden diet, were canker-ridden and blackened through neglect. Most of their missing neighbours had been removed by the 'string-in-the-door' technique, for the old man was not a one for dental surgery and only the anaesthetic provided by constant alcoholic refreshment prevented him from ever suffering toothache. He pointed his knotted market stick at the young couple in a threatening manner; an appurtenance, which had been cut from the hedgerow during the same period that signalled the demise of so many of his teeth. Teeth, tongue and physically threatening blackthorn augmented an attitude that would have caused a saint to flinch, but Mary and Woody bravely stood their ground.

"Well, I daresay you wasn't, but it didn't look like that over the varm." He cast an eye at Mary, the tongue in and out; still pointing the stick. "An' does your mam know you're 'ere with this boy? I reckon 'er don't. An' what would 'er think if 'er did?" He dropped the stick to his side and leant back on the gate; his sickly smile vanishing. "Course 'er don't 'ave t' know I reckon, unless someone d' tell 'er. An' 'oo'd do that, I wonder?" He toyed with them: the very worst of cats tormenting two vanquished mice. "Why there's only me uz knows 'sides you two, ent there?"

The dreaded smile resurfaced and a wad of Condor sliced came out of a faded leather pouch. With maddening slowness, Charlie rolled his own; the tongue travelling west to east in between his ill-directed attempts to lick the cigarette paper. Pipe tobacco in a cigarette, achieved after much fumbling and lit by a Swan Vesta.

Woody had gone the colour of butter beans. "You won't say anythin' to are mams, will y', Mr Watkins?"

A billow of smoke, a flick of ash disregarding the fast ripening barley; the stick once more raised horizontally at Woody.

Charlie paused, unconcerned; using delaying tactics, playing the feline with the quivering hind quarters and ready to pounce.

"I'll 'adda think about it, but then, it'd 'ave to be worthwhile for old Charlie not t' say summat. I means, it'd adda be worth it, like, fur me t' kip quiet."

Near to tears, Mary implored, "please, Mr Watkins, please don' say anythin'. Me mam's ever s' strict an' me dad 'ould get is belt off to me. 'ee don't believe in treatin' girls no different than boys an' we ant really done nothin'."

A hardened hand came over the gate and landed none to softly on the girl's shoulder and its owner engaged in a change of tactics. Nothing fazed the resident blackbird, who just went on warbling exquisitely; impervious to the playlet that was being acted out on this broad stage and not for the first time puzzled why these alleged stewards of the earth could not be as content as he was.

"There, there, don' you worry, my little beauty. What I reckons iz you two young 'uns ought t' come an' 'ave a drop with owld Charlie in iz caravan over there." Emerging from the smoke, the serpent's tongue looked like lava from a volcano, which had lost its equilibrium. "I got a good flagon 'o the 'ome made uz wants drinkin' an' it wouldn't 'urt y' t' try a drop. Nobody d' come 'n' zee owld Charlie Watkins these days." He became increasingly maudlin. "Don' know why, really. 'spect I's because 'ee's a bit of an owld windbag! Anyway, you two young uns 'd be welcome. What d'y' zay?"

Woody did not like the sound of it and he sensed Mary felt the same. He knew they should be returning home by now, but was at a loss to know how to turn down Charlie's invitation. Mentally maturer, as well as physically advanced, Mary thought the matter out constructively. If they refused Charlie's offer, he might tell all and she was terrified at the prospect of her parents being told a load of blatant untruths by the old man.

"Le's go, Woody."

"Well, I don' know..."

"Come on. We wunt stop long."

"Okay, then." Not knowing what else to do, Woody complied. "But Charlie, we ent drinkin cider. We'll 'ave to 'ave lemonade or water or summat an' we can't stop long. I 'ave t' be 'ome by eight, 'n' i's gone seven now." The volcano coughed and spluttered, throwing the cigarette stub down to be crushed by the blackthorn. He lit another one, leant on the gate and carelessly let the still lit match drop into the cornfield. Youth went off with the serpent, the mouldy teeth and the stick; leaving a rustling sea of yellow, the invasive poppies and the single- minded blackbird.

A wisp of smoke took to the air; tiny, but growing by the second. Besmirched like an artist upsetting the wrong colour on to an already finished canvas, the prevailing yellow was soon to change to amber.

TWENTY

Double decker buses ran every hour from Gloucester. Pamela and Tom Donaldson caught the nine-fifteen and hoped it would not meander along at a funereal pace as it was sometimes apt to do. The news concerning William Johnson was of a very mixed nature. His recovery was assured, but he would probably have to give up the farm. He made no bones about the fractured relationship with his wife and maintained that it was only habit that kept them together. He had been brought up to view divorce with anathema, but he'd had enough of Lizzie's shameless philandering and the current malaise, he avowed, might work out for the best in the long run.

This presented a dilemma for the Donaldsons. It looked as though they would have to up sticks and move. Any new owner would more than likely want the cottage for a worker or caretaker and Tom was unsure how secure they were and if their tenancy was protected by law. He supposed he'd have to find somewhere else to live pretty quickly. With the prevalent housing shortage, the chances of finding somewhere else were not good and his laissez-faire temperament rebelled at the thought of what it involved.

The ageing double decker lurched round a

corner, causing Pamela to slide along the all-in-one front seat; right into the window-hogging Tom.

"That's nice," said Tom. There was nothing quite the same as riding upstairs in the front of this four wheeled charger; a modern equivalent of the old mail coach; particularly on a country service. It was said that before one of the company's double deckers was allowed to travel any route, a 'special' had to be despatched to clear overhead branches and other impedimenta with an almost uniquely designed power saw attached to the outside of the nearside roof. People who used buses regularly - and that was the majority of the populace - came to know drivers and conductors as personal friends. A bus would often wait at the outlet of a country lane for an early morning worker and consternation would be expressed by the conductor or conductress ('clippie') if Ted, Bill or Diana didn't turn up as usual. If you were an inveterate bus passenger, you often learned far more about other people's business than you should have done; including all the petty ailments experienced, the alienation of close ones and the state of your neighbour's dog or pet orangutan. If the 'Mrs' had managed a baby or fallen for one (sometimes by somebody else!), you learned of it and if a cataclysmic happening like the cat contracting fleas occurred, all sorts of remedies would be proffered and all the information and advice usually volunteered and received in a convivial and light-hearted manner.

People would travel on the same bus, sit in the same seat and follow the same route for a decade or more, before a different job or even death took them elsewhere, either on another bus or off this mortal coil. A reliance on omnibuses engendered a dependence on your fellow man. This enabled you to remove yourself from your often restricted environment to a place of work, or to see a far-flung relative, or helped in the on-going emancipation of the fairer sex by allowing them the unrestricted freedom to indulge in a shopping expedition to the nearest city; a liberty only dreamed of by their trodden down forebears. It was true that you were not able to travel exactly when you wished, but rather had to bow to the will of the majority, not a perfect way of managing things, but a very much improved and democratic one.

A car overtook on a dangerous bend and elicited a few gasps from the top deck passengers.

"And I'm very much afraid that's what it's coming to. Tin boxes on four wheels with a lunatic behind the fifth inside."

"What are you talking about?" Pamela sometimes worried about her husband.

"The Coming Thing. Everyone's Instant Transport!"

"Oh, why worry about it? I'm quite sure we'll

never have one."

Tom gazed across the slopes of the famous Blaisdon plumb orchards, which could still be discerned in the July twilight. It appeared that every mortal this side of that geological oddity, May Hill, grew plums. Quite a number of the larger growers in the area had amassed a tidy amount from the Blaisdon plums and a walk on a fine September day through the May Hill cutting would reveal several stall holders all trying to attract the passing traveller with the graphic invitation to purchase 'RIPE PLUMS'. Something endemic in the soil, strangers were informed, and if in spring they had recourse to come the same way 'something in the soil' caused them to be immersed in and lured insidiously into buying the area's other prolific natural products, daffodils or narcissi. This was truly a fecund little patch in the world's garden and with misgivings; Tom baulked at the idea of living elsewhere, away from this beauteous spot.

"Well, I don't know what we're going to do." With some irrelevance, Pamela voiced the thing, which had been on her mind for the entire journey.

"About what, my gorgeous one?" Tom was still entrenched, his mind still subservient to plumbs and daffodils.

"Oh, Tom. You are hopeless!" She tried not to get irate, though found it difficult not to become impatient with this delightfully unconcerned, but obdurately head-in-the sand man. He compounded this by throwing his head back and taking the wind out of her sails by criticising himself.

"Hopeless, hapless and helpless!"

Here starteth the admonishment proper, she thought, thinking that she shouldn't have to do this. "How useful to be a dreamer like you, Tom. You pretend you don't really understand or don't want to and you buy time by pretending to be confused." Here she smoothed her long auburn coloured hair and moved sideways to look him in the face. "You know full well what I'm on about. Where are we going to live?"

"There's no real hurry..."

God help her, she'd strangle him in a minute. "You say that, but there bloody well is! You won't bloody well do anything until you absolutely have to, then it'll be too late!"

"William won't throw us out. He wouldn't dream of it." There was a lack of conviction in his voice. Exasperation overcame Pamela and she none too gently took hold of his chin in both hands. She held him firmly and tried to control her mounting anger.

"He won't, but the new owner might. Tom dear, you must try and find somewhere right away."

Tom shrugged, gently disengaged her hands and put his arm round her. What a caper marriage was. The perpetual struggle and it seemed if you were the breadwinner, the more you did, the more they expected you to do. He decided to reveal something he'd known for some time and hoped it would not cause an explosion.

"I had a letter the other day. From my uncle in New Zealand." Her reaction was milder than he anticipated.

"Oh Tom! You are a close person. Why didn't you tell me? We're not supposed to have secrets..."

She sat forward, her indignation blunted by the knowledge that Tom did not usually hide things from her, but for reasons ostensibly known only to himself, had an odd idea of what was and what was not important for her to know.

"I just didn't want to do anything premature; not to be too hasty..."

To his surprise, she laughed; the last thing he expected.

"What you mean is, you don't want me to push you into anything. Yes, I know I'm impetuous, but you'll have to spill the beans now." She eyed him expectantly and a short pause ensued. He seemed reluctant.

"Well?"

"Well what?"

"What did he have to say? How is he getting on? You are infuriating!"

Tom shrugged his shoulders and tentatively

felt inside his jacket. They were descending the slope to Leadon, the village before Waterton and he caught sight of a reddish glint in the sky over Waterton Hill. He pulled his uncle's letter out and handed it to his wife.

"Uh, here you are then. Read it. But what's that over there? That glow over the hill. Hell, I hope it's not a fire?"

With remarkable and uncharacteristic restraint, Pamela put the letter from Uncle Charles of the Antipodes in her handbag. She liked to appear to be perverse and unpredictable occasionally and with atypical feminine guile, reckoned it kept her husband on his toes. The letter was probably only purveying a lot of old nonsense about stocks and shares and sheep with the odd photograph thrown in and she would read it later at her leisure. She did wonder what decision Tom might have to make about it, but she knew from past experiences that it was no good rushing him. Procrastination was his middle name. He hated making decisions and if nagged into making the wrong one, could quite easily turn round and blame her for the disaster, which might conceivably happen as a result of it.

They alighted from the bus at Waterton Cross to witness pencil slim Miss Emily Ward talking to undeniably rotund Mrs Taylor.

TWENTY-ONE

The latter lady was, for her in a voluble and highly excited state.

"I sin three fire engines go up the lane an' Ted Lewis 'oo come down jus' now reckons they wunt 'ave it out before mornin'. They don' know 'ow it started, but i's destroyed that cornfield in front of Morris's. My ol' man's jus' gone up there now!"

As if somehow affected by the mere thought of the inferno on the hill, the worthy lady frantically wiped her brow with a large gentleman's handkerchief, returning it at intervals into the pocket of a voluminous floral pinafore. And all the while, the elegant, passive Miss Ward; a simulated expression of concern on her still only slightly furrowed brow, interjected with mild non-contributions such as 'really' and 'well, fancy' and 'oh dear'.

The night had suddenly drawn in and a motley collection of individuals emerged in the pool of light cast by the Horse and Jockey from over the road. Boots clattered across the tarmac and loose-tongued voices saluted the bus stop quartet.

"Night Tom, night Pam. Night Mrs T, night Miss Ward. We're off up the fire. They wants beaters." Garth Wood, he of the fecund loins, was their spokesman and announced this with the panache of someone about to attend a gladiatorial contest.

It was perhaps not too far from the truth for Tom Donaldson imagined it was probably the most exciting spectacle that had happened in Waterton since the Romans had invaded and built the nearby town of Ariconium. This was a settlement now buried beneath the fields of the hamlet of Byeford, but still a site where coins and artefacts of the period would occasionally come to the surface.

Without loitering, this disparate party of Waterton's manhood, torch beams to the fore and with some regrets at having to leave the public house before closing time, set off uphill; bolstered by their martyrdom, yet resolved to come to the rescue of the hard-pressed Hereford County Fire Brigade.

Mrs T was doubtful and contemptuous. "Fat lot of good they'll do," then abruptly," I'll be goin' now. Got t' get that boy o' mine a bit of supper. 'ee allus like a bit of bread 'n cheese before 'ee goes up the 'ooden lane. Cheerio."

The lady nodded a perfunctory farewell. It was long past John Taylor's supper-time and his illness had not taken away his healthy appetite.

"Goodnight, Mrs Taylor." Tom Donaldson hailed the lady's back, which was just disappearing from the light cast from Miss

Ward's shop window. These hasty departures were a well-known facet of Mrs Taylor's character. Similarly, she did not welcome guests at inconvenient times. She was not one to pretend in the middle of cake making that a visitor was wonderfully welcome. She was not a 'how-nice-to-see-you' person and tact was not a virtue where she was concerned. After sitting uncomfortably in the little kitchen amidst a feast of freshly made and impeccably 'ironed' pastry for ten minutes, the unwanted intruder would be dismissed with something akin to 'I jus' wunt t' put this lot in the oven. You can see your way out. I ant got time t' talk. Ernest 'll be 'ome soon an' 'ee'll expect iz tea on the table.'

At other times, the same visitor who had previously left the Taylors' feeling guilty at ever having had the temerity to darken the doors of 3, Temperance Cottages, would return some weeks later to a comfortable chair, a large cup of tea and an overly-proportioned slice of homemade cake. You never quite knew with the enigmatic Mrs T, but when the chips were decidedly down, there was no better person than her to suddenly metamorphose into the 'salt of the earth'.

Perhaps realising she had scarcely acknowledged the arrival of the Donaldsons, Mrs Taylor turned about at the sound of Tom's voice.

"An' 'ow's that babby of yourn?"

"Fine thanks, Mrs T. She's with Mike's mum at the moment." Pamela answered this eleventh hour enquiry.

"Well, Gran Fryer's alright. Makes good ellenblow (Elderflower) wine. Beat mine at the Leadon Vlower Show this year." Having satisfied herself that the Donaldson's heir was in good hands, Mrs Taylor nodded, this time with approval and went on her way.

"I think I'll go and join those fellas," said Tom. "Sounds pretty serious to me."

The quiescent Emily Ward voiced approval, and Pamela, disapproval. Tom's timorous revelation of the letter from New Zealand rankled.

"I'm not walking home at this time of night on my own and if we'd been more alert we'd have got off at the end of the lane instead of here."

"I thought you wanted a drink," said Tom hopefully.

Pamela tossed her finely sculptured head and laughed derisively. "You mean you wanted one!"

Emily Ward, turning a key in the shop door, had discreetly left them and the young couple, a torch lighting their way, walked home in silence.

A grey, impassive old woman, Gran Fryer came to the door.

"You sure you won't have a drink before you go, Mrs Fryer?" Tom offered, but knew that his offer would be rejected. He noticed that the food on the supper tray provided had not been touched.

"No thanks. Never eats nor drinks before I

goes t' bed. Sometimes 'as a cup o' cocoa." A slightly contradictory statement. "Goodnight Mr Donaldson, Pam."

Footsteps across the yard, another door opening and Gran Fryer had left them alone.

Pamela caught Tom by the lapels and dragging him with her, flopped on to the couch. "Go on, you great ninny, take the bike. Have a drink and then go and have a look at that fire! Don't be too late!"

"Are you sure...?" Another unpredictable woman, thought Tom.

"Yes, bloody well go on. I want to read that letter from New Zealand."

Tom hesitated, then searched frenetically for his bicycle clips; his wife still sitting there and looking upon him with mock pity. He kissed her, was tempted to stay, but a minute later was pedalling furiously towards the Horse and Jockey. His luminous watch showed twenty-past ten. Precious minutes passing as he desperately attempted to succeed in his quest for liquid refreshment. On the main road he encountered a bike going in the other direction and to his dismay, the rider dismounted and hailed Tom to stop.

"If I wa'nt tired, I'd book y' fur not 'avin a back light, young Mr Donaldson. But I ent goin' to. So you'd better get 'im fixed uz soon as possible, if you please!"

"Sorry, Constable. I suppose you've been

at the fire?" The guilty party was all obsequiousness and to his chagrin, the local law in the form of PC Adam Walters, was disposed to talk.

"I 'ave, an' they 'ave only just sent out a car from Leeside to relieve me." He went on bemoaning his fate for an infuriating amount of lost drinking time and then said, "Anyway, you'd better 'urry up. I'll 'ave you fur drinkin' adder time, else." With this sardonic parting shot, he re-mounted and if a policeman can 'plod' on a bike, wended his way to where the police house stood on the left, on the straight after the bends towards Gloucester.

Tom was penitent, but too late and hoped that Phil Arnold was in a generous mood and would take a lax attitude to his arrival after legal hours.

TWENTY-TWO

The Horse and Jockey had been in the Arnold family for several generations and was not yet afflicted by city dwellers who alleged that they knew what a proper country pub should look like. It still sold crisps with screwed up blue greaseproof salt packets and visitors had to be content with the only dish of the day, a recent venture deliciously cooked by Mrs Phil and dished out to first- comers until the capacious, but not bottomless pot was empty. Horse brasses and servile labradors had not yet invaded the place and pickled eggs and onions still took their place on the bar, along with the inevitable barrel of strong draught cider, which one unwise individual had once dismissed as being 'cloudy'; a cosmetic indication of its undoubted potency. Having had it explained to him, the guileless gentleman from somewhere in the capital city, was persuaded to partake and a couple of hours later staggered down to the River Hotel near Caldersley Lane and from all informed reports, did not move from his bedroom for the rest of his holiday.

Apart from a few obvious visitors in the lounge bar, the place was practically deserted, or at first appeared so and Phil Arnold was going through the preliminary motions of closing down for the night. He did not comment on Tom's late arrival and had already taken the top off a bottle of Guinness in readiness.

"Sorry," said the latecomer in what he imagined might be a contrite timbre, "I've been to see William Johnson and got back late. I imagine they're all at the fire?"

"S'alright, me boy. Glad t'see you. Bin a bit quiet in 'ere t'night."

Just at that moment the bar door swung open again and sensing an opportunity, Charlie Watkins lurched in, looking, if possible, even more unkempt than usual. His fly buttons were undone and the agitated tongue feverishly darted in and out without respite.

"'ow about a quick one, Phil," he whined, "go on, jus' a quick un? I'll be off then, ol' mate."

From behind the bar, Phil Arnold towered over his clientele and his intimidating bulk and presence was usually enough to rebuff and vanquish even the most awkward of customers. His reply to the old man's sycophantic request was unequivocal.

"No, bugger off 'ome, Charlie. You've 'ad far too much already an' I aint puttin' up with it no more!" A basso profondo admonishment which, had they been the butt of this big man's chastening vitriol, would have caused most of the armed forces in the world to retreat.

But the indomitable Charlie wheedled on. "I'll pay y' t'morrow, Phil, my ol' mate, honest!"

An uncomfortable bystander, Tom downed his stout quickly and invited Charlie to walk with him up Church Lane. He sought and received permission from Phil to leave his bike at the Jockey.

The acute landlord was not slow to intervene. "This is Tom Donaldson," he quickly said. 'ee's goin' up t' the fire. You go with 'im, Charlie."

Tom began to usher the drunken old man out, winked at Phil and promised to get his charge safely home.

But Phil was not yet finished with the old aged reprobate. "Oh Charlie," he thundered," just a minute!" Clutching the still open bar door, Charlie peered unsteadily back into the inner sanctum. He could just discern the massive blur of Phil leaning on the bar with a slight indication of amused tolerance on his face. Though his senses were decaying and dulled by the 'fermented apple', Charlie was not slow to seize upon the remotest chance of further imbibing. The stick pointed and the tongue hissed and he took one step forward and two backwards before having the monstrous temerity to try again.

Sadly for him, the unmoved landlord was not having any. "You can bugger off, Charlie!" he shouted. "An' while you're at it, do your bloody flies up." And here he paused for effect. "'cos we don' want y' frightenin' anythin' in th' 'edge, do us?"

TWENTY-THREE

Charlie had not, he convincingly declared, any knowledge as to the origins of the fire and after a horrendous and winding journey up Church and Wood Lanes and helping the old soak into his serendipitous, cluttered caravan, Tom sauntered over to view the serious fire, which now raged on Waterton Hill. The flames had destroyed the barley field, devoured the hay stored in a now skeletal looking French barn and were now busy ominously whetting their appetite on the fringes of the perilously vulnerable woodland nearby. Three scarlet fire engines spewed gallons of precious water in what, until now, seemed to be an unavailing deluge. The trees immediately fronting the beleaguered cornfield were, as luck would have it, mere saplings. They'd been planted as replacements a couple of years previously, after felling of their predecessors by timber merchant, Philip Latham and although the flames had already encroached by some hundred yards; the fire chief had an hour previously set every available man to work with an axe; the object being to fell those further back before the fire's omnivorous progress burst disastrously upon and destroyed the maturer and often ancient trees in the main wood.

Upon reaching this denuded swathe, the

flames would either have to jump or die and in order to enhance the chances of this happening, the enlightened fire chief had recruited two bulldozers from the Forestry Commission to follow the felling and to finish off any standing foliage; hopefully pushing it round the trees already burnt and to the edge of the blackened cornfield. The axe men returned to knock out any obdurate saplings and then a tractor pulling a water spraying cart drove round several times to wet the all-pervading bracken.

At the scene with his gleaming sports car, Philip Latham had been horrified at this deliberate destruction, but it had been not too politely explained to him that the entire Waterton Wood could be lost if this action were not taken. They had tried beating but it was not that effective; the fire grew more rapacious by the minute and whilst they had enjoyed brief success in containing it to the edge of the cornfield, it had evaded them in several places and entered the woodland.

Tom Donaldson had bumped into Bob Allen, Mike Fryer and a group of villagers with whom he was not all that well acquainted. Mike Fryer had his hand on the handle of an axe and looked exhausted. No-one knew how the conflagration had started, but Bob Allen said you could see the glow from Leeside and pointed out Mr Jeremy's now half floodlit 'dig' in the next field along. The fire chief had not been concerned about it and after a visit to the Langdon's over a school governor's meeting, Mr Jeremy had seen the iridescent sky above the hill and was now a lone figure, pacing up and down the fresh earth mound, which had been formed by the soil removed from his disappointing archaeological investigations. At various times bystanders had detached themselves from the scorching main attraction and climbed the gate to the headmaster; their sole intention to have a friendly word, but the normally charismatic Mr Jeremy made it quite plain to these amicable souls that their presence was not welcome. He did not seem at all his usual self and the well-meaning interlopers were given a curt, snappy dismissal; enabling the solitary figure to go back to his perambulations on the earth mound in peace. The site took on a decidedly telluric eeriness in the reflected light and once or twice Mr Jeremy's tired legs failed him and he stumbled. Startled, he soon corrected himself and carried on, hoping that nobody had noticed

Casting his eyes on these adjacent goings-on, Bob Allen supposed archaeology 'buffs' were a zealous and jealous lot. Mr Jeremy and his entourage had been working hard on the project most of the summer. This enervating toil had not been helped at weekends by aimless spectators. Too many people were willing to watch; there were not enough helpers and the watchers - as they usually did when witnessing any skilled enterprise they didn't understand - asked all the wrong questions. Bob Allen had been a guilty party himself and had not the demands of his recent recruitment by Waterton Cricket Club and other things got in first, he would have gladly offered to help. But schoolwork and other things seemed to take priority and much as he would have liked to support his enthusiastic headmaster, his time was limited and he had to draw the line somewhere. Suddenly, he saw the figure on the mound bend down to pick something up. It cannot have been very big, for the headmaster appeared to put it in an inside pocket and having done so, resumed his endless pacing up and down.

Despite the strenuous efforts that had been made to stop it, the fire had continued to traverse the exposed bracken and was now dangerously near to the main wood. It was beginning to take its light from the fields and no-one had seemed to notice the disappearance of the stars.

Awesomely, a gigantic boom from over Ross way announced a dramatic change in the weather and Bob Allen expected the fire chief to prostrate himself towards Mecca or otherwise make obeisance to some other deity. This indeed must be divine intervention and manna from the Gods. At first a slow trickle, the rain gradually increased in momentum until great hailstones began hitting the fire engines and bouncing off into what was left of the blackened barley and sodden bracken. Seemingly impervious to the unremitting deluge, Bob Allen stood looking at the three fire appliances, a trio of behemoths amongst a panoply of the elements; earth, fire and water. Yellow oilskins now gleamed on the scurrying bodies of the firemen and at a signal from the fire chief, the fire engines disengaged and were now slowly crawling from the cornfield and making for the lane. Lightning seared the sky and the rain came down in torrents, tropical in its intensity, unremitting and saving the day.

Most of the spectators and helpers were now safely accommodated within the spacious and sturdy confines of Morris's ancient cowshed and this is where Bob Allen supposed that he too, should make his way. He caught up with Tom Donaldson, a fellow dreamer who, transfixed by this great act of nature, had realised too late that he was now saturated. Running for cover was a little like shutting the stable after the horse had bolted, but they reached shelter to find the milking parlour well-occupied and home to a hive of conversation.

"'s bin a sultry ol' night."

Midst the overall cackle, the sodden schoolmaster detected a familiar monotone. Roadman par excellence and weather prophet extraordinaire, Mr Brain was holding the floor. The same Anton Brain, that is, who hailed from that bit of Waterton that bordered the forest, but somehow looking different than Bob Allen had ever seen him before. It was the cap or rather, the lack of it. The roadman was bald and evidently the protector of Waterton's greatest secret had been sacrificed in the conflict. Sad though it was, perhaps some person unknown would find it one day: a quintessential piece of the village's historical and sartorial history. It would be a matter for conjecture, but Bob Allen wondered how far that lost piece of corduroy headgear had travelled during its owner's perambulations round the parish.

Someone was brandishing a large torch, the beam of which from time to time alighted erringly on the sterling roadman's hairless condition. But he was not fazed by this blatant exposure and continued to address his fellow parishioners in his inimitable style. "I told thick fire chif it wunt a'gwowin' t' stay fine, but there wuz a yup o' people chopsin' to un at the time an' 'ee didn't take no notice of I. Still, I darezaiy 'im yunt too un'appy about it now. Which iz more 'n I cun saiy fur ol' Bill. I daime (imagine) 't'was the only bit o' real good cereal 'im 'ad got on th' 'ole varm."

The 'Bill' referred to in the roadman's justification of his weather prognosis, came in just then with a couple of Tilley lamps and after depositing them in a position to fully illuminate the building, mentioned something about a power cut.

"We seems t' be 'avin it all t'night."

Denis Smith, builder and cricketer, a black smudge across his forehead, spoke to the strained looking farmer.

"I shouldn't think it'll be too long."

Bob Allen turned round to observe the dog collar behind him. So the local clergy did work on odd occasions and here was the local priest to watch hypocritically - the schoolteacher thought - over his flock or, bearing in mind the current location, should it be 'herd?'

Come to think of it, where else would you find such a gregarious, but odd selection of bedfellows? Not in the pub; not at a village meeting - nobody went to those if they could help it - not at a village soccer match or, for that matter, a village anything else. However, they were nearly all here in the cowshed. The church, the medical profession, the master builder, the roadman, the bank clerk, the carpenter et al. Even he, the frequently harassed and sometimes reviled schoolteacher was here. They could re-build the Morris 'ranch', doctor, his wife - a creaking gate if ever there was one - solve his financial problems, educate his growing grandchildren, preach at him, keep his ditches clear and now Phil Arnold was come, serve up his homemade cider.

Large earthenware mugs of cloudy potency, administered by the willing landlord to the populace. Mike Fryer, Ted Lewis and a few others were acting as waiters and dishing out the country 'wine'. Phil Arnold, who had divested himself of his waterlogged shirt leant, muscles rippling, coaxing the golden liquid from the barrel and overly-exciting the one or two members of the fairer sex who happened to be present.

It was inevitable that the bad fairy should turn up at this convivial gathering and indeed, another familiar figure lurched through the half door with an expectant look in his eyes.

"I got woke up by the thunder," announced the newcomer and Phil Arnold laughed. More a subterranean chortle, remarked the amused Reverend David Oliver to Bob Allen and Tom Donaldson.

"You must 'ave a conk on you," said the landlord, addressing the dishevelled village drunk. "Fancy smellin' this barrel o' goods frum over that ol' caravan. Still, since you've sobered up a bit, Charlie, y'can 'ave a 'alf. y' are!" A big paw, which would have deterred any aggressor or intimidated the most ardent tee-totaller, handed the mug to his usual bête noire. He wondered what had possessed him to do it, but in doing so, he showed a good deal of heart and compassion. Even the village drunk, observed Bob Allen.

Though he was the village drunk, Bob Allen understood Charlie was the world's greatest authority on chickens. If any of the local farmer's wives wished to buy a breed of fowls or had any other problems concerning their clucking charges, Charlie Watkins was the man to consult. Even the vet from Ross had been known to consult Charlie about a singularly unfortunate specimen of the breed, who had contracted an unknown disease. The vet did not know if it was contagious and Charlie had taken the bird in; cosseted it, filled it with his own herbal concoction, which he spread on its feed and cured it. In gratitude the chicken's owner had given the bird to its amateur 'physician', but fate decreed a fortnight later that of all the chickens, Freddy, the predator fox could have taken, Clara was his chosen one. This caused the old man lamentations and provided an excuse for him to go on even more of a 'bender' than usual.

Bob Allen felt something soft rubbing against his legs and looking down, was confronted by two bold emerald eyes. Sam, the Morris household's favourite feline, purred generously at him and a cat lover, he hoisted the animal on to his shoulders. Tom Donaldson tickled the creature's chin and Sam, appreciative of so much attention, jumped from shoulder to shoulder.

"If we're in here, where are the cows?" asked Tom.

"By some 'edgerow, I shouldn't wonder. Anyway, there less likely t' catch pneumonia than us, I reckons." Mike Fryer answered the question.

Over by the door, Doctor Langford was in earnest conversation with the vicar.

"How d'you get a night off?" enquired the clergyman.

"My calls get switched to Ross. Even so, it's not a thing I can do more than once a week. It's quite a large practice and I really shall have to think about taking on a younger man. Looking after seven scattered villages besides Waterton, takes a bit of doing."

He has eight parishes to my one, thought the clergyman. Some people worked hard for a living. With some bitterness, he was beginning to think it was more rewarding to tend to a man's bodily needs than his spiritual ones. Everyone admired the doctor, whereas his own standing in the community had fallen to a nadir. He mentally cursed the day he had met Lizzie Johnson. How could a man minister with such a flagrant, apposite private existence to hamper his endeavours? He supposed the old maxim 'don't do as I do, do as I say', could vaguely apply. He wondered how many of them knew? Probably most of the village. Perhaps it would not be long before he received a deputation led by the churchwardens. He could sense the lack of respect now being exuded by some of his parishioners. Meanwhile, the Reverend David Oliver chatted to all and sundry and drank his cider with the best of them. And the more cider he consumed, the less troubled his conscience became.

The storm began to abate and one or two cars containing one or two wives began to arrive. Exhausted by events, a fireman entered the cowshed and sat, head in hands on a manger until someone tempted him with a glass, which he shouldn't have accepted, but to which the fire chief would have probably turned a blind eye. Someone called for Dr Langford. His wife had arrived in the Rover and oblivious to the exigencies of the fire, was champing at the bit with impatience. The doctor reluctantly left the goodly company to join an irate Maude Langford; a barrage of enquiries rending the inside of the large saloon as it trundled down the muddy lane. The questioning was interminable and not for the first time, Henry Langford speculated as to why the Gestapo hadn't employed his wife's interrogatory powers during the Second World War.

Why had he gone? What a silly man he was and he needn't expect her to nurse him if he caught 'flu and in that circumstance, what would happen to the practice? She had her beloved and enervating dogs to attend and Janet would not be home from her exclusive ladies' college to help et cetera, et cetera; the woman's tongue was indefatigable, and this ceaseless verbal onslaught eventually served to foster rebellion in the good man. He resolved that at long last, he would put up with it no longer. He had noticed that the fire was nearly extinguished. The fire brigade was now clearing up. The inevitable black Wolseley belonging to the police stood by the farm gate, which denoted the last exit on the lane and a policeman he vaguely recognised from Ross waved the Rover to a halt. He came round to the passenger window and the doctor wound it down. It had stopped raining and in the driving seat, Maude Langford fidgeted impatiently, anxious to be away.

"No casualties, sir?"

"No, officer. It's all in order. No ambulance needed, thank heavens."

"Right, sorry to stop you sir. G'night!"

Maude let out the clutch and they slithered on through the mud to the accompaniment of his wife's high-pitched harangue. Dr Langford felt exhausted; a couple of decades exhausted and took the bull by the horns. 'Cometh the hour...'

"My dear..."

"Yes, Henry?"

He composed himself and addressed her with surprising vigour.

"Shut up!"

Faced with this enormously unexpected affront, the woman hardly knew how to react.

"I beg your pardon?!"

"I said for God's sake, shut up!"

This was perhaps the first time in her life that Maude Langford had been shocked into silence and her husband suddenly felt less weary. It would have been a good notion; he realised, to have used this tactic on his wife aeons ago.

Following the doctor's departure, the cowshed gradually began to divest itself of its human inhabitants. Some went in cars, some on bikes and some on the trailer pulled by Bill Morris's old green Ford tractor. Bill Morris a somewhat inefficient farmer, even in his misfortune, had proved a courteous and grateful host.

Eventually only Bob Allen, Mr Jeremy and Mike Fryer were left watching the firemen concluding the mopping up operations. The headmaster had an excited air about him, but Bob noticed that to talk in his usual animated style, he had to sit down on an old seed drill, sodden from the downpour and covered in grasses from the uncut verge; a condition, which did not seem to deter or inhibit him in any way whatsoever. He was fervently clutching some object in his right hand and there was a miniscule tremor in his left one, not something his faithful minion, Bob Allen, had ever noticed before.

"I didn't want to produce this in front of all those people, but I believe I've made a remarkable find. It's extraordinary it wasn't noticed before. I picked it up, just like that! Off the earth mound."

By the light of his powerful torch, Mike Fryer looked down at a small ivory plaque, little more than five inches in height, which showed a tiny, bare-breasted goddess. On either side were two horned goats.

"Hmm," commented the eager Bob Allen, "that can't be Roman. Looks Grecian or even earlier in style."

"I don't think it's either." The headmaster liked nothing better than to enlighten people. "I know history's your forte, Bob, but I think it could well be Phoenician.

Bob Allen did not wish to pour cold water on the head's theory, but felt he had to make a point. "What would a Phoenician relic be doing so far inland in this barbaric - sorry, what was barbaric - country? I don't see it. I know the Phoenicians are supposed to have traded pre- and during the Roman era, but surely they didn't get much further than the south coast settlements?"

Mr Jeremy was not to be denied. "Not at all. What about Hadrian's Wall? Roman soldiers could have been posted anywhere in the Empire. This figurine could have been purchased in somewhere like Iberia or Carthage or any of the former western or eastern Phoenician cities, or merely exchanged from one legionnaire to another in this country. And what was there to prevent a soldier from Ariconium from visiting what we think was a temple up here and losing it?"

"In which case," persisted Bob Allen, "who is the figure depicted on the plaque?" Have you any idea?"

"I think it may be Asherah, Baal's mother figure and sometimes consort. She was known in Babylon as Ishtor; in the Bible as Ashtoret and of course, in Greece as Aphrodite. Amongst other roles, she is usually recognised as the fertility goddess."

Bob Allen never failed to be surprised by his erudite headmaster's broad knowledge. There was no better exponent of religious instruction and it was obvious that Mr Jeremy's studies had also taken in the ancient, pagan beliefs and practices as well.

"So Baal's lady has come to Waterton," declared Bob Allen flippantly, "and it appears Baal may have been around tonight with his fire and water. You do, I presume, mean the Old Testament Baal? You know, he who caused goodie Elijah enormous palaver?"

Amused by his young colleague's ability to turn most subjects into facetious wordage, Mr Jeremy indulged in a wan smile before continuing. "Yes, Bob. I do mean all-purpose, awesome Baal. God of energy, light, storm, fire, strength; anything in that line. He also has various guises in a variety of civilisations and was far more in vogue and allegedly powerful than the Bible suggests. Whatever he's called in different climes, he's usually found to be the same old, corrupt, amoral, terrifying Baal!"

Mike Fryer was lost. "I'd better be goin'," he

said. “I wunt say nothin’.” And bidding the two schoolteachers goodnight, he mounted his bike, pedalled past the still stationary police car and made his way cautiously down the mud-strewn lane. As he passed the black Wolseley, he noticed Philip Latham talking to the police and caught the words ‘not necessary’ and wondered what prompted the timber merchant to question the fire chief’s handling of the inferno. He rather thought it would boil down to a question of financial loss, which was typical of a man who could not be grateful for what had been saved and was therefore, decidedly purblind. All that talk of gods and goddesses was beyond him. He planted things in the soil and generally speaking, they grew. He never recalled praying to any god about it, although he did go to harvest festival once a year. *We plough the fields and scatter.* That was a good old harvest hymn.

Half an hour later, Bob Allen and Mr Jeremy - the latter clutching his precious relic - climbed into their cars and made their separate ways home. It was well past midnight and the only onlooker left was a marginally sobered-up Charlie Watkins; standing in the frame of his caravan door, another cigarette between his lips, glowing in the darkened night. He turned, unwittingly slammed the caravan door and still under the influence, reeled on to his shabby couch and as he fell, managed to stub the offensive weed out on a tobacco tin lid, which served as an ashtray. He had either entirely forgotten or conveniently expunged from his consciousness that early evening fag, which he'd smoked by the gate to the cornfield.

TWENTY-FOUR

Never hailed for his underwhelming reticence, Woody could not keep it to himself. Playtime at Waterton found him, Martin Lewis, Dudley, Arnold and a few other small beings, engaged in juvenile rapport and rustic repartee near the Boys' toilets. At present the village did not have a sewerage system and the pong caused by massed defecation into primitive buckets, though not desirable, did not seem to affect the boys, who were as likely inured to it by the fact that most of the time they did not smell so good themselves.

Today 'The Fire' was the predominating topic. How it could have started, an exaggerated estimate of the damage done, who had been there and all this frequently distorted knowledge gleaned from tired parents over the breakfast table.

Woody hesitated, but discretion was not his second name. "I reckons I knows 'ow it started."

The conversation ceased. Here was the news they'd possibly been waiting for. Woody went on and had not the nous to realise that he could be about to hang himself. "I went fur a walk up the 'ood last night round seven, an' ol' Charlie 'ee wuz 'avin' a pee against the five-bar gate. You knows, that un what goes in t' the cornfield up there. 'ee finished 'avin a leak, then lit a fag. Then 'ee went down the lane. 'ee didn't see me. I wuz up a tree, y' know, the oak by Morris's 'ouse."

"Y' couldn't climb that tree!" interjected Dudley. "You ent no good at climbin' trees!"

Morris's oak was generally reckoned by the boys that knew, to be the most difficult tree to climb in Waterton. The intrepid Arnold had once managed to scale its heights, but it was extremely unlikely that Woody could have managed to conceal himself in the lower foliage as he had asserted. Woody was well down the tree climbing rankings and his deliberate fabrication had landed him in hot water.

"I'm tellin' you buggers the truth!" insisted the unrepentant boy. "I can climb that bloody tree any time you like!" He squared up to Dudley but Arnold, more sensible, stood between the two antagonists.

"Cut it out, you soft sods. It aint worth fightin' over an' if it comes t' that, we'll go up there tonight an' see if Woody can climb it. I don' reckon' 'ee can, but that's the only way t' find out."

A silent figure and until now only on the periphery of this scintillating debate, John Taylor stood with his friend Spencer, watching the animation of the older boys. He did not wish to gate-crash and though aware of the unofficial pecking order, which applied within the tribe, wore a slight smile on his face and courageously decided to have his say.

"Excuse me." There was no harm in being

deferential. "But Woody didn't climb that tree. I know, 'cos I followed 'im t' Morris's last night. I kept well outta sight and I wuz collectin', I wuz collectin'..." and here Taylor, unused to the limelight; went crimson, "wildflowers from be'ind the 'edge in Coningby-Wilson's orchard an' I sin 'im run up by. So I followed 'im..."

As if he knew he had perhaps said too much, Taylor clammed up. He hadn't made himself known to Woody at the time lest the would-be macho male ridiculed him about his gentle hobby and condemned him for being somewhat epicene in character.

Furious at being rumbled, Woody was about to direct his violent attentions to Taylor, but was again restrained by Arnold, who could not be argued with and had grown at least a foot in height during the last four months.

"You leave 'im alone. 'ee's bin ill an' let 'im finish."

Taylor cleared his throat. He did not want to tell the next bit and wished he was back home with his mam and the cat. "Then a few minutes later, Mary come out of the wood and I..." Here a small lacuna occurred and Dudley promised to buy Taylor a gobstopper if he continued, whilst Woody threatened the younger boy under his breath and squirmed with embarrassment.

Taylor did not wish to admit curiosity on his part and was beginning to wish he'd kept right out of it.

"What did y' do when Mary come?" enquired the understanding Arnold.

"I went back 'ome," replied Taylor lamely. This was not what he had done. He had watched the young couple dismount from the gate, noticed the repugnant old cider drinker emerge from his caravan and sensing something unpleasant was about to happen, had beat a prosaic hasty retreat.

Never slow to take advantage of an opportunity to debunk the hapless Woody, Dudley instigated a cruel chant.

"MARY, MARY. MA-RY, MA-RY. WOODY LOVES MARY." A cry which was taken up by most of those present and caused Woody to hang his head in shame, not knowing what to do or how to combat it.

Anxious not to make any more indiscreet revelations, Taylor crept away and was joined in this defection by Spencer, who was anxious to have a game of marbles before it was time to go in.

His eyes brimming and suffering acute embarrassment, Woody took an aggressive stance and hit out at Dudley and anyone else within range, until Mr Jones stepped in with the whistle, which meant lines before lessons. Mr Jones had taken over the top class from Mr Jeremy who'd wanted a rest from their boisterousness and he set them a task about the geography of Australia. He then went off to see Mr Jeremy about some internal matter and during his absence, uproar ensued. This was singularly unfortunate for Woody, as most of his adversaries were in this class, as were Mary and her friend Marion. The playground chant revived itself, augmented by the bitchiness of some female voices; the owners of which were maybe not as pretty as Mary. Some distance from one another, the two juvenile lovebirds tried to get on with their work, but tears soon began to course down the young girl's cheeks. Disconcerted by her friend's distress, Marion marched to the front of the classroom and stood on Mr Jones's chair. She had a surprisingly powerful larynx.

"Shut up, you lot! Leave 'em alone. They can't 'elp it. 'ee like 'er an' she likes 'im. What's wrong with that?"

"When y' getting' married?" Bradley, a boy who managed to be both fat and tall, smirked; going bright red in the process.

"Shut up, Braddie!" bawled Marion. But her efforts were to no avail. The class remained chaotic until Mr Jones briskly returned and with her back to the door, Marion did not see him.

Mr Jones had no illusions about his chosen profession. Fifteen years of teaching, only interrupted by the war had taught him that children, when you left them to their own devices, did not stay mute. But he was still surprised to see Marion isolated upon his chair.

"And what indeed, are you doing up

there, young lady?" The Welsh inflexion, lyrical and prominent, was much in evidence; softly mocking, but always kindly.

Marion dismounted guiltily. "Tryin' to kip 'em quiet, sir." She'd thought quickly and decided not to reveal the real reason for her lofty position.

"Thank you Marion, but much as it is appreciated, I don't think I need your help. There should have been no noise and a good deal of work done by now." Mr Jones scratched his head. "Let me see, Woody, come out here and bring your book, boy!"

It was not Woody's hour and understandably, he hesitated.

"Come on boy, I'm waiting!" Clutching his geography book, Woody trailed miserably to the front. He placed the book gingerly on Mr Jones's desk for the teacher to examine with his myopic gaze.

"Hmm." Mr Jones leant back in his chair and surveyed Woody for at least ten seconds. Silence reigned and was only broken when the teacher blew his nose and addressed the hapless boy. "I see that apart from the title 'Australia', you have managed to pen two words in quarter of an hour. Namely, 'The Aborigines', spelt incorrectly into the bargain. The rest of your opening page is, regrettably, pristine white; which suggests that either you are using invisible ink or you were involved in the likely furore, which took place during my absence." Here the kindly schoolteacher looked directly into Woody's face and noticed the tearstained condition of it. "Go and sit down, boy. If I cared to look round, I imagine I could find others with even less thoughts about Captain Cook's great discovery than you. However, Marion, please come here again. It does not seem to have been a normal disturbance and I would like to know what really happened when I was out of the room?"

No tell-tale, Marion came forward, trying to think of a story. She had no need, for frightened that her friend was about to reveal all, Mary burst into tears and left the room. Disconcerted, Mr Jones stood up and faced the class.

"Marion, will you go and find Mary and bring her back, please." He became very positive. "The rest of you will get on with your work and Doris, would you go and ask Miss Barnes if she'd come and see me for a minute."

The infant teacher with the winning manner, Miss Barnes, came and after a whispered conversation with Mr Jones, took the returned but distressed Mary back to the infants', where the poor girl poured out her sorrows; being careful not to divulge anything concerning the previous evening's tryst with Woody. A homely, dedicated spinster of some forty years, the kindly infant teacher put her arm around the girl and tried to comfort her.

"If it's just teasing dear, the best way is

to take no notice. They'll soon get tired." She was not convinced that Mary had told her the whole story, but who knows what girls attaining puberty imagined to be the truth? To them, there is often a thin division between reality and fiction. Miss Barnes wiped away her tears and sent her back to her class. Mr Jones motioned her to sit down, made no further comment and discreetly returned to marking some papers.

Emboldened by Miss Barnes's encouraging words, Mary applied herself diligently to the task in hand, paused in her efforts, waited until she thought Mr Jones was engrossed in his marking and to everyone's surprise, gave Woody a bewitching smile. Initially dumbstruck, Woody eventually returned the compliment and unsure that he'd done the right thing, blushed deeply and lifted his desk top to hide.

Five minutes later the bell signalled the end of lessons and the intoxicating smell of Irish stew tantalised throughout the building; tormenting young appetites and suggesting that dinner was about to be served.

During the dinner hour break, the considerate Arnold decided that Woody had endured enough taunts and took it upon himself to see off any threats to his friend's peace of mind by displaying his talent as the toughest fourteen year old in the school. Antagonists were given short shrift, sore earholes were acquired and in gratitude, Woody took Arnold off to the woodshed to apprise him of last night's happenings truthfully and as it were, straight from the horse's mouth.

"I only give 'er a kiss," he maintained and trying to disguise his embarrassment, nonchalantly propelled a stray cob across the blackened floor. They were sitting on an upturned wheelbarrow, which was used to transport fuel in winter from the shed to the old-fashioned stoves. Another week and they would not have been able to get into the place, for the autumn term's delivery was due and several tonnes of coke would fill it to capacity.

"You soft bugger." Arnold did not mince words and was still apt to opine that football or conkers were far more worthwhile pursuits than consorting with the other sex. He reckoned that 'once you'd felt one girl, you'd felt the lot' and he'd once overheard his scurrilous old Grancher say 'wimin wuz all the same with a flour bag over their 'eads'; a dubious homily he did not comprehend, but one he knew must be correct, because his Grancher was very sanguine and as a result, usually right over most things.

"I didn't do nothin' like, you know, like..." avowed the hole-digging Woody. "It wunt 'ave bin right with 'er."

"Well, tell me what 'appened when you went into Watty's caravan? You didn't 'ave nothin' t' drink did y'?" Interrogator Arnold was a chip off the old block and although brought up in a pub and perhaps because of it, had little time for those that imbibed too heavily.

Woody became scornful. "We wuzn't there a minute before 'ee looked out th' windda an' 'ustled us out the back door! I reckon 'ee must 'a sin smoke 'n realised what 'ee'd done and didn't want us t' see it. We went down Beavan's rocks way an' 'ee folled us. I reckon 'ee wuz frightened some un 'd come and ask un occard questions. All the way down, 'ee wuz pantin' 'n wheezin' an' 'ee couldn't kip up. Said 'ee 'ad summat called an-an gina an' 'ee did look pasty. When us got t' the bottom, Mary went up Caldersley Lane to 'er place an' I went along the main road with Charlie. We got to your pub an' 'ee went in an' I went on t' Byeford. I wuz late 'ome goin' that way and me mam give me a clip round the ear'ole."

This was a long and manful speech from the rejuvenated lad, but Arnold was not satisfied.

"Did anybody see y' climb the fence on t' th' road?

"No, we waited fur the traffic t' go, then got over. We sin one or two az we wuz walkin' along the road, but I think they wuz only visitors from th' 'otel out fur a stroll." Woody was positive on this point.

"Tha's good," observed his friend, 'cos y' know what you two are, don' you?"

"What, me and Mary?" Woody was uncertain.

"Yes, you two."

Woody looked perplexed and just then a patter of rain hit the corrugated roof. It seemed the fine weather had broken for good. Small hands thumped the door, seeking shelter, which Arnold had denied them by turning the rusting key in the lock and had removed it before entering; a wise precautionary measure, for to have left it in would have invited some gleeful antagonist to incarcerate the duo without fear of ever being apprehended. It had happened to Dudley and him a little while back and only a session of good, honest down-to-earth verbal terrorising had enabled them to escape. It had taken a good half hour for them to persuade some mortal to unlock the door and apprehensive that someone might 'welch' on him, Martin Lewis had only done so when threatened with the prospect of having the two small spherical portions of his anatomy removed by horrendously amateur surgical methods.

Ignoring the entreaties from outside and thumping the corrugated iron roof in defiance, Arnold steadfastly resumed his assessment of Woody and his pretty girl.

"As I wuz sayin. You knows what you two are? Yer witnesses, th'as what y' are. You 'n' Mary sin old Watty light a fag, smoke it 'n' drop the dub in the cornfield." Arnold's voice became Stentorian as the banging on the door became more persistent and someone started to belabour the roof with a stick or some other equally peace- shattering type of implement.

"Bugger off!" bawled the incensed juvenile counsellor.

"Come on, Arny." Woody recognised Dudley's voice. "Let uz in, it's bloody pissin' down out 'ere!"

"You sod off under the bike shed. Go on, this iz important. Bugger Off."

There followed a lot of mixed falsetto-basso grumbling - in the manner peculiar to boys of that age - and the would-be stormers of Arnold's near impregnable stronghold left to clatter across the playground and seek shelter elsewhere.

"So, if I wuz you, I'd kip them big chops o' yourn shut. You already told 'em all a bit on it; although y' wuz lyin'. It wuz a bit too near th' truth from what I can see and you needs t' watch it. Ol' Charlie can be nasty when 'ee's 'ad too much cider. When 'ee can afford it he gets that 'Strongarm' in t' 'im an' me dad says it d' take the varnish off the tables 'n' 'ee should know. ol' Watty can be an occard un when 'ee wants, n' I reckon 'ee'll want t' kip you quiet one way or t'other."

Woody briefly looked bothered by this sage advice, but had an answer.

"I don' think 'ee's worried 'bout us tellin'."

"Why not?" queried Arnold.

Moithered again at the thought of his sweetheart, Woody told Arnold that Charlie had said that if either of them so much as mentioned being in his company on the night of the fire, he would approach their parents with his version of the confrontation, and this was something they wanted to avoid at all costs.

"Y' only give 'er a kiss, didn't y'?" said Arnold bluntly.

"Yes, but 'eed probably say we wuz doin' more..."

But his friend was avidly re-assuring. "Y' great, doolally girl's blouse! I'd say if y' kips quiet, you'll be okay. Jus' kip that big trap o' your bunged up, thas' all!"

"Thanks Arny," said the relieved Woody and gave his friend a friendly punch on the arm; the only sign of affection that was ever permitted and practised amongst boys in the school.

A whistle blew - Bob Allen's, which had a different tone to anyone else's - and the temporary inmates of the fuel shed, emerged into the renewed sunlight. It had been a short shower and during lines, the resentful Dudley dug Woody in the ribs.

"MARY," he hissed. MA-RY, MARY, MA-MARY!"

Woody thought quickly. "I ent goin' with 'er no more."

"'oo are y', then?" whispered Dudley,

"Arnold," replied Woody and applied his fist deftly into his inquisitor's ribs in reprisal.

TWENTY-FIVE

Back from one of her hypocritical and sporadic visits to see the still ailing William in hospital, Lizzie Johnson addressed the Donaldsons in their small cottage. Pamela Donaldson had always been taught never to trust people who did not smile with their eyes - a hangover from days spent with her ancient and superstitious grandmother-and since old indoctrinations die hard, she felt Lizzie filled the bill. The farmer's wife had glinting black eyes, dominated by a perceptible coldness that belied her excruciatingly cheery manner, and this undeniably lent veracity to old Gran's questionable words of wisdom.

"So I'm afraid that's it. You'll have to go. We'll be putting it all up for sale. A man from Crapp and Kennelly's will be here tomorrow to look the house over and, of course, he'll want see the cottages as well. Mike will probably be alright, because whoever buys the place will doubtless want labour. But as for yourselves, well, I'd advise you to start looking right away."

"That won't be necessary," said Tom Donaldson quietly.

Lizzie's features contorted into more of a scowl than a frown. She did not comprehend.

"What do you mean by that?"

Tom resolved to make the bitch wait and lit a cigarette. "It won't be necessary because I've already taken steps to get us out of this fuckin' mess!" He was almost enjoying this and revelled in the fact that he'd had the balls to use a bang up-to-date expletive; one he'd only heard in a slightly seedy, but earthy local public house recently. He was uncharacteristically agitated and drew heavily on his Craven A; a throat burning apology of a fag that he'd lately taken to smoking.

"Tom..." Pamela tried to intervene and Lizzie looked shocked.

"There's no need to use lang..."

But he was having none of it and ploughed on regardless. "It had occurred to me that a selfish bitch like you might not concern yourself overly with our welfare and, as Pam knows, I answered a recent letter from my uncle in New Zealand. He's offered me a job and is sending us the wherewithal to get there. We've decided to accept and with any luck, will be leaving this bloody God-forsaken village as soon as possible! I can't see us getting any help here. I've asked around, but the word 'homeless', far from receiving sympathy, seems to rankle with people. You certainly find out who your friends are when you need a roof!"

Though not quite vanquished, but appalled at the unrestrained vitriol emanating from this normally easy- going personality, Lizzie shrunk towards the door; unwilling to capitulate, yet ready if necessary to escape from his clutches. Her voice sunk in a harsh glissando from a dubious bel canto into something akin to the harsh utterances of a wizened and time served old crow.

She almost shouted at her accuser and the motionless eyes were now two pools of near hysterical tears.

"I let you the bloody cottage in the first place, didn't I? Is that all the gratitude I get?" she raved. "To hell with you and your cosy little marriage, if that's your attitude! I don't give a damn what happens to you. You've a large chip on your shoulder, sonny boy. You go to bloody New Zealand to your ever loving uncle! You won't get on any better over there. You've got about as much drive in you as a wet weekend!"

Furious, Tom crossed the room to within a foot of the philippic mouthful being directed at him and motioned Lizzie towards the door.

"Get out, Lizzie!" The words were spat out from between clenched teeth. "Get out of my sight! I can't stand you and the dislike appears to be mutual. Leave before I do something I regret, there's a good girl. Just go!"

The sound of the front door being abused reverberated round the echoing yard and a whimpering from upstairs indicated that the furious verbal contest had caused a disturbance of another kind.

Exhausted, Tom slumped into an armchair by the window. The still blazing August sun dominated this first Sunday afternoon of the month and proud of her man, Pamela came over and spread herself on his lap. She could feel him shaking and in an attempt to quell this tremor, planted a kiss on his forehead.

"Well done," she said, her face wreathed in a serene smile. He was not too enervated not to make hopeful explorations under her skirt and she had unfortunately to deter him in order to go upstairs for the baby.

TWENTY-SIX

A car crunched up the driveway to the farm and slid into the yard. Bob Allen, the roof of his convertible down, vacated the vehicle, walked to the brightly painted door and knocked.

Outwardly unruffled by the recent hostile encounter with Lizzie Johnson, Pamela invited him in and took him to the front room where her husband was fully occupied in nursing and making appropriate noises at the infantile Sarah. Tom was pleased to see the schoolteacher and baby in hand, arose to greet him.

"Sorry, Bob. I almost forgot you were coming. We've just had licentious Lizzie here and..."

"Tom..." This from a concerned Pamela.

"That's okay," said Bob agreeably, taking the proffered chair. "I'm familiar with her unsavoury little habits - not personally, I hasten to add. Anyway, tell me the latest tidings. Is it as you thought?"

"Quite as we thought." Tom elucidated and excusing herself, Pamela made her way to the kitchen. Affected by Lizzie's rancorous intrusion, she too had forgotten that the schoolteacher had been invited to tea.

"And there's more," Tom continued, flippantly bringing into play his past experience with a local amateur dramatic society. "I have to inform you, dear boy that we're off to the Antipodes!"

"Good Lord! What brought that on?" Astonished, Bob took the familiar green packet out of his pocket and lit up. Tom explained about his uncle.

"Are you sure you're doing the right thing?" Bob tried not to pour cold water on things, but could not help voicing his concerns over this earth-shattering news. "Phew, it's a hell of a long way and things are improving here, albeit slowly; even for bank clerks."

Tom placed the placid baby in a high chair, where she proceeded to hit a row of small wooden animals with a desert spoon. He accepted a cigarette from his guest, lit it with a fuel-driven lighter and inhaled deeply.

"Not in the way of housing," he explained. "I can't buy a place, it's almost impossible to rent with a baby and I don't fancy a council house."

"Well, is it a good job he's offering you?"

Tom stood up and in his enthusiasm, began restlessly to peregrinate round the room. "That's just it. It's a damn good job. He's got two thousand acres, millions of sheep and not much of a head for figures. My Aunt Rosamund has been doing the financial side of it for him for years, but she's not that fit and with no children, I was always in the reckoning. I don't remember them that well. I was only two when they left for the great unknown, but he's done very well.

Pam's dead keen on the idea."

"What about your parents?" Bob Allen resisted the temptation to intimate that the grass might not be any greener in New Zealand.

"Both mine are gone and Pam's mother would probably come with us. Her mother's separated from her stepfather."

The schoolteacher made a wry face. "Is that wise to take mother-in-law along? D'you get on well with her?"

This did not seem a problem for the potential immigrant. "She's a sweet old girl. She doesn't interfere over Sarah, yet she'll always help. She rents a place in Hereford, mind you and whether closer proximity would enhance or detract from our present amicable relationship, I don't know. Still, I don't see how we could leave her behind and, anyway, I don't think Pam would go without her, so we haven't much choice."

Bob Allen laughed lightly. "Oh well; I don't know why it is, but whenever I meet someone interesting, they up sticks and vanish from my life for ever! I've only just got to know your lovely self and your devastatingly beautiful wife and here you are, calmly proposing to up and leave me. It's a great shame!"

Tom absent-mindedly stubbed his cigarette out on a highly decorated dish, which perched precariously on top of an old Singer sewing machine, and walked over to the window.

"I shall be sorry to leave England in many

ways," he averred. "In fact, I shall probably miss it like hell. However, one place I shan't miss is this bloody village! It has a strange alien air about it. Almost pagan. I'm a dreadful cynic, but there have been too many odd happenings just before and since we arrived. I told you about the wax doll. Then there was the fire and before we came, Mike's poor wife and that sad devil; what was his name? Peter something uh-or other...?"

"Trout," supplied an outwardly unfazed Bob Allen. His mouth had gone dry and he was desperately trying to suppress the turbulence, which threatened to overcome him.

"That's it," blundered on Tom, completely unaware of the emotions he had aroused in his comparatively new friend. "Peter Trout, oh - and that lad Taylor. It makes you wonder what's going to happen next."

Bob Allen had recovered. "Coincidence, dear boy. Pure coincidence."

"I'm not so sure," murmured Tom, almost to himself. "The whole atmosphere of the village seems tainted. Probably living next door to Lady Lizzie doesn't help." He raised his voice to an audible level. "Her and the vicar, so I've heard. He must be a damn fool!"

"It's virtually common knowledge." Bob Allen saw no harm in confirming Tom's suspicions. "I had the chance of an exploration with that party on one particular occasion, but the mere thought of venturing where so many other penises had penetrated, repulsed me and I took myself off to be sick somewhere. Some would have said something apropos to gift horses and mouths, but I'm sure it would have been far too daunting an experience for an innocent young bachelor like me, don't you think?"

"Tea up." Not choosing to question the cause of the gales of mirth she'd just walked in on, Pamela swayed elegantly in with a tray and proceeded to unload a sumptuous selection of sandwiches and cakes on to the table. Tom went to fetch the teapot and some cups and baby Sarah's vitals and with everything in place, they helped themselves to the food.

"Just carry on, Bob, we don't stand on ceremony." She gave their guest a questioning grin. "I don't suppose you'd care to give Sarah the occasional spoonful or two? I know it's feasibly beyond your remit, but you never know when it might come in useful! How's Mr Jeremy, by the way? I was sorry to hear he's poorly."

She was right. Feeding babies was not a thing he'd ever made a habit of, but he took the teaspoon in good grace and eating with his left hand, managed to locate Sarah's mouth on one or two occasions with the other. Proving that men can multi-task, he also contrived to answer her query vis-a-vis Mr Jeremy at the same time.

"Not too well, I'm afraid. Doesn't look as though he'll be back for the start of term."

The schoolteacher anticipated what his host was going to come out with next.

"Another coincidence? Can you tell us what the medical profession have found concerning him? Is he liable to get worse? I know what it sounds like to me..."

Throughout the rest of the meal Bob Allen was strangely reticent and to change the subject, made an enormous fuss of the Donaldsons' daughter. He had his doubts about Mr Jeremy and hoped the illness would not prove fatal; but had a gut feeling that it might.

He had vivid recollections of his time as a small boy in Shropshire and of being transported every Saturday to visit an ailing Grandmama who lived, pallid and distressed amidst the Clun Hills. From Onibury by train into the black and white quaintness of Ludlow, then a rambling bus trip to the back of beyond. Here they found Granny languishing amongst the cushions on the hard leather sofa and arthritic Grandad struggled to make tea with water from the bubbling kettles, which sat permanently simmering on the big, black range. Apart from the verdant countryside immortalised by AE Housman, Mary Webb and others, everything in Shropshire in those formative years, appeared to be tarnished with a black pallor. Black hats, a black cat at Gran's called Sooty; black cows, black-and-white houses, which correctly, should have been brown and white; an ebony dresser;

a hideous Victorian flower-patterned papier-mâché table and to crown it all, the high-collared black dresses, which Gran always wore. It could be that he'd been mistaken and not all things in this, one of the least known counties of England were of a funereal hue, but in the dismal light of Gran's ever worsening illness, it just seemed like it. When in later life he came to explore the bracing and beauteous hills of Clun and Clee and been awestruck by the Long Mynd, he had to admit that his clouded childlike impressions had been well wide of the mark. They had faithfully visited Granny every Saturday for three months; a period which to the young Bob Allen felt more like three years. Sadly, with no palliative care practised in those days, Granny eventually died in pain, but uncomplaining to the end.

Mr Jeremy was now afflicted by the same yellow pallor that Granny had and Bob Allen was sure that the genial and compassionate Dr Langford knew full well what it was, but being obliged to respect patients' confidentiality, was not prepared to divulge anything.

From somewhere the Donaldsons had acquired a large ornate antique wall clock, which with a sonority that would not have disgraced Big Ben, chimed the hour of six o'clock. This was the signal for the now slightly fractious Sarah to be deposited in bed and after being changed and exhibiting a small protest, she went off peacefully enough and was soon slumbering deeply in her innocence.

Tom Donaldson and Bob Allen talked of politics and idiot politicians until half past seven, by which time the schoolteacher began to get restless. He rose from his chair and with profuse thanks to his hostess, intimated that he should be going.

"Splendid tea, Pam. Sorry can't stay longer, though you've probably had enough of me! Got some marking to do..."

This didn't ring true and the real reason for the schoolteacher's proposed departure was, to Pam, pretty obvious. She smiled and confronted him.

"Would you mind Tom accompanying you? I'm sure he'd be agreeable to such a liaison."

Bob Allen raised his eyebrow in mock surprise and gave a reciprocal chuckle.

"How did you guess?" he parried badly and commented further, "thy sins will find thee out!"

"Everywhere outside a pub to a man is an arid desert and you intended going to the oasis. The Horse and Jockey is a good watering hole and Tom, also, is something of an Arab. So I suggest you both get in your motorised camel and hive off across the dunes. I, of course, will be the little woman and stay home to do the ironing."

Pamela dredged up a huge sigh and Tom smacked her bottom. Bob Allen wondered if this was an appeasing gesture exclusive to married couples, or if anyone else could join in. He dismissed the notion as unworthy and tried to concentrate on what Tom was saying.

"If I know anything about it, there's probably a rotten play on the radio. In fact, her own intellectual desert. She never reaches an oasis like William Shakespeare. She's content to remain in the sand with her bucket and spade; perpetually thirsty, but enjoying herself!"

Pamela went to fetch the iron and returning, had the last word. "Go on out with Bob, clever knickers, or I'll brand you!"

TWENTY-SEVEN

Confirmation. The organ, complete with ciphers and Mr Jones manipulating the two manuals, sang out *Jesu Joy of Man's Desiring*. This disturbed the snoring mice who inhabited the instrument and caused the resident woodworm to scuttle to the mouths of their homes to witness a scene of pomp and splendour that had not been seen in St Lawrence's for some considerable time.

The equable Welsh schoolmaster had been co-opted for this service; taking over from the worthy Mrs Gubbins who, though very loyal, could not use the pedals and considered herself not competent enough to accompany such a grand occasion. Thus, the parasites who had spent happy years manifesting themselves on the massive wooden Bourdon pipes, found themselves assailed by sudden, unaccustomed gusts of intermittent air; a stuttering invasion of their normally inviolate space, both disconcerting and thoroughly uncomfortable. Even cousins in the upper reaches reported more activity than usual and without further ado; all the prevalent little pests emigrated to the vulnerable tracker action where with the exception of the odd occasional horizontal ride when Mr Jones pulled a stop out, they were able to forage relatively undisturbed for the duration of the service.

An ailing beast, St Lawrence's church organ was still hand blown and Spencer, assumed to be musical and therefore interested and reliable, had been commandeered by Mr Jones to 'blow' or pump the handle of this ageing musical conglomeration. Hidden from view, Spencer had to keep his eyes on a vital tell-tale, which indicated how much air there was in the bellows and if you 'blew' too hard and the wind chamber became bloated, the organ tended to hiccup. Conversely, if you allowed the brass weight to ascend and reach the dreaded word 'empty', a banshee wail would herald a complete musical collapse akin to an air-raid siren subsiding into nothingness and peeping round the side of the organ casing, the stranded organist would give you a dark look.

His brow currently furrowed beyond his years and furiously masticating on a piece of tasteless chewing gum, Spencer endeavoured to steer a middle of the road course. *Jesu Joy* was okay, but heaven knows what he'd do if at the end of all the sacred fun-and-games, 'Jonesy' went to town with something like the same great composer's *Toccata* and *Fugue in D Minor*! It was heavy work for a small being and with understandable misgivings; Spencer just hoped he would be able to cope.

Splendidly attired in newish robes, the choir entered and to his surprise, to the basses were attached Woody and Arnold and to the sopranos, the rubicund-cheeked Mary and her ripening extrovert friend, Marion. Spencer was sure that these school colleagues had not been part of this saintly canto when he'd last reluctantly agreed to blow the organ and wondered what inducement had persuaded such an unlikely quartet to strengthen - or possibly - weaken it. In his naïve way he thought the inculcation of Christian values to which they had all been ceaselessly subjected to at Waterton School, might have influenced them - plus Reverend David's engaging personality - or maybe they just wished to be present to witness others suffer as they themselves had suffered the previous year. It was beyond Spencer's comprehension to explain Woody's presence in particular. Either the vicar had not auditioned him or he'd been included to make up the numbers for the bishop's coming. Mary and Marion, he was aware, had dulcet voices - he'd heard them in assembly - and after months of see-sawing, Arnold's had sunk to a rustic basso profondo. But though also broken, Woody's still resembled that of an unmusical corn crake and it was perhaps fortunate that when arriving at the chancel, he went to sit in the furthest place on the back row of the choir stalls.

Following the choir, a covey of confirmation candidates - mostly young ladies - huddled together in their quest to receive the Holy Ghost and bedecked in pristine white, felt suitably dressed to do so. Spencer could never understand the necessity for this mysterious member of what was called the Trinity, which Mr Jeremy, in his wisdom, had imposed upon them. How could anything be three and yet one? Spencer believed in God and Jesus - this you were compelled to do if you attended Waterton School - but he found the Holy Spirit largely an unfathomable and unnecessary addition to the revered and sacred duo. It was like having a third parent, as if you did not have enough keeping out of trouble with the other two, but he consoled himself with the thought that if his near omnipotent headmaster said there was a Holy Ghost; a Mighty Rushing Wind; A Baffling Ghost of Goodness; then who was he, a boy of but double figures, to question it?

With some amusement, Spencer reflected that it was all 'wind' in here this afternoon. Here he was straining to maintain a 'mighty wind' in the decrepit organ for the sake of the Holy Ghost, whilst emitting the results of a heavy Sunday meal from his nether regions! And immersed as he was in the subterranean gloom of the organ bowels, it was a delicious luxury to be able to let rip in an unrestrained and unobserved manner without having to suffer the usual rebuke which, when grown-ups were around, inevitably accompanied such indiscretions! Spencer knew that it was impolite to break wind in church normally, but freed from parental shackles and away from the 'common herd' he managed to indulge in some gloriously fortissimo explosions. He then was able to remain blissfully unconcerned as the accompanying smell caused by these emancipated detonations dispersed and wafted harmlessly up into the mellow diapasons. Spencer wondered if the artful Woody was letting off silent ones midst the choir stalls or whether the nearby presence of his girlfriend had caused him to opt for discretion.

Here came the Lord Bishop of Hereford with his brightly robed retinue; the Reverend David Oliver, the Reverend Michael Cannington, Rural Dean of Ross and Archenfield; Canons, Chaplain and lesser minions.

The bishop, resplendent in purple, jewels reflecting light from the stain glass window of Christ in agony; a crook to guide his followers and a mitre of religious authority on his head. Never mind that there is a record of the ancient Etruscans first using these religious symbols when paying obeisance to their ancient Gods, the bishop was tall, popular and benign. He strode with steady ease to his appointed seat near the altar and one of his minions removed his mitre.

David Oliver announced the first hymn and Mr Jones pulled out all the stops, very nearly catching the flatulently inclined Spencer unawares. Recovering from a small operation, Mr Jeremy had made a redoubtable effort to attend. It came as a relief to sit in the sanctity of the church after the heat outside, but he found it an effort to stand for the hymns. He was grateful for the presence of his wife and the support of Bob Allen - a confirmed atheist if ever there was one - on this, the acceptance into God's kingdom of some of his students. Candidates had also come from several villages around, but the biggest contingent, nine in all, hailed from Waterton. Mr Jeremy liked to think this was as a result of his influence and the cynical Bob Allen had to concede to himself that it probably was. The headmaster noted the Ward sisters, handkerchiefs to the fore in the moment of 'laying on hands' and Dr and Maude Langford assiduously observing the form of service. All the parents, scrubbed and neat; the several landowners; even Philip Latham, whose daughter, though at private school, had come home to be 'done' in her own parish church. Noticeably alert, Sir Arthur read a declaration from the Old Testament. Now devoid of its former alcoholic induced slur, his was a true aristocratic accent; unexaggerated, concise and clearly audible, without undue emphasis having to be made on his part. Tired and trying hard to keep alert, Mr Jeremy listened to the impeccable diction, which broadcast the experience of Elijah ascending in his chariot of fire. A strange choice, he thought, though perhaps vaguely appropriate to the supernatural aura of the proceedings. The headmaster's fertile mind wandered. Elijah and Baal. Formidable opponents. Baal allegedly defeated. Was the occult ever defeated? Where did a mythical man-made deity like Baal stand in relation to God and the Devil? Surely anything opposed to God was of the Devil? And what of the other great religions? Despite his outward and enthusiastic show of Christianity, Mr Jeremy could never honestly believe in the concept of millions of Moslems, Hindus or Buddhists being cast into hellfire. And yet Christ had said 'unless ye believe...' Christianity was not a religion of compromise. No 'live and let live' policy could be pursued. Christians had to be right and the vast multitudes of non-acceptors, patronisingly and sometimes smugly disregarded, left to accept their fate. The essence, the guide-rope of this stern doctrine was conversion leading to salvation. You had to accept Christ or perish. In their naïve conceit, Christians claimed they were saved and that the great unwashed mass of unbelievers would be doomed. At best these unfortunates would be left to wander aimlessly round the universe, lost souls in a spiritual galaxy; whilst the favoured Christians ultimately reaped the benefit of their constant faith.

But then, what sort of Christian did you have to be to qualify? A spectrum of divergent viewpoints was thrown at you, from the deepest intransigent Roman Catholicism to the meanest, closest, almost masochistic interpretations of the Brethren. Interpolated, there was the laxity of the Church of England; the perverted misquotations of the Jehovah's Witnesses and any number of non-conformist dogmas; some fervent; some tepid and some bugged by a peculiar insistence that a particular vice was unacceptable. No drinking; thou shalt not smoke; thou shalt not wear a hat in God's presence; thou shall have an altar; thou shalt not have an altar... and all for poor Jesus Christ, His sake.

Alarmed, the sick headmaster wondered why he was suddenly embroiled in these doubts. He felt faint and well below par. His shirt clung uncomfortably to him and he was just conscious of the bishop ascending to the pulpit for the address. Mellifluous tones from a convinced mind soothed Mr Jeremy's troubled thoughts. Here was the voice of unwavering certainty. The man was a formidable orator. Also capable of talking to young people in an acceptable, though authoritive voice. The Bishop of Hereford did not talk down to his congregation and could be clearly understood by both young and old alike. Even the cynical Bob Allen found himself becoming enmeshed in this spider's web of verbal dexterity. If only he could have a woodbine, he thought, he'd be prepared to shift his standpoint on such matters to a sort of right-wing agnosticism or - perish the unheard thought! - left-wing Christianity.

Back behind the organ, Spencer flexed his muscles and peeped anxiously round the corner at Mr Jones. The 'deputy' organist beamed and Spencer applied himself with vigour. Mr Jones opened the swell box for a hymn and a deluge of sound encouraged the choir to lead the congregation in what passed for a joyous and laudatory noise.

Mr Jeremy tried to stand, but had to remain seated. Globulets of perspiration trickled down his forehead and the stained glass Christ swam before his eyes. He would miss the first communion of some of his pupils... blackness... the encroachment of night... a pit of unwelcome unconsciousness.

Motivated by Dr Langford, Bob Allen accompanied a Mrs Lowe to her cottage, which sat just by the Lychgate opposite the church and his 999 call for an ambulance was answered within fifteen minutes. Necks had strained to see Mr Jeremy carried out and after a short lacuna and a few words of condolence, the bishop announced that the communion would take place as the headmaster would have wished. After the service and still unobtrusive behind the organ, Spencer heard Bob Allen apprising Mr Jones of the situation. Whilst still at the affable and compliant Mrs Lowe's, a phone call had come through from Dr Langford at Ross Cottage Hospital to say that Mr Jeremy had recovered well. It had been a slight relapse, but as a precaution they were taking him to Hereford General for a further examination and more tests.

Having satisfied his colleague, Bob Allen conducted him down the aisle and Spencer followed at what he considered to be a discreet and suitably servile distance. Spencer's innards were directing him with everyone else to the village hall, where to his knowledge and in the words of the cerebral Sir Arthur, 'a goodly feast' was to take place. With John Taylor in tow and on a similar quest, he walked down the familiar church meadow to the school and turned right up the lane that led to the hall and the cricket ground.

Considering herself a quintessential part of anything of any importance whatsoever that took place in the parish, Maude Langford was now trying to impose her will on the already well-organised village ladies who were serving the tea. She thought them ponderously slow and could not be persuaded that, had she chosen to let them, they could well manage the whole thing perfectly well on their own.

There was an understandably subdued atmosphere at this sweet and savoury repast, partly through anxiety over the stricken Mr Jeremy and partly due to the awesome presence of the Bishop of Hereford who, to his credit, went out of his way to thank the choir and organist and even congratulated the uneasy Spencer for - as he put it - 'feeding the ailing monster' so ably. At this point, Taylor had winked at Spencer and the organ blower, pleased but flustered, grinned self-consciously back. In a corner, Woody flirted quite openly with Mary and Arnold could not get away from the flamboyant Marion; not that he really wanted to. He had belatedly noticed across the chancel that her cassock jutted out promisingly at the top. And here, in close proximity and attired in a thin blouse, he could see closer evidence of her ample bosom. He was just beginning to realise that there were perhaps other things in life worth pursuing other than football, cricket and 'ooding. It had taken him longer than Woody to assimilate it, but Marion, he reckoned, was certainly possessed of a 'nice pair of tits'.

Things began to run smoothly when the unique Mrs Taylor, fully exercising her innate ability to get round Maude Langford, eased her out of it and took over running the buffet.

Secretly glad to be relieved of the responsibility, the doctor's wife breathed a sigh of relief and buttonholed the unfortunate bishop. David Oliver had to suffer his Rural Dean and as a result of these pairings, Bob Allen found himself confronted by the undesirable Lizzie Johnson; a circumstance he would have liked to have obviated like the bubonic plague.

"What a hoot!" An unsmiling opening

gambit from the insensitive woman.

Slow off the mark, Bob did not comprehend.

"I'm sorry?"

"Mr Jeremy, I mean."

Bob Allen pulled what he imagined was a disapproving face.

"I'm afraid he's a very sick man."

"Oh," said Lizzie. "I thought he'd just fainted. Seems to me the whole place is dying on its feet one way or another. What with my William and the headmaster... Won't you have a piece of fruitcake?"

The school teacher had been about to enquire after William Johnson, but his lips formed the unspoken words, 'callous bitch' instead. He loathed fruitcake and took a piece of Battenberg. He felt sick at heart. He felt it in his bones that it would shortly be the end for a good man and here he was cornered by this vixen of a woman. David Oliver passed by, pointedly and awkwardly avoiding Lizzie and with relief; Bob Allen brought the Reverend Michael Cannington into the conversation. The Rural Dean still looked like an outcast from the fishmonger's slab, but never had the schoolmaster been so glad to welcome a visitor from the deep.

After a decent interval mainly spent in mediocre small talk, Bob left the incongruous couple to it, nodded a farewell to various others and made a swift escape. He drove the convertible slowly down the lane and paused at the school, guiltily feeling that he ought to spend some time there before the holidays ended and he would be fully occupied with teaching and not have the time to sort out one or two of the more mundane aspects of the job. It had become overcast, there was now a slight nip in the air and he knew that was only to be expected; it being the dog days of August with autumn beckoning and a new term in the offing. Transformed from the nascent and pallid green of spring, the leaves on the vast ellipse that was Waterton Wood between the Hill and Ross-on-Wye, were now of a darker more effulgent colour and yet he still could not hack the miracle of their sudden change of hue. True, they would die and be resurrected, and where had he heard that before? And dozens of heretics had been crucified by the two Iberian nations in South America. Some died and some were taken down and lived. So, he thought, go tell that to the marines. It was difficult to know what or what not to believe and maybe he should go see a shrink or something? Wasn't that what they called the men in white coats nowadays?

Soon Ross, with its giddily dominating spire appeared and anticipating his arrival, Mrs Adderley opened the door for him. The lady was plainly agitated. Her grey bun bobbed animatedly as she talked and she seemed unusually excited. She nervously clasped and unclasped her hands on her garishly striped pinafore and was ostensibly eager to tell him something.

"That lady you used to teach, Mr Allen has come. You know, that Margaret Trout. Said she wuz stayin' with 'er brother. She left a note. I put it on the mantle in the front room. If you 'angs on a minute, I'll go an' get it."

And a moment later, here it was. A big brown envelope. A delightful big brown envelope with Margaret's distinct and delightful handwriting on it. He was conscious of Mrs Adderley just standing there, all eyes as he read the contents.

'Dear Bob,

I don't know whether you want to see me, but I'm home, I hope, for good. I've not really had enough of France, but enough of France on my own. I am at present staying with my brother in Tillett Street. Come round if you like, when you like.

Lots of love,

Maggie.'

Apologising to his understanding landlady for leaving her so quickly, he astonished her by giving her Maggie's missive to peruse and went straight round to Tillett Street.

He returned five hours later and going straight to bed, wept into the night. He wept for joy and sorrow. The day had been too traumatic. He would gain Margaret and lose Mr Jeremy. He was sure that the appalling disease was incurable. And that was life to a tee. Most of the bastards survived with impunity and the good ones died young. He gave up any thought of sleep, heaved himself out of bed and opened a bottle of Irish. He switched the radio on low and half way down the bottle fell asleep, fully clothed.

TWENTY-EIGHT

The final days of August could well have conspired with one another. In unison, they assailed the perspiring inhabitants of Waterton and elsewhere with intense humidity, sleepless nights and heavy, sunless days. A pretty sight in her simple summer dress, her hair brushed and neatly falling to her shoulders, Mary came down from Caldersley Farm through the foxgloves, the hawkbit; bedstraw, proliferating gorse and bracken. A modern Juliette, she walked straight and proud and sometimes pondering, on her way to choir practice.

Pigs squealed in their cots behind Caldersley farmyard - some squabble over swill a likely cause - and sheep bleated 'hallos' across the surrounding pastures. A large Hereford bull eyed Mary with what may have been admiration. Showing no fear, she went over to the hedge and further pacified him by scratching his white face, that 'white face', which has spread and can be seen peacefully grazing all over the world. Hercules had been around on the farm for as long as Mary could remember and it was one of her delights in life to lead him by the nose when he needed shifting, usually with his attendant harem, to another part of the extensive acreage that her father farmed. There had never been any question of her being apprehensive of him and at the tender age of four, and to her mother's consternation when she learned of it, her dad had put her up on the placid beast and taken her for a ride round the farm.

She did not think it was her imagination, that when she patted him a fond farewell, he shook his great head in acknowledgement at the gesture and let out a great bellow as she continued on down the footpath into the lane. She hurried on until she came to the main road and turning left, made to walk briskly towards the village.

But her progress had not been unobserved. Her walk had not been unobserved almost from its inception. Her intended trip to choir had been keenly viewed by a pair of rheumy, bloodshot eyes, the owner of which sat behind the hedge quietly contemplating an approach.

"Ah now, young missy. Can ol' Charlie 'ave a word?"

Brought to a halt, her well-being shattered by this sudden incursion, Mary felt her heart racing and stood, desperately wondering how she could escape the attentions of the frightening old drunkard. She hadn't seen the 'Serpent' since the fire and had tried to dismiss him from her thoughts.

"I can't stop, Mr Watkins," she beseeched him. "I'm off to choir practice and I'm already late."

Charlie made a great show of disappointment and to the girl's disgust, assembled a great gob of spittle within his mouth and spat it out on the tarmac. He came a little way down the hedge to a gate and surprisingly quickly, opened it and like some rudderless duck, hobbled across the road to confront her. He thrust the blackthorn stick at her and with little option but to stay where she was, she listened to what he said with mounting trepidation. "I ent astin' y', young missy. I'm tellin' y' an' I don' want no argument!"

Inwardly quailing at this onslaught, Mary nevertheless had the courage to try and defy him.

"I mustn't stop, Mr Watkins. Me mam likes me t'get t' choir 'n' back quick as I can. So please, if y' don' mind, I'll 'ave t' be goin'."

At this, a look of sheer malevolence covered the old man's face, then changing tack, he began to wheedle and cajole.

"Aw, c'mon missy. It ent uz if ol' Charlie d' zee many pretty young uns like you up 'is way," - and here his face became harsh again - "an' y' wouldn't wan' 'im t' tell that mam o' yourn 'bout that little boy friend of yourn an' what you wuz doin,' would y'?"

Displaying resilience beyond her years, the young girl fought back and treated the smelling miscreant of an old man to a 'chopsful' in the vernacular. "We wuzn't doin' nothin' wrong, 'onest we weren't, Mr Watkins." Though still bravely resisting, Mary brooked at the thought of disclosure and even though what Charlie would reveal to her parents would be untrue, she did not want to run the risk of raising his hackles for fear that he might persuade them to believe it.

To further enhance his threatening talk, Charlie began to swirl his blackthorn, much in the manner that Terence Stamp as the villainous Sergeant Troy was to do in the television adaptation of Hardy's Far from the Madding Crowd. Petrified, Mary yet managed to remain almost statuesque, as the rustic rapier flashed round her head and prodded her shoulders and it was only when he became tired that he lowered the weapon and emitted a maniacal chuckle.

"Well now, young missy," he said, "it's only a small favour I'm astin' you, Mary, my love."

The frightened girl flinched and felt nauseous at what might be coming next. She had been well tutored about nasty old men and was already poised to raise her foot and give Charlie something to permanently to remember her by, but fervently prayed that it would not come to that. Her face conveyed utter distrust and repulsion towards this decaying example of prematurely aged manhood. But the snake's tongue punctuated the rambling preamble and the blackthorn once again touched her body and roved round her solar plexus region in short, quick playful bursts. With a limp attempt at a final flourish, the potentially deadly miming antics came to an end and the senile 'fencer' dropped his guard to continue with his verbal ramblings.

"Y' know 'ow ol' Charlie is fond of iz drop an' zummat now n' agin, like? Well, I wuz wonderin' if you'd 'elp 'im get 'old on it now ol' Phil Arnold up th' pub 'ave took a dislike t' ol' Charlie?"

Staunch Phil Arnold up the pub, had indeed declared that the putrid caravan dweller would not be allowed to enter his premises ever again. The previous Sunday the sodden old toper had more than blotted his copybook. The Sabbath had seen him blind-drunk in the lounge in front of visitors and furthermore - as mein host had succinctly put it - 'smellin' fit t' stink them pigs up at Caldersley outta the pigsty!' - as a result, the incensed landlord had escorted the incoherent chicken minder out of the pub and told him not to apply for a re-entry ticket. Normally the most tolerant of men, Phil Arnold had had enough.

"Was' that got t' do with me, Mr Watkins?" Not too young not to be equipped with some feminine wiles, Mary backed away from the old man, but this just seemed to induce a resumption of the harassment she had already suffered. Charlie prodded the ground and lifting the stick, began all over again. Fortunately, he could not keep it up for any length of time and he flourished the blackthorn in a u-shape, from his victim's right foot, bringing it over her head and landing it perilously close to her left. He droned on. "I knows y're getting' t' the end o' yer 'olidays, young lady, an' I wants you t' go t' that cellar o' Phil's what the brewery drayman rolls them beer barrels down, n' liftin' up the flap, fetch ol' Charlie a vew flagons o' zider. You can do it in the addernoon. Ol' Phil slips then an' 'is missus goes shoppin'. I 'ave of'en thought o' doin' it, but I couldn't manage them steps. It's round the back an' if y' goes careful, like, you ent goin' t' be sin. You could take that boyfriend of yourn with y' an' an' yer mam's shoppin' bags t' carry the bottles in. 'er ent goin' t' miss 'em fur a while."

Whilst not being as horrendous as Mary thought it might be, this ultimatum took Mary aback. She was being asked to steal and this for her was not an option. But the alternative was to have this pestilential old relic of an old man tell her parents some dreadful tale about her and Woody and she thought quickly.

"But wunt it be locked, Mr Watkins?"

This, apparently, would not present a problem. "That flap ent got a lock on it. I went out th' back way last week an' I did see it. It'd be an easy ol' job for y' 'n' young lover boy. Y'd jus' 'ave t' nip down an' get me a drop" - and here a lascivious sneer accompanied his instructions - "providin' of course, y' didn't stop t' 'ave a cuddle an' show 'im yer knickers or something..."

Appalled, Mary cast her eyes down and near to tears, murmured a barely audible reply.

"I ent doin' it," she murmured, half-choking. "I ent stealin' for you or nobody else."

Like a ship changing to leeside, Charlie affected deep hurt and though Mary could not have known it, the old devil in him still had a smidgeon of decency and this prevented him from chastising her in any horrendously physical way.

"Thas' a pity," he wheedled. "Poor ol' Charlie, 'ee don' get no 'elp nowhere. 'ee's all on 'iz todd with them fowls an' 'iz thoughts. 'ee ent got no money left an' 'ee can't cadge a drop no more." Here he stepped forward and cupped the young girl's chin in his gnarled and unwashed hands; causing her to struggle in horror. "An' 'ere y' are, my little missy, wi' th' means t' 'elp ol' Charlie an' y' wunt! Nevermind, I 'spect 'ee'll manage." His voice became glutinously self-pitying. "Never done no 'arm 'ave Charlie, an' 'ee can't even 'ave a 'armless drink no more." It was becoming quite maudlin and she was noting the ominous change of tactic with dread; expecting a reversion to antipathy any minute.

Not, in the local parlance, being 'tuppence short of a shilling,' she had a sudden flash of inspiration.

"Mr Watkins, I might be able t''elp, but I'll 'ave t' see what Woody says."

Her tormentor let go of her chin, but with the same two horny, calloused hands grasped her shoulders, making sure he still remained the focus of her attention.

Now fully reduced to cascading tears and trembling, Mary was tempted to scream and hoped that someone would pass by.

He callously ignored this reaction and rambled onerously on whilst still holding her by the shoulders. She would have to consult Woody and they would both have to meet him here under the chestnut tree with the bottles the following night, a Saturday night. She was not to speak of it to anyone else and if she and Woody did not appear, he would grass on them to their parents. They'd have to get to the pub after half-past two and making sure they were not observed, do the dirty deed.

Mary was now 'a good 'un' and no harm would come to her if she did as she was asked. He had to have the cider. He let go of her shoulders and at last her dreadful ordeal came to an end, leaving her shaken, but free to resume her belated way to choir.

TWENTY-NINE

Woody was adamant.

"I ent doin' it!"

"But Woody..."

He and Mary were strolling down Church Lane together after choir, a few yards ahead of Marion and Arnold. Marion was clucking away aimlessly to a disinterested Arnold and neither of them could hear or particularly wished to hear the conversation of the couple in front.

"'ey, Arnie, come 'ere!" Woody beckoned at his friend and his girl vainly protested at the prospect of their discussion being thrown open to a third party.

"But I promised 'im, Woody. I promised!"

"W'as the matter?" The concerned Arnold caught them up, trying to sound manly, but displaying his not too distant boyhood by kicking the detritus of an empty can and used cigarette packet off the path.

"But Woody," Mary pleaded.

"Aw, shut up, will y', leave this t' me! I ent frightened o' that dirty ol' sod. 'ee can't 'urt y'!" The words 'chauvinist' and 'pig' were not in near conjunction in those days and had they been, Mary might have applied them to Woody. She was still suffering from the humiliation she had suffered at the hands of the old man and was alarmed at what might happen if Charlie became aware of her broken promise. But Woody would not listen and dismissing her near hysterical objections, told Arnold of Charlie's proposal to Mary.

Arnold pulled a face and thought for a minute or two. Then shrugging his shoulders, he flatly stated that he imagined Woody and Mary had nothing to worry about.

"Why's that?" Through her tears, Mary seemed consoled by Arnold's reassuring attitude.

"Simple," said the makeshift confidante and counsellor, sitting down on the bank and dangling his legs into the ditch. "If 'ee threatens to tell on you, you tell on 'im. I reckoned 'ee'd be frit to death."

Mary had thought it best not to fully reveal the treatment the old man had subjected her to, in case Woody attempted to be physical and came off worst against him, but she still look worried.

"'ee might 'urt us!"

This was no problem for the towering Arnold. "Not if I d' come with y'!"

So after further discussion and some dissent from the alarmed Mary, it was agreed that the foursome - Marion had to be included because of what Arnold ungallantly referred to as her 'big chops' - would meet the old man at the appointed time and having said their farewells at the main road, Woody walked with Mary as far as the Chestnut tree, which now displayed its abundant fruit at the bottom of Caldersley Lane. They could not have been the first couple who indulged in an awkward embrace under it and Woody reflected afterwards that the thing they didn't tell you about girls in school was how much softer and warmer they were to anything else living and breathing and how much tastier they were - say - even than his mam's Sunday dinner.

THIRTY

Sauntering idly up Church Lane, Taylor paused to follow the path of a squirrel as it scurried up a tree. The rodent - for in Taylor's view, being grey, it was undeniably a tree rat - clutched possessively at something and unfazed by the boy's interest, suddenly stopped to sit on a bough to observe him; returning the compliment. It sat eating something for a minute and when sated, resumed its frenetic progress until it vanished into the topmost regions of the sturdy oak.

Taylor's father, who was rarely wrong about such things, had reckoned on an early winter, but with the sun beginning to emerge through the overcast clouds for almost a couple of weeks and humidity high, Taylor could not see the justification for this prognosis. It would be a strange winter at Waterton School if Mr Jeremy did not return for the new term. His mam, who did not believe in calling a spade anything other than a spade, had told him that the headmaster was now pretty ill and had been sent home from hospital. She had tried to explain what this meant, but he found it hard to contemplate learning without that avuncular personality to cajole; to humour and to emphatically lead the entire proceedings in the close-knit village seminary. And this was also Taylor's scholarship year. He had made rapid strides since his illness and if he continued this excellent progress, Mr Jeremy had even promised a shot at a free scholarship to a nearby public school.

It was funny to think that only a year since; he had been nearly struck out of existence by the hand of fate. But he had recovered beyond his and others' wildest dreams. Unless the Deity or some hidden spiritual force intervened, he knew that his beloved headmaster would not and he could not understand why life appeared to be such a lottery. He could not comprehend the pseudo-sagelike wisdom of the not particularly intelligent villagers who smiled to themselves knowingly when they encountered him and talked naively of miracles, but conceded that there was no hope for Mr Jeremy. Why, pray, a miracle for an innocent, immature boy and not a saintlike headmaster?

Already the possessor of an open, fast maturing and agile mind, Taylor freely acknowledged that the medical profession had conquered his polio, but would not achieve the same success with Mr Jeremy's illness. Whilst the spiritual side of him wished to genuflect before the Lord in grateful obeisance, his practical nature appropriated his recovery to the skill of his fellow men and perhaps sadly, a nascent inclination to reject the idea of anything supernatural was beginning to take hold. Once, during the holidays he had bumped into David Oliver in the churchyard and put the whole question to him. With practised ease, the clergyman had neatly sidestepped the issue by asking Taylor if he knew from whence the medical profession acquired their knowledge and skill, if it were not from God. And Taylor had replied that it was probably just a question of research and training; a reply that ensured that the debate ended in an uneasy stalemate.

Directly across the lane opposite the church grew the Coningby-Wilsons' unique orchard of greengage plums. This year, these succulent, juice-laden fruits hung down in invitingly large clusters and were well within the reach of anyone who might climb the gate to illicitly partake of them. It could not be long before several young relatives of the Coningby-Wilsons - as they usually did -came to harvest them and despite the consumption of an easily digested breakfast, Taylor did not baulk at supplementing it further with a small hors-d'œuvre. He took a furtive glance around, tentatively mounted the gate; the most physical action he had attempted since his recovery and finding it easier than he had imagined, stretched upwards for the largest greengage he could find. Just as he had managed to grasp it, he became fearfully aware of a motor of some sort taking the turn from the main road and fast coming up the lane towards him. In haste, he became ponderously slow and he was still standing on the penultimate bar of the gate as the unwelcome police car slithered to a halt. A constable he vaguely recognised from Ross wound down the window; a broad grin on his face.

"Caught in the act, young un," he said.

"I only had one," replied the near mortified Taylor. "Honest..."

The policeman smiled again. "T'aint you we're after, me boy. It's a Mr Charlie Watkins. Adam, your local plod, tells us 'ee lives in a caravan up the top there, near the farm. Is that right?"

"That's right." Taylor was mightily relieved and happily informative.

"Right, and while you're at it, my mate and I wouldn't mind one or two of those, so hand a couple down will you?"

With some hesitancy, Taylor obliged and with another re-assuring wink, the officer wound the window back up and in a flurry of gravel, shot off in his quest to question the unsuspecting Charlie Watkins. It was a possibility, Adam Walters maintained, that the old boy might know something about the origins of the fire and it was an avenue of enquiry worth pursuing because, according to the local bobby, Charlie had been very cagey when previously interviewed and might reveal something quite useful if questioned further.

Somehow feeling unreasonably wicked; Taylor laboriously climbed down from the gate and quickly made for the churchyard. He pushed through the moss-laden lych gate, by-passed the tombs of various village ancestors and came hastily out the other side into Church Meadow. Someone had now obtained permission to run ponies with the Friesians and while the bovines stood watching him, the invasive equines came forward, expecting to be fussed as he went as fast as he was able down the well-defined path at the side of the field. He ungraciously ignored them - not a thing he would ever do normally - and continued to the stile at the bottom, where an assemblage of small humanity had gathered to exchange news before the new term began. The junior bush telegraph had worked well, for amongst their number was Woody, Dudley, Martin Lewis and Spencer, who had cycled out from Leeside on an ancient bike to save bus fares. The only reason he could ride this archaic machine was because, although it was too big for him, it was of the ladies' variety and had no cross bar. This impromptu meeting, possibly owing its instigation to Mr Jeremy's plight, was a curiosity in that its participants would otherwise never have dreamed of congregating here in holiday time, but might have been brought on through a desire that, when the normally dreaded time arrived, the school would be open for business as usual.

Almost inevitably, the 'chopsy' lovebird, Woody, was holding forth. It was cricket versus football, always a keen near autumnal argument and when the intrepid Spencer mentioned a preference for conkers he was mercilessly howled down. A late arrival, Taylor had not said anything, but when asked his opinion, altered the conversation by mentioning the police car and the object of its visit.

Woody went milk white. "I didn't tell, 'onest..."

Though tired from doing late night things under his bedclothes, this prompted Arnold to wake up.

"Shouldn't worry. Prob'ly only wanted the old bugger fur questionin'" - and aside to Woody - "an' don't say nothin' else, y' silly sod!"

"For what?" said an uncomprehending Martin Lewis. Not trusting Woody to keep quiet, Arnold took over.

"Questioning," he repeated. "They takes you in a room an' drops water on your 'ead fur 'ours and 'ours 'til you tells 'em what they wants t' know."

"Why pick on 'im?" enquired tall and fat Bradley.

"Simple," went on the legal expert, confidante and counsellor. "'ee's th' only un uz lives up there besides Morris's and 'ee might o' sin summat. Some un might o' done it fur arson!"

"W'as 'is arse got t' do with it!" interjected Martin Lewis, assuming a bellicose laugh, which no-one else in the small gathering shared.

"Daft sod!" snorted the belligerent Dudley. "arson is when you set fire t' somethin' on purpose n' why would old Charlie or anyone else want t' do that to Bill Morris's barley field?"

"But'ee didn't..." began the guileless Woody, momentarily forgetting the trouble his previous revelations had caused.

Dudley turned on him scornfully. "We knows y' saw 'im light a fag when Taylor saw y' doin' summat t' Mary..."

Face the hue of ripened tomatoes, Woody frantically interrupted. "I wazent doin' nothin' t' Mary!"

"But th' police don' know that, do they!"

"But I wuzant!"

"I wuz talkin' 'bout the fire!" riposted Dudley.

"Why should they think 'eed light a fire on purpuss?" put in Bradley; the last syllable sounding like the substance of a boil on little Reggie Morris's neck. Reggie was a grandchild of the fire-smitten farmer and it didn't seem from the boy's tendency to contract boils at frequent intervals, that the Morris family as a whole enjoyed a lot of good fortune in life.

"Zum people can't 'elp it," said the dogged Dudley, glad to be still holding the floor. "They're comp-com-comp - *(he couldn't manage it)* - they can't 'elp it, so my dad says."

"Will they lock 'im up?" Martin Lewis had been to see too many cowboy films and was already on horseback pulling the bars out of

Gloucester Prison.

"They can't prove nothin'," stated Dudley with an air of finality and after a few desultory and pointless words on the subject, they decided to retire to the cricket ground at the top of the lane, where they were allowed to play impromptu games on the outfield, well away from the sacred square. Arnold and Dudley picked up sides and with surprising equanimity, the fearless Spencer stood up to face Waterton's latest demon fast bowler and promising all-rounder, Arnold.

"Tell you what," said the unfazed Spencer, "you be Lindwall an' I'll be Len Hutton an' I bets I hits you for six!"

Of such things dreams are made and whilst he did not hoist the embryonic speed-merchant that was Arnold for six, Spencer more than held his own and as he adored the game, determined that one day, he too, would undoubtedly play for England.

THIRTY-ONE

Mary had risen early on this Saturday morning. It was still barely light as she collected the eggs; first from the hen coop and from all the several places she had come to know where they inconsiderately laid at random. Once when Marion had come to play, they had discovered a whole cache of uncollected eggs in the haybarn and after breaking one to find it rotten and the stench unbearable, they bombarded the rest with stones and had to retreat outside in a fit of nausea to get away from the dreadful smell.

Mary loved the farm. She could ride - something taught her a while ago by Janet Langford - and was a regular competitor at local gymkhanas where she had won a number of prizes. Her father, a stern disciplinarian with ideas as to how children should be treated, had threatened her with his belt if she ever tried his patience too much, but this was an action on his part that was never realised. In truth, he would no more of touched her than hurt a fly. It was not often that she goaded him, which made it desperately important that he did not find out about her and Woody. As she put the last eggs in her basket, she worried grievously about what might transpire down by the old chestnut tree that evening. She delivered the eggs to her mam, who was surprised to see her about so early and was busy in the farmhouse with all the chores a farmer's wife was expected to do. Although this was an age of slowly emerging mechanisation, life was only just beginning to be made easier for the farmer and his often harassed wife.

Bert Beavan had arisen even earlier than his daughter and she knew that after a few jobs like feeding the impatient pigs, he would bring the cows in and after milking had been completed, let them out and come in for a relatively late breakfast. This was the pattern on most farms. You roused yourself early, did what was necessary and having done so, come in to break your fast. Gone were the days, thank heavens, when the water was so awful, you downed Hardy's fabled pint of mead for this first meal of the day, and Bert's 'good woman' - as he called her - always contrived to have enough bacon and eggs on the table to sink a battleship and feed both him and his two labourers several times over. Mary especially enjoyed these mealtimes and already hungry at the thought of it, decided to go and feed her pony, Aneurin, who was named by Father after a well-known politician of the day. Mary had wanted to call the pony Dewdrop, but her father wouldn't hear of it and she had no alternative but to comply.

Unusually for a farmer, Bert Beavan was a staunch socialist and he thought his namesake was a great man. As he had tried to explain to Mary, 'the man has found shelter for the workers, arranged free glasses, universal health treatment' and was, in the enthusiastic farmer's opinion, one of the most honest politicians the country had ever produced.

Behind his back, the local farming community despised him. They hunted, attended balls and tried hard to maintain the status quo. They labelled him a mountebank and a traitor to the cause, all of which did not disconcert him. He maintained that changes to society were inexorable and it was them and not he who would have to mend their ways if they were not to become dinosaurs.

The early chores done and breakfast over, Mary was asked by her mother to go to the village shop for one or two things that were needed and was a little taken aback when the girl at first, demurred. The promise of a Fry's creamy chocolate bar changed her mind and the fear of meeting the dreaded Charlie Watkins en route soon diminished as the sun made an appearance and she reached the shop without incident. She had to wait for the deliberating Mrs Taylor as the tubby lady took an age to pick what she wanted and was startled to hear that the police had just recently gone up in a squad car to fetch Charlie for questioning about the fire. She knew this because they'd called in to purchase some cigarettes and in her gently persistent way, Miss Ward had somehow elicited the information from them. Agitated by this unwelcome news, Mary hurried home and that afternoon, to keep her mind off the evening's tryst with the old malcontent, went for a long ride on Aneurin.

She had tea and after applying the very little amount of make-up she was allowed to wear, informed her mother that she was going to meet Marion; a statement that was not wholly untrue and which only merited an admonishment to try and be back before it became too dark. In those innocent times, country children were allowed to wander almost anywhere at will and Mary knew that even if she got back after dark, providing it was not too late, it would arouse little comment from her parents. With some trepidation, she bid them farewell and made for the footpath, which with such disastrous and frightening results she'd taken the previous evening. This was quicker than going down the farm track to a point three quarters of the way up Caldersley Lane, where you turned and walked three quarters of a mile down to the main road and the chestnut tree where the dreaded meeting was to take place.

Marion lived some quarter of a mile from the top of Caldersley Lane and the plan was for her and Arnold to walk down it and hide behind the hedge as Mary and Woody confronted the contentious Charlie. Arnold was not clear when or if he was supposed to intervene, but with the optimism that was his natural trademark, he'd convinced himself that he could cope with any situation that might arise and had supplemented this bravado by augmenting his armoury with a large pot of black pepper, which he had filched from the pub larder. He had thought of bringing along the mettlesome canine, Mugsy who, since the arrival of a new baby sister for the disinterested Woody, had spent most of his joint ownership at the Horse and Jockey. But he had come to the conclusion that a snuffling, welcoming dog would not put the fear of God into anyone and finally decided to depend on just his own physical prowess and proved resourcefulness.

As promised, Woody was already there when Mary arrived to join him under the chestnut tree and with mounting apprehension; they waited for the villain of the hour to put in an appearance. Mary was assured by Woody that Arnold and Marion were in the vicinity and she only hoped they'd arrived in time. On hearing the 'serpent' hopefully condemning himself with his own words, the other couple were to emerge from behind the hedge in support and threaten Charlie with the police. They hoped that, confronted by two more witnesses, he would back down. Of course, the old miscreant could always turn nasty with that stick of his and spooked by this thought, Mary involuntarily shuddered. The whole thing was repellent and she almost rued the day she had agreed to meet the injudicious Woody on that fatal night of the fire. Yet she knew she had to go through with it.

In the embracing pallor of coming dusk the clock of St Lawrence's intoned the hour of seven. The evening was becoming chilly, a departure from the recently experienced humidity and Woody felt drawn to his girl for warmth.

"Woody," she murmured shyly.

"Yes?"

"Woody I..." Whatever it was did not come easily.

"What??" He was losing patience.

"Y' promise not to laugh...?

"Get on with it!"

"Promise...?"

"Aw, shit. I s'pose!" He wasn't prepared for what was coming and did not have time to react to it as he would have liked.

"Well, I-I-I love you." Mary confessed this in what her father would have termed her gymkhana voice. He maintained she spoke two dialects; the posh one at horsey events and what he called 'dead 'ereford' when with the village children. They had tried in vain to quash the latter one, but all to no avail, except on this occasion when the overcome and besotted Woody thought she sounded like a heroine from a stilted English 'B' movie.

Woody had no time to react, as the outpourings of a late rising and mediocre pseudo-cockerel - played by Marion - warned of

Charlie's approach. Heeding this hasty warning, they looked to the fence over the road where the figure of Charlie Watkins could just be discerned in the gathering gloom, grunting its way over the gate, which gave access to the main road. Shambling across the tarmac, he made for the chestnut tree and leant unsteadily against the fence before the young couple. It was obvious from his condition that he had reached a nadir. He snarled and attempted to poke at them with the blackthorn through the bars.

"Bloody pol-polis'," he slurred. "Bloody polis' 'ad me t'day! You musta told 'em. What did y' tell 'em, y' young buggers!"

His heart thumping, Woody stood his ground. "We 'an't told 'em nothin', Mr Watkins. An' me an' Mary talked about getting' the cider fur you an' we 'an't done it an' we ent goin' to!"

A deranged volcano erupted in the intoxicated and enraged old soak. He rose to his not inconsiderable height, the tongue going like an emancipated whiplash and brought the blackthorn down with a mighty blow on the topmost bar of the fence. The stick shattered, flying in all directions and the two subjects of the old man's fury were lucky to escape harm; largely to the quick thinking Woody, who brought Mary to the ground with an ungallant, but timely rugby tackle. They crouched there in a terrified embrace and their assailant then proceeded to accost them with further accusations, whilst trying to climb the flimsy barrier, which was all that kept him from them.

"An' what did I ask y' t' do, y' little hussy! Jus' take a vew bottle o' zider fur ol' Charlie! Why, y' young buggers, y'd better look t' yerself!"

Arnold, who had been hiding as the plan demanded, suddenly arose above the hedge in the lane and bawling at the beleaguered couple, instructed them to make for a gap where they could join Marion and himself and with luck, escape their pursuer's hideous clutches. This they did with alacrity, but they had not accounted for the latent energy still prevalent in their adversary. Charlie summoned up unexpected mobility, abandoned his attempt to scale the fence and uttering countless blasphemies, made for the lane with astonishing rapidity. He was not far behind the fleeing foursome and continuing to spit out appalling oaths, threatened dire consequences if ever he caught up with them.

Marion and Mary began to whimper, but the gallant boys dragged them on.

And then a strangulated cry preceded a cessation of the heavy footsteps behind them. Arnold halted to look and the others followed his example. A perfunctory glance was not enough and gave no clue as to what lay in the gathering gloom some eighteen yards away. But they all knew and with internal sledgehammers for hearts, they crept back down the lane.

Charlie Watkins lay on his back with his mouth open. He had fallen slowly to his knees and in a last convulsion, thrown himself backwards in death on to his skull. A red substance seeped through his matted unwashed hair and trickled down the camber of the road into the verge.

'Doop-da-doo.' A grey tawny owl, ghostly in the failing light, took wing from the chestnut tree and skimming the hedge, alighted on a ditching post nearby; adding a fifth living pair of eyes to those that were reluctantly surveying the repugnant corpse.

Marion fainted, being caught by Arnold and Mary heaved her insides out into the ditch.

Woody stood transfixed, hands thrust in hole-ridden pockets, rivulets running unchecked down his ashen face. Talking to no-one in particular he could not take his eyes off the crumpled old man.

"T'wasn't are fault, Charlie. y' just drunk too much cider, tha's all. Y'just drunk too much cider!" His voice tailed off; sibilant and ending in a bout of uncontrolled and almost hysterical sobbing.

Though badly shaken, Arnold began to gently slap Marion's cheeks and with a slow moan, she gradually revived to the nightmare. Weeping, Mary came over and put her arms round Marion and the rapidly maturing Arnold was just wondering what to do next, when the sidelights of a sleek motor came under the railway bridge half way up the lane and in the still encroaching darkness, stopped within feet of the corpse, where its headlights were switched on.

The occupant skipped out, noted the body lying there and shuddered.

"Good God, how horrible!" A matter of fact, rasping female voice. Lizzie Johnson, hands on hips, took in the ghoulish scene. The four scared children and the hand of death hovering over the splayed being that had been Charlie Watkins, one of the world's greatest experts on Galicean creatures; a fount of knowledge on all that appertained to them. Otherwise a man of little consequence in life, 'made equal' in death; killed by a cruel, insidious product of nature, the yellow wine of Herefordshire. Putting a dainty foot beneath the dead man's torso and pulling a disapproving face, Lizzie rolled the deceased Charlie down the camber and as if belatedly stricken by a sense of decency, pulled a blanket from the car and flung it distastefully over him. It did not occur to her that there might still be some semblance of life lurking within him and before diverting her attention to the children, she addressed him in a demeaning and thoroughly unpleasant manner.

"There you are, Charlie. What an end! Still, I can't say the world will fall off its axis when hearing of your demise..."

She turned to the children and gave them what she imagined was a consoling smile. Enigmatic and often blatantly selfish, there was a compassionate side to her, which most of the time, struggled to rise to the surface. She went over to the two girls, who still sat numbed and shocked and hauled them gently to their feet.

“Right, Mary, I think I’d better take you all up to your dad’s and we’ll phone the police and ambulance from there. I hope nobody comes along in the meantime, but there’s not a lot I can do about that.”

THIRTY-TWO

The police came and the medics and Dr Langford, who true to local tradition and practice, could not, in Bert Beavan's opinion, be left out of anything like this. The doctor, aware that there would probably have to be an autopsy, nevertheless unofficially attributed the old man's demise to probable heart and kidney failure and pointed out that he had been treating Charlie for angina for some time and it was just unfortunate that tablets and excessive alcohol were a deadly concoction and the patient had been told this many times, but had not heeded the warnings.

Safely back in their own homes, all four children told the staggering truth to their respective parents and though upset, their elders did not think any further action on their part was appropriate. Mary cowered before her father and confronted by her trauma, he surprised her with a degree of compassion of which she thought him incapable. The sexual implications of Mary's relationship with Woody were answered quite simply by the girl, who stated that Woody was just a friend and that - in 'gymkhana English'- nothing occurred between them on this or any other occasion. The fact that it nearly had on the Friday when Woody escorted her home from choir, still did not detract from the veracity of her explanation and drained by the whole extraordinary happening, she had to have her father sit by the bedside until she entered a troubled sleep.

Perhaps affected by the macabre scenario even more than the others, Woody spent that night and subsequent nights the victim of horrendous nightmares, until Dr Langford had to be called in to see him and prescribe a sedative. Not something the good man liked to give to a child and not a treatment he acquiesced to without a lot of forebodings.

After a not very decent interval and allowing the children little respite, the police did ask questions, which thanks to the discretion of Bert Beavan and a surprisingly amenable Lizzie Johnson, absolved them of any part in Charlie's death.

A small headline in the *Ross Gazette* announced 'FARM LABOURER COLLAPSES IN LANE' and with characteristic and inappropriate facetiousness, Bob Allen wondered who was to pay for the funeral.

Earlier that infamous Saturday evening, having for the first time gained an honourable draw with his illustrious opponent, Dr Langford had left the gracious Elizabethan pile for home, happy in the knowledge of his achievement and richer for the winning of a two ounce tin of Gold Block; which the generous knight insisted he accepted to mark the notable occasion.

THIRTY-THREE

The autumn term started with the usual reluctance by the kids to go back and this dissent was exacerbated by Mr Jeremy's notable absence and the fact that the not so popular Mr Jones was in charge. In consultation with the rest of the staff, Mr Jones had decided to play down Mr Jeremy's grave illness and had mostly managed to evade direct questioning from anxious pupils. But the tragedy of the head's plight was never more evident than during assembly. Each day they would pray for his recovery and each day he grew a little worse. Barring a miraculous amelioration - and who countenanced such a thing in the twentieth century? - there appeared to be no hope.

Although having to comply with his colleague's views, Bob Allen's attitude towards the situation was a minority one. He reasoned that sooner or later the inevitable would happen and that the children should be prepared for it. Pretending that a recovery was possible would not prepare them for the stark, bald announcement that would eventually have to be made; engendering unbridled grief and numbed disbelief.

He accepted and put in jam jars the posies of wild autumn flowers they brought him;

the abundant seasonal fruit and pitiably, the well-meant cards and often badly conceived letters. There were not many evenings that he and Margaret did not go to see the doomed headmaster and although re-assured by her that he was doing the right thing, he still felt guilty about not delivering the often handmade 'get well' cards. It was a curiously bittersweet passage of time for the two of them. Their relationship was no longer a secretive, furtive affair and with a staff shortage, 'Jonesy' was adamant that he wanted Margaret back to make up the numbers; a request that the Education Authority could hardly refuse and into which role she fitted with grace and consummate ease.

Despite the mantle of responsibility, which had been thrown upon him, the deputy head still managed to retain his dry sense of humour and delighted that Bob Allen was ostensibly 'getting the girl', had the temerity, tongue-in-cheek, to ask him where things were leading. Bob Allen imagined they would lead in a contrasting way, like Mr Jeremy's impasse, to an inevitable conclusion. It would have to be given much thought. How many of his friends were now snarling at one another 'midst the dirty nappies? He wryly posited to himself that before marrying, all couples should live together with a three-month-old baby borrowed for the duration from a relative. After the ceremony was too late. Still, not all marriages were disasters. Look at the

Donaldsons. Oh yes, he was aware Pam could be alarmingly impetuous and the laissez-faire Tom sometimes ineffectual, but they were preparing for their Antipodean venture with surprising resolution; strong in their dependence on each other and filled with unbending optimism. He privately thought the New Zealand decision could be a purblind one, but he admired their courage and though the expedition might fail, he was pretty convinced that the marriage could withstand it.

Fortunately, Margaret, whose first attempt had been such an unqualified disaster, was in no hurry and for the moment, they were just deliriously glad to have become an item again. Bob could see the time coming when marriage would not be a necessity, children would no longer be born 'out of wedlock' and in the playground the word 'bastard' cruelly applied to those that were, would hopefully fall out of usage. Bob Allen had spent the last few weeks as if on drugs of mixed parentage. There was the sweet narcotic of Margaret and the bitter, fatal pill of Mr Jeremy and from this contrasting cocktail he had also gained another hugely beneficial bonus. Gently supported by Margaret, not a solitary woodbine had defiled his person for what seemed like a decade and despite loss of custom, even Miss Emily Ward at the village shop had noted his progress and with great generosity, had been one of the first to compliment him upon his splendid effort.

At last the school day came to an end and they could all go home to their respective 'eyries'. Not that everyone lived in an eyrie, but those that did, usually wended their way uncomplaining and studiously ignored the world's problems. Most had too many worries of their own; others wore blinkers and a considerable number were only interested in accruing wealth through the sweat and toil of their fellow men and frequently did not care how they did it. In the words of the controversial song: 'you and me, we sweat and strain, while the white-upper-class folks play'. Would it ever change, Bob wondered and if it ever did, how long would it take?

A man-of-the-world had once tried to tell him that he should 'look after number one' first. Idealism did not pay. You just ended up crucified. To which the ideological schoolteacher had declared that if the world had a few more idealists, then perhaps a larger number of the planet's population would be getting enough to eat.

This brought a prompt rejoinder. "Who do you think you are?" said the man-of-the-world, "Jesus Christ?"

Now driving towards Ross, the sun glinting low over Waterton Hill, a bibulous bird noise sounding even over the engine, Bob Allen chuckled. In truth, it was too cold to have the hood up, yet the schoolteacher was quite enjoying the early autumn air. When he arrived, Mrs Adderley was sitting in the kitchen talking to Margaret who, with half a day a week off, had called round to ask about a recipe and received a warm welcome from the culinary expert.

"I've been invited to tea," she said cheerfully.

You never knew with Mrs Adderley. She was cousin to the stalwart Mrs Taylor and as with her contrary relative, her attitudes to things and people varied from day to day. Once you were in, you were in; except sometimes you weren't and there was nothing you could do about it.

THIRTY-FOUR

The death of Charlie Watkins had provided much scope for conjecture in the village shop for a couple of weeks, but had now been superseded by sensational news. No-one in the village had really noticed Janet Langdon's absence from the place during the long August vacation. When the baying female hoards that gathered there thought about it, they realised that there had been no sign of the doctor's scatty daughter since Easter.

A sixth form student, the skittish young thing could be anywhere, but one worthy lady whose duties included attending to the cleaning of the medical household and surgery had, in the absence of Maude Langford, taken it upon herself to sign for a sturdy cream-coloured pram, which a delivery man had brought to the back door during her polishing operations. As a result of this revelation, it would be a fabrication to say that speculation was not rife.

Mrs Taylor, whose propensity to call a bucket a bucket and not a water-bearing receptacle has been related before. She had bluntly asked the mistress of the house who 'that big pram wuz fur' and had received the curt reply that it was for a relative and would she be so good as to put the kettle on and then go and let the dogs out.

Standing her ground, Mrs Taylor had asked how Janet was and stated that, corpulent as she was, there was no way she was going to let 'them Great Swedes out'. The darn great lummocks' 'd 'av 'er over free uz look, an' Mrs Langford - with all due respect - 'ould 'ave t' let 'em loose 'erself.'

To the cleaning lady's surprise, Maude Langford made some vague remark about Janet and thinking better of her refusal to attend the dogs, Mrs Taylor muttered disparagingly under her breath and went off to see to them as requested.

As protocol demanded, Miss Emily Ward presided over, rather than took part in this cauldron of currently breaking village news. At the moment she was demurely prompting the excited conversation and though no vilifying rumours could be heard emanating from her lips, yet she it was who encouraged and quietly enflamed the proceedings.

"Fancy," she'd mildly exclaim to an intrigued Mrs Marshall and "really and don't you think..." to Mrs Wood of the many progeny and to the original bearer of these latest tidings, Mrs Taylor, she was saying in hushed tones, "I can't think it's for Janet, but you never know. There's seldom smoke without fire..." At which the recipient of this last homily lapsed further into the probability of it all being a calumny caused by the licentiousness of the students at 'that girl's college of 'ern, little 'ussies uz they most likely wuz'.

The party broke up with the entry of a remarkably spry looking Sir Arthur Wilton who, having acknowledged the deeply ingrained and centuries-old obsequiousness of the 'peasant ladies', asked the fluttering Miss Ward for two ounces of Gold Block. He dutifully enquired after the health of the spouses of those that remained and also their offspring; doffed his hat like the true gentleman he was, and went on his way.

The doctor, of course, was calling in sometime and there was nothing like bribery for getting him to prolong his visit.

THIRTY-FIVE

"I suppose, Henry, you realise it's your fault?"

Maude Langford sat interviewing her husband in the kitchen.

"My fault?" Had he had more than two eyebrows, he would have raised them all. "Why should it be any more my fault than yours, or anyone else's, for that matter?"

Maude braced herself for another onslaught. "You spoilt the child right from the start. My God, if only the wretched girl had come to us in the beginning, you could have done something!" Looking like a refugee from a Noel Coward tragi-comedy, Maude sought succour from an ebony cigarette holder; a habit she only just formed due to the 'stress' of what she termed 'this bloody disaster'.

The doctor could not believe his ears. He was in the business of preserving life; not destroying it and to have acceded to Maude's monstrous suggestion early on in his daughter's pregnancy, would have gone against everything he believed in. He let go of his cup with a clatter into the saucer. He had, he decided, to be firm with this woman, his wife, the potential grandmother of the baby. He leant forward and launched into quite a dominant peroration.

"I most certainly would not have done

anything, my dear and I resent your imputation that I would. I cannot envisage a time when abortion could ever be an acceptable part of human experience. At present it is wholly illegal and to suggest such a thing could have been a 'get out' for my own daughter, to my mind is preposterous and wholly immoral!" Since the night of the fire, the doctor had refused to bow to the browbeating of his wife and so far it was standing him in good stead.

For once, almost mollified, Maude Langford sighed and returned to the attack. She tried to ignore his comments, but he knew he'd be able to gain the upper hand, when her voice veered towards the querulous.

"Fancy going to a party, getting drunk and allowing, well - really! Where have we failed her, Henry?"

Henry Langford gladly noticed the shift of emphasis to dual responsibility. He cleared his throat. Maude was not going to relish what was coming next.

"My dear, I have decided not to take the pram to Aunt Jane's, I've decided to send for Janet instead."

Maude looked aghast. She flicked non-existent ash into the ashtray and shoved Tobias, one of the fawning household moggies off the table. Although aware that he should not have been there in the first place, the startled creature could not understand why he should suddenly have become the butt of such ungracious treatment and giving his irate mistress a filthy look, slouched away to devour the remnants of his late breakfast.

The words that burst from his mistress's mouth were indicative of the outrage she felt inside; a low sibilant utterance.

"Did I hear you aright, dear?"

"You did, dear." He did not hesitate in his determination.

His wife lingered in order to light another cigarette. She inhaled deeply and snorted smoke through her lengthy nasal passages. Truly a dragon, thought the doctor and had she possessed artillery, she would have ordered it to open fire on him.

"You mean she is to come here and make me, the president of the WI, a member of the Gladsbury-Frocester family, a rural district councillor and magistrate, a laughing stock!? You do realise the baby is due on Monday? Good God! Whatever will the village think? And what if there are complications?"

This did not seem to present a problem and the doctor produced his tobacco pouch before answering.

"Won't be the first babe born at home and I can always get her into the Cottage Hospital, if required."

"You do realise, Henry, that I shall never be able to show my face in public again!" And here to her husband's astonishment and partial gratification, she burst into tears.

He found himself self-consciously putting an arm round her shoulders, a gesture he'd not made for years and he searched hard for words of comfort.

"Don't get upset by it, my dear. There will be the vindictive ones and the generous-hearted ones. I think the village as a whole will accept it more readily than if we attempt to hide it away. Times they are a-changing. I think we need to take the bull by the horns and look the world in the face. What terrible thing has the girl done, anyway? Just succumbed to a natural desire."

Maude Langford sat up straight, endeavouring to control herself.

"Henry, I can't believe you said that, but if that is the way you feel, then I suppose I must be a martyr. And when shall you fetch Janet?"

Dr Langford had expected greater opposition, but sensed that his wife was torn two ways. Furtively pleased at the thought of becoming a grandmother and at the same time not reconciled to the fact that the baby would be born 'out of wedlock'. He sensed that the concerns of motherhood had overridden the folly of false pride. Here was a new role. A chance to play the 'Lady Bountiful'; to display a hurt, but forgiving nature; to surprise, shock and ultimately gained admiration for her modernity, from an initially hostile populace. Perhaps he was being too cynical. Resigned to her new role, like any so- called 'legitimate' granny, Maude began to make plans. She'd ring Aunt Jane in Oxford, who would think them crazy and the local hospital up there would have to be informed.

Dr Langford mentally heaved a huge sigh of relief and lighting his pipe, retreated to the security afforded him by his *Times* newspaper. The customary monologue began and it was oddly re-assuring to have to once more tolerate it. Cots were mentioned and spare rooms; also Mrs Taylor would have to be squarely looked in the face and told. They had just seven days to prepare and she hoped the child would not arrive early.

"You didn't answer my question, Henry."

He was far away. "Uh - what question was that, my dear?"

"Henry, you are so utterly exasperating sometimes. I asked you when you were going to fetch Janet. Are you going to ring Aunt Jane, or shall I do it? The sooner, the better. You don't want the child to be born en route!"

"Tomorrow, dear."

"What d'you mean, tomorrow?"

"Well, I arranged it all some time ago," he said sheepishly and waited for the storm to return.

"D'you mean to say...?"

But he wasn't listening and with feelings

now bordering on panic, she quit the room to phone Aunt Jane in Oxford.

THIRTY-SIX

They met in a milk bar down the bottom of Southgate Street; the not-so-salubrious bit where it merges with Bristol road.

He did not beat about the bush. "D'you think he'll come this time?"

"Who knows?"

"Why d'you think he didn't come last time? Did he say any more about it?"

"Well, yes. But can't you see it's a bit of a quandary for him?"

"Huh, why should it be a quandary?"

"Surely, it would be an extraordinary defection?"

"Why? His religion is built on paganism. Mary only became the 'Mother of God' in AD 435 at some Catholic shindig or other and that was only to supersede Diana, the ancient Virgin Goddess. The pre-Roman Etruscan priests wore mitres and carried crooks in several hundreds of years BC. So there's really nothing very original about modern Christianity. There's no real demarcation line and anyway, it's worked for you, hasn't it?"

His companion was inclined to demur. "Hmm, almost."

He knitted his brows together and slapped the table with his one bejewelled hand in a gesture of slight annoyance. He was an imposing figure and not the type with whom it was easy to argue. She felt half-afraid of him.

"That's why we need to take it a stage further. You can't expect to receive without giving something." He leant forward and the intelligent brown eyes seemed to bore right through her. "Now tell me, is the other thing possible? I mean, can I leave it to you?"

His question made her blood run cold, but she answered as evenly as she could.

"Quite possible. In fact I think we now have an easier alternative."

They were not far from the level crossing, an anomaly that often brought the traffic to a standstill in this city of two adjacent stations. She could hear a steam train negotiating the crossing and this everyday incursion of normality somehow re-assured her.

This appeared to satisfy him. "Well, I won't ask why. I'll leave it entirely to you and Milo, I take it you'll telephone him?"

"I'll do that."

He bent to rummage in his hessian bag and favouring her with a look somewhere between a smile and a grimace, pulled out a small parcel.

"I'd like you to wear this. You should wear it on the night."

She smiled in return and asked, "what would this be, I wonder?" She fumbled with the string and losing patience, he produced a Swiss Army knife, took the parcel back and severed it in one stroke.

Revealed, the object was precious and fragile and glinted in the feeble light of the shabby milk bar. Apart from the seedy looking proprietor, who was heavily engrossed in the current edition of *Exchange and Mart*, there was no-one else in the place and since he had no eyes for anything other than the special Cotton motorcycle advertised within the magazine, she rolled up her sleeve and tried the bracelet on. Decorated with two snakes, their tails intertwined in a Herculean knot, the bracelet had a garnet in a bezel setting and must have been horrendously expensive.

"This, I take it, is antique? I'm afraid I can't accept it. It must be gold and look at these stones!"

To her consternation, his face became almost menacing. "You will accept it! It is vital that you do so. And furthermore, you must wear it on the night."

You could not show dissent when this powerful man spoke in the authoritive tones with which he seemed naturally imbued. But she knew the bracelet was right out of her league and would surely find a way to give it back after the ceremony without offending him. She kept it on and he showed tacit approval.

"It's a finely made replica." That frightening smile emerged again. "And I also have something else for you to wear, my Jezebel."

She showed cautious indignance. "Hey, just a minute. Are you saying..."

Unusually, he laughed. "If the coat fits..."

"Not sure I like that. Are you saying...?"

"Not to worry. There will be other females doing the same thing."

Anxiety overcame her. "Will that be necessary?"

"Most certainly."

"But surely..."

"We have to give one hundred per cent. This must be no mealy-mouthed supplication." Incongruously, he sipped his lime milkshake, a ludicrous drink for a person of his stature and focused his gaze upon her for an uncomfortable length of time.

"I take it you didn't tell your friend where it's to be held, as instructed; since the rule is to conduct people to the ceremony and he didn't come."

Guiltily, she tried to squeeze another drop of the execrable coffee out of her cup and having failed, decided to lie.

"Of course not."

"I sincerely hope not and you'll take him there this time?" He didn't look as though he believed her and this only added to her internal discomfort.

"I'll do that." Unconvincing, and she hoped she wouldn't have to offer excuses again. The followers didn't take too kindly to being let down and what punishment she would incur if it happened again, she could not imagine. His expression had changed and he was now looking at her expectantly. A look most men were capable of and for once she did not want to acquiesce. But confronted by this staggering male's naked lust, it was nigh impossible to resist.

"You'll come round to the flat before you depart?"

"Uh, yes. We'll go in my car. It's about time I moved it and it's easier to park round there." She knew this sounded trite, but as the area round the park would be relatively free of vehicles, she preferred to do this. She did not want to take his arm and he did not object, heaving his vast bulk into the passenger seat and waiting for her to fire the engine.

His flat was one of several in a large Victorian edifice and she found it possible to park outside it without difficulty. The outside of this large pile did not auger well for what might be inside, but having visited numerous times before, she was aware that the rich furnishings and tastefully sited artefacts would impress anyone who cared to venture within. The place oozed wealth and his acceptance of this largesse as an almost inalienable right, disconcerted her and with a sudden quirk of misplaced humour, she wondered what would happen if she spilt the contents of her glass of sherry on the lush,

Middle-Eastern carpet. His warped smile was unnerving and he lit an invigoratingly scented cigar as he sat down beside her. She mused that it would be worth it for the luxurious bed, which had a mattress to dream of, containing feathers that enveloped you and could easily induce untroubled slumber. She was quite used to fornicating with what she called the 'filthy sex' and persuaded herself to enjoy what was coming.

He stubbed his Dutch cigar out and stood. He none-too-gently hauled her to her feet and making no comment, led her firmly to the bedchamber.

He drove someway up the lane and parked in a gateway. He walked back under the railway bridge and keeping out of sight, noted the idyllic scene in the garden. The weather continued fine and it was comfortable to walk around in his grubby blue shirt. As he had been informed, he did not have to wait long. His informant had done the homework and as described, the elderly man came and unwittingly removed what could be the obvious encumbrances to his proposed plan. Having satisfied himself that the thing would be a piece of cake, he resolved to come back and carry out the job in a day or two. He walked back up to the gateway and instead of turning the car round, drove on to the mock castle at the top of Green Lane, and from there made his sinuous way down to the main road.

THIRTY-SEVEN

There is nowhere a small-minded quango than that which exists within the confines of an English parochial boundary. The solid condemnation of a coterie of good village ladies can be likened unto the vituperative cacklings of Madame Defarge and her consorts in witnessing the blood spilling of revolution. In Janet Langford's blatant exposure of her 'wrongdoings' they found something, which offended all the tenets of accepted motherhood. In the immediate postwar years, unmarried mothers were still stigmatised. They were something to be discussed with overt disdain. It was not that uncommon in a community like Waterton, where young people are closer to the earth than their urban cousins; embraced by nature and inspired by the morally unfettered copulating of the animal world, for accidents to happen and for thus impregnated daughters to be cruelly 'sent away'. On one or two occasions which suggested an attempt at a more liberal attitude, the 'little stranger' had been brought up by their Gran, a bold step for those days; but nothing compared with the decision of Dr Langford to acknowledge his illegitimate grandchild to the world at large.

There is, however, something primeval and

irresistible about the cry of a new-born babe. Biologists can tell you how, but not why. Any more than scientists, who have a great understanding of the universes, can really fathom the reason for their existence. Simple and not so simple-minded people are willing to accept heaven, but what if there is a land before birth inhabited by people waiting to be born? A 'before life' as well as an 'after life'? Is it any more of a ludicrous conception than any other?

Despite a determined display of complete indifference, Mrs Taylor found herself weakening. Another beautiful autumn day, blessed with warm weather, found a pram mounted between the prominent pillars of the Langdon's square Georgian residence. The doctor's surgery was in the back of the house and to reach this, a gate in the hedge gave access from the lane, which contained amongst other places, the Horse and Jockey and further on up, the vicarage; also the cottage owned by Mr Jones, now acting head of Waterton Primary School.

Like sentinels, two great dogs, their bellies displayed for the sun to caress with its still moderately strong rays, lay either side of the newest inhabitant, virtually ensuring no encroachment by anyone unauthorised. An occasional bird rustled within the clinging ivy and some bees were still busying themselves about the bushes. Maude Langford had insisted that the man that came in to help with the garden leave it much as it had always been and as a result, it still had old roses with intoxicating perfumes, giant hollyhocks, a multi-coloured heather bed and a fine bank of rhododendrons and hydrangeas. In the spring, the daffodils magically emerged once more and beyond the surgery at the back and below the railway embankment, grew rows of vegetables, planted with almost military precision.

The Langfords' garden did not harbour elves, sprites, goblins or shepherds and shepherdesses; or even Pan with his mellifluous pipes. None of these could be viewed, except in the imagination of those that chose to see them; but if peace and beauty are a prerequisite of Arcadia, then this was certainly a peculiar English one.

Leaving somewhat late for her own home, Mrs Taylor could not resist a look at the slumbering newcomer. She could not constrain a smile and bearing her bulk surprisingly unobtrusively, tip-toed slowly past the pram. John Taylor's tea was a priority and she'd had to outface the demanding Maude Langford in order to get away. No, she would not stay on to deal with the nappies. 'That lazy Janet could do 'em instead of playing the pianna most of the day.' Therapeutic it might be in her father's eyes, 'slummocky' it was in his daily help's. 'er 'adn't 'ad a rough time, so 'er should get on with it 'erself!'

Significantly, the birth of Paul Henry

Langford was still attracting more attention in the village stores, than the demise of Charlie Watkins.

"Ol' Charlie 'ad bin astin' fur it fur a long time an' iz insides musta looked like th' insides of a cider press!"

Mrs Taylor collected her ordered two pound loaf and made to resume her progress towards the provision of her son's tea.

Deft in her verbal dexterity as usual, Miss Emily revealed a thought that 'someone had told her that nice Mr Allen was perhaps-uh-considering a permanent liaison with Mrs Trout'.

"Better late than never," opined Mrs Taylor caustically, at the same time making her exit in the grand manner and with a rare attempt at jocularity.

Bob Allen, whose ears were not burning, sat with his intended in Mrs Adderley's kitchen. His landlady had seen fit to make it a royal repast. Game soup, a fish starter, a roast, Baglioni's ice-cream from Baglioni's ice-cream parlour - served by Mrs Baglioni's house-bound henpecked husband and to Margaret's astonishment, a glass of Champagne. Consumed by the spirit of overwhelming hospitality, Mrs Adderley insisted on pushing the boat out upon being told 'the news' before anyone else and any plans the couple had had to dine out were quashed by the sheer enthusiasm and goodwill of the lady.

"After all, 'and't Mr Allen bin like a son to 'er an' 'twas the least she could do, an' I 'opes you'll both be very 'appy."

Bob Allen squirmed with embarrassment and valiantly tried not to succumb to the promptings of his back passage in its desire to emit a little wind. A sumptuous spread like this was worthy of an uncontrolled bout of unrestrained farting and he was finding it quite painful to resist the temptation to let rip regardless!

Only one thing clouded the horizon. Very shortly, he and Margaret were to make their usual visit to Mr Jeremy. It could not be long now. Whereas it was not long since the headmaster had been accustomed to receive them in an armchair, they now had to mount the stairs to his bedroom. On each visit they had noticed an odd desire on his part to retain the Phoenician plaque as a feature of his décor. Whether in the kitchen armchair or on the front room couch, the object moved with the man. Bob Allen had once asked him if he should take it to the Hereford Museum, but the headmaster had changed the subject hastily, as he had also done with David Oliver and members of the Ross and District Archaeological Society. One of the society's more determined 'moles', upon encountering Bob in Ross, had intimated that Mr Jeremy be persuaded to hand over the relic, but on being quietly pacified by the schoolteacher, agreed to await events and for the time being, no more was said on the subject.

That Mr Jeremy took communion and was obliged in this by David Oliver's ministrations, gave the sick man the opportunity to harass the clergyman with some perplexing and dark questions. This was known to the wry agnostic, Bob Allen and he wondered how you reconciled such a stricken man to the dreadful final act that he would somehow have to endure. But Mr Jeremy was intelligent enough to realise there would be no recovery and knowing his undoubted resilience, Bob was confident that he'd cope with it with dignity and courage.

The young schoolteacher had quite often heard the head's explanation of Christ's alleged miracles. No more convincing speaker for Christ to children had Bob Allen ever heard and now, after a lifetime of unstinted belief and persuasion, it seemed that Mr Jeremy wasn't quite sure any more. The perversity in Bob's nature had raised its dubious head. As a last and possibly hypocritical resort, he found himself praying.

Throughout his career the teacher had nearly always assumed an antagonistic stance towards any all-embracing religion or dogma. Confronted, say, with a rabid Marxist, he would refute the theories of true communism and conversely, a head on collision would occur if someone attempted to impose narrow religious premises on his person. This deliberately contentious pose concealed a troubled mind. He often thought people with bigoted ideals must be of a happier breed than himself.

In the same way that the inhabitants of a small village used to enjoy birth, work, play and death in their one accustomed and familiar part of the globe, then people with doctrinal and religious blinkers might better equip themselves to deal with the harshness of life. There was a danger in being too rational.

Perhaps this was why he, Bob Allen, was now praying for Mr Jeremy. However, this prayer was not a supplication for Mr Jeremy's fortitude when the end came. If it were possible to offer up a secular prayer, then this was it. Bob Allen wanted a miracle. He wanted this saintly man back in his rightful place. Orating to the peasant children. Head of a house of learning. What use was death and some vague promise of afterlife to an erudite man of fifty and to those he had served so ably?

Bob Allen wanted Mr Jeremy to partake of the fruits of the earth. To once more fire the imagination of his pupils. To carry on captaining the ship and to have his chance of senility or an acute old age, whichever.

This stark felling of a scarcely matured oak boded ill for any successor who attempted to explain the miracles and mysteries of

Christianity to his young charges.

Bob Allen could almost hear the question. "Please sir, what about Mr Jeremy?"

He was quite sure they were all still praying. Praying for a miracle, and who was he to knock it?

THIRTY-EIGHT

As a diversion after surgery, Dr Langford in turn slipped by the baby carriage and collected the two Great Danes with the object of taking a walk. This was something he had taken to doing quite recently and ensured he practised what he preached in at least having a reasonable amount of exercise.

The large bay window of the front room was open and he could hear his daughter, not the most talented of pianists, struggling with the complexities of a Beethoven Sonata. He stuck his head through the opening to inform her that he was taking the dogs out and receiving no more than a grunt of acknowledgement in reply, went on his way.

Afternoon surgery had been a particularly long and gruelling session. A 'bug' throat was the prevailing malady in Waterton and the surrounding parishes at the moment and the doctor had grown weary of endless Johnnies and Anns and Willys and Deborahs; all of whom had to be prescribed a mixture, which would enable them to return to school in due course. He had also interviewed a curiously wan and listless Woody, who's mam expressed understandable anxiety over the boy's unaccustomed lassitude. A hard case if ever there was one, Mary's dad had forbidden any out of school fraternisation between the two youngsters and as his mam succinctly put it, 'the daft boy was pinin' away'. She had tried to interest him with various masculine attractions and amongst other things, bought him a model aeroplane. Encumbered with yet another new baby, she could not really afford this and horrified, watched helplessly as her gentle and well-meaning husband spent their last halfpenny on a serviceable bike as a replacement for the brakeless, tyre- shredded machine Woody had been riding for the last few months. He scarcely went out, save to school and even there, Mary was too frightened to speak to him. Not that his parents disagreed with this action on her father's part. A fourteen-and-a-half year old boy with an unhealthy interest in a girl of a similar age and disposition could not be a good thing. It had to be 'nipped in the bud' before 'summat 'appened' but 'please, Doctor,' how could she buck him up?

Doodling with his pen on a notepad, Dr Langford had mulled the problem over. He was not sure it was a problem. A boy of very tender years lovesick prevented from seeing his amore? He supposed it was not unknown. Romeo with a Herefordshire accent. "Where y' got to, Julie?"

In the end Doctor Langford had advised a holiday. He would drop a note over to Mr Jones's cottage and Mrs Wood, who had been frantically worrying about the cost, suddenly remembered a cousin in Burnham-on-Sea. Woody quailed inwardly at the thought of a week away from Waterton in an alien environment without even a sight of Mary; but as the times were well before the age of teenage disobedience, there was no question of dissent and he would have to go.

And now a pipe and two Great Danes were fitting company for a mentally-jaded man. The doctor took his favourite walk under the railway bridge where he paused to let his charges refresh themselves at the water trough which caught a bubbling little stream as it emerged from the bank further up. This was the same watercourse that flowed through his garden and except in times of extreme drought, permanently overflowed the manmade trough, before inexorably continuing down a culvert under the hedge until it broadened out into a loop and left the Langford's domain, flowing onwards towards Gloucester. Higher up, he noted the absence of a car at the vicarage and took the footpath on the right, which led to The Green. He passed the French barn and dismissed any rumours he'd heard about the vicar and Lizzie Johnson pertaining to it. He had enough worries, the woman was a hussy and David Oliver, if guilty, a fool.

A Red Admiral precariously flew round the head of Hetty, causing her to snap at it with little chance of success and the doctor had to drag the noxious Hamish into the meadow before he defecated on the footpath; an alarming prospect, for a full-blown Great Dane foetus is something not to encounter or behold! He had beseeched Maude not to have these massive creatures and although through their sustenance his wallet was now mostly on empty, he had warmed to them and it did mean that he now felt physically healthier than he'd been for some time.

THIRTY-NINE

White-faced and gibbering, Janet Langford burst in upon her mother who sat within, she thought, the sanctuary of her own small study-come-sewing room.

"Mummy, he's gone! Paul's gone!"

It didn't at first register. It was probably just another of Janet's panicky approaches to something trivial and putting her sewing down, Maude removed her glasses and prepared to deal with the situation.

"What's that dear?"

"Mummy, someone's taken the baby! Do listen!" The girl was near hysterical. "Oh God, where is he? Where is he!?"

The pram was agonisingly empty and Maude Langford tried to calm her daughter down. She tried to think of a simple explanation. Could Henry have taken the baby with him? It was feasible, but he hadn't taken the pram and he surely would have said. Was there anyone else? Could someone have wandered over from the pub and whisked Paul Henry away to show him off to the punters? Again, inconceivable, but what had happened to him?

She wasted no more time and rang PC Adam Walters who, as luck would have it, was at home in the village police house. Within ten minutes he and Dr Langford arrived simultaneously. Their first port of call was to the Horse and Jockey and despite the obvious concern of big Phil Arnold and his wife, they got no joy there and with Janet taking a pill prescribed by her father to sedate her, Adam Walters decided to call up reinforcements. Soon a couple of black Wolseleys arrived from Ross and by six o'clock the hunt was on in earnest. The divisional superintendent appeared, summoning up tracker dogs and spread a vast map of the area on the kitchen table. Hetty and Hamish did not like this invasion of their territory by 'alien' canines. They'd caught the whiff of 'dog' and for quite a while regaled the company of police and civilians with incessant noise, until frantic with worry, Maude Langford shut them up and fed them an extra portion of their normally, strictly regulated ration of food.

But there was one beneficial side to this concern over the probable abduction of Paul Henry. The hostile attitude of disapproval towards him and his mother in the village, melted like fat in a saucepan and the matrons of Waterton sat inwardly grieving, regretting their animosity and praying that the babe be found soon. Not knowing what else to do, their perplexed menfolk hived off to the pub; talked morosely to one another and fruitlessly speculated over what could have happened. Discussion of soccer and such luminaries as

Stanley Matthews and the 'Lion of Vienna' - free-scoring Tommy Lawton - was out and for a while they did not know what to do to help.

Arnold and Dudley, who were engaged in propelling an old laced football around the car park, were very excited when the police made yet another unaccustomed visit to question the clientele and with their numbers slowly increasing, the force began house to house visits. A full-scale search ensued and as on the night of the fire, the men were eventually co-opted to help. The wood was soon crawling with searchers and the superintendent, though burdened with thoughts of needles and haystacks did his best to encourage his troops and remain optimistic. Janet had been assigned to the front room couch by her mother and Mrs Taylor, upset and generously philanthropic had come back in to furnish tea and coffee to those that wanted it.

The enemy of darkness ultimately curtailed the action and though a few of his officers carried on with torches and the dogs, the cause seemed hopeless and the superintendent sent the majority of people home; with most of them agreeing to return to resume the search for Paul Henry at first light on what would then be Saturday morning.

FORTY

The affluence of Clifton appealed to him and his mother was always welcoming. One day he resolved to forsake the mistake that was Waterton for a city parish. But for the moment he was just glad to escape the insatiable clutches of Lizzie. Over the last week he'd vowed to wind up his affair with her and making arrangements for the parish with his churchwardens, had decided to visit his widowed mother for a couple of days without saying anything.

Arriving on the Friday morning, he took her to lunch at her favourite restaurant in Whiteladies Road and afterwards took the opportunity to visit Churchill's music shop in Park Street. Park Street was known as Bristol's 'Bond Street', running steeply upwards towards the university and in snobbish fashion, closed on a Saturday afternoon. All the staff in Churchill's knew mother, who often went in the place to try out whichever piano she fancied and then spent hours foraging in their extensive sheet music department. She usually ended up buying stuff that she seldom played and knowing of her considerable musical knowledge, they'd once offered her a job. She'd declined because money was not a problem. Her husband, David's father, had left her well-off and she had enough to occupy her in supporting the local church, doing her garden and playing whist to a pretty high standard. David's parents had always been very supportive. He went from prep school to Clifton College, on to Lampeter, where he'd jived and drunk with the best of them, and eventually fell off this educational conveyor belt to become a 'clerk in holy orders'. After surviving this - not to him particularly invigorating experience - with a minimum of effort, he hugely benefited when an older cousin in Bath died and left him an almost obscene hoard of money. This did not sit too easily with him and as a salve to his limited conscience; he still decided to pursue a life in the ministry. As a callow curate, he tolerated a rigorous initiation into the way the other half lived in St Paul's and after this, moved to run his own parish in the more conducive climes of Taunton. Several passive years elapsed and a chance meeting with the Bishop of Hereford brought him, fatally, to Waterton.

The Luftwaffe had not spared Bristol and the modern buildings erected to replace the bombed ones, David condemned as an eyesore. But like St Paul's cathedral in London, the gracious church of St Mary Radcliffe had survived inviolate and in the evening he took his mother to the beautiful service of compline. In his detached enigmatic way he did ask for forgiveness and fervently hoped that his resolve over Lizzie would remain steadfast.

Dawn on the Saturday brought rain and if neighbouring Wales suffered more than its fair share, then the ancient city of Bristol was not far behind. The outlook was gloomy, but with the weather improving, they went for a stroll on Clifton Downs. Mother's large ginger cat, Rufus, followed her everywhere and his presence caused no surprise to the customary dog walkers who were, ostensibly, perfectly acquainted with both cat and owner.

Clifton suspension bridge always took his breath away and tales about it were legion. Like the lady who jumped off it in a crinoline, which became a parachute carrying her safely to the ground and the dubious one about the elephant from the nearby zoo who defied the weight limit and walked across without paying; a tale concocted by his late father, who was famous for his distorted sense of humour and had he been well enough, would have probably died laughing!

Mother insisted on him having lunch and unlike some cossetted sons he knew, she did not make a fuss when he broached the subject of departing. She did not question him as some might have done and this forbearance on her part induced him to tell her more than he may have otherwise done. He needed to get back to visit Mr Jeremy, whose demise he knew was imminent and by four o'clock he was motoring up the Gloucester road out of the city. He'd not opted to use the ancient Aust Ferry, for there were often delays and having crossed that way before, he hadn't felt safe and was not prepared to risk it.

Soon reaching Gloucester with its looming cathedral, he contemplated visiting the apparently improving William Johnson, but since he and a succession of forerunners had been cuckolding the man in taking advantage of his wife's promiscuous habits, he thought it might be unwise and certainly very inappropriate. Not yet fully encircled by its complex traffic system, Gloucester could be a bottleneck and going through the docks took some time. He decided to abandon the idea of calling in at the vicarage en route and with time pressing, made straight for Ross and the Jeremys'.

Passing through the village he noticed two police cars parked in the pub car park and another outside Langford's'. There would be plenty of time to discover what was afoot after he'd seen Mr Jeremy and the awful thought struck him that in the latter's case, he might be too late. He carried on into Ross and took the turn up Copse Cross Street to Halford Road, where the Jeremys, to no-one's surprise, lived in a white, flat-roofed, art deco house. His subdued knock was answered by the attractive headmaster's wife and after politely refusing her offer of a drink, he made his way upstairs to the bedroom.

Mrs Jeremy was upset. Her doctor had been. The end was near. They were to take him in tomorrow for palliative care. He was delirious and did not always recognise her. This would probably be the last time and did they wish to see him like this? She preceded them to the bedroom where they found David Oliver trying to talk to the failing patient. He welcomed them and withdrew to the window where heavy curtains kept out the brightness.

Mr Jeremy did recognise them and with a tremendous struggle, was trying to say something.

"Bob, Bob, sorry..." The head fell back on the pillow.

"Bob..."

Bob Allen found himself holding the dying man's hand. Tears could not be checked and Margaret had to avert her eyes.

"What is it?" he asked gently.

"The figurine. Smash it... go Waterton and..."

"Gently..." This from David Oliver.

The ashen features had left the pillow and the imploring eyes beseeched Bob Allen. Slowly, two words, slurred and almost inaudible, escaped the arid lips and then it was all over.

"W-Waterton...in-fanticide..."

A scythe clove the heart of Mr Jeremy and in that instance Bob Allen knew what to do. He'd helped in the search for Paul Henry last night and unless he was very much mistaken, he now had a clue as to where the babe might be found. He left Margaret to console Mrs Jeremy and to call the doctor and with David Oliver, covered the journey to Waterton in record time. It was near to seven and with the sky overcast and the late September darkness descending, there was no time to be lost. On the way, to his increasing incredulity, David Oliver divulged all and when they arrived at the Langford's, Bob Allen allowed the cleric to talk to the superintendent without interruption.

The superintendent looked utterly enervated and was prepared to try anything. The extraordinary theory propounded by this distraught clergyman could scarcely be given credence, but since no other avenues had opened up, it could be a remote possibility. David Oliver was convinced they should move in straightaway, but influenced by other police officers, the superintendent was slow to move. How did he know the vicar was telling the truth; why was a man of the cloth mixed up in this sort of thing anyway and what if he, the superintendent, deployed his entire force on a wild goose chase? The thing was scarcely credible and this contentious schoolteacher was getting on his nerves with his adamant persistence that he/they were right. The man was nearly going berserk and faced with this pressure, he gave way and authorised the proposed raid.

It was now half past eight and as the hour of nine approached a net began to spread itself around Waterton Wood, concentrating on the part where it became absorbed into the Forest of Dean; an enmeshment of black uniforms and concerned civilians. The neighbouring Gloucestershire Constabulary had been contacted to cut off any escape into their territory and the superintendent only hoped that he'd not been misled and that the whole thing would not turn out to be a huge mistake and an inglorious waste of time.

Bob Allen was an important yarn in this encirclement and he only hoped they were not too late. As the prime instigator of this intensive action, he took his seat in a squad car, which almost flew to the western side of the wood. Here was the hamlet of Byeford, a rough track from which led to Marling Meadows. At the end of it, stood the two cottages belonging to the Brain and Wood families and hardly waiting for the car to come to a halt, he leapt out and impatiently hammered on the roadman's front door. His torch highlighted the flaking paintwork and there was little response to his peremptory summons for quite a while. Whilst he waited more cars and a Black Maria pulled up, disgorging featureless black figures and finally, the dogs arrived, straining at the leash, but well-trained and gently quieted by their handlers.

The Brains were by nature not ones to be hurried and growing more impatient by the minute, the schoolteacher repeated his action; applying an impatient fist to the ailing door again.

"Alright! Alright! I be comin'!"

And come Mr Brain did, expressing mild annoyance at Bob Allen's untimely intrusion, but not put out by the sight of a goodly number of Herefordshire's police force outside his door. Bob Allen noted that even in the house, the roadman wore a cap; a newer, smarter version of the old one adorning his bald pate, to replace the one lost in the fire.

His stolid deliberation was never more an irritant than now and the superintendent came forward to see what the delay was about.

"Yes, thair be a vew caves up there. Thou'll 'ave t' walk, mind. You d'go over thick meada 'n skirt along t' th' left o' the rocks, turn right up th' rise, through a gap in the broom at the top, 'n thee'll find 'em."

In reply to the superintendent's question as to whether he'd seen anyone pass his cottage and go up that way this evening, the roadman shook his head and made his own attitude quite clear.

"But there be a back waiy, but I wunt go up thair meself, back nor front, it ent a good plaice to be!"

Some age-old suspicion kept the locals away from that part of the wood. Wild garlic flourished there and virtually attached to the forest, it still had a reputation as being a habitat for wild and unknown creatures, and had a mysterious aura, which even the most intelligent and sceptical of the local villages' inhabitants did not dismiss out of hand.

Bob Allen had no time to loiter in conversation with Mr Brain. He and the law abandoned their vehicles and raced through Marlings Meadow, torches picking out the rocks, then up through the broom to their objective, the caves, which they stumbled upon quite quickly. The superintendent had played his all and a pallid light coming from one of them caused the schoolteacher's heart to race. As far as he knew, there were no other caves this side of the wood and knowing of them, the natives - for a number of deeply embedded reasons - would not go near and it was therefore a good place for anyone to meet unobserved.

FORTY-ONE

She went as his Jezebel and found the place lit by candles. There were very young girls dispensing favours, wearing headdresses, bracelets and very little else. She wore the bracelet and the incredible gold tiara style headdress, feeling like her ancient biblical counterpart and crazed with drugs and potent wine. The priests wore rich purple robes and carried croziers and were not so far removed in their mode of dress from modern bishops.

They chanted and sang a travesty from some musical work she was not knowledgeable enough to recognise.

"Baal, we cry to thee, Baal we cry to thee. Here and answer us!"

She did not know what the supplication was for, but knew she'd have to throw herself wholeheartedly into the ceremony for it to be effective. She was past caring as she gave herself to yet another naked man and was startled when someone lit the brazier which, primed with gathered fir cones, caught well. All of a sudden a great cry went up and a tall, awesome figure, his features obscured by a great bull's head, came slowly and steadily from the back of the cave. His minions and acolytes - bare breasted girls in white robes - parted to make a pathway for him and a great cry went up from all those present.

"Sakkunyaten! Sakkunyaten! Blest art thou with our Lord Baal! Bring us the sacrifice that we may one day pass into eternity!"

A pause ensued and this was followed by the appearance of a young girl entirely bedecked in wildflowers, who made obeisance to Sakkunyaten and when she had done, showed him what she held in her arms. The followers began to dance, a curious shuffling motion and a low steadily increasing hum, a crescendo of sound, emanated from their lips.

The young priestess, for that is what she was, joined the dance and slowly took Paul Henry over to the statue of Moloch and the lighted brazier. Sakkunyaten raised his bull's head to reveal his radiant features and placed it before him. Hands extended, he incited his people and they responded with an incomprehensible cry in an incomprehensible tongue. For one brief moment, the utterly despoiled Jezebel was assailed with doubts and was tempted to intervene as the young priestess showed Paul Henry to the followers. But the moment soon passed and after presenting the babe to Moloch, the priestess steeled herself to commit the final act of sacrifice.

FORTY-TWO

Bob Allen reached the entrance first and with a sickening jolt, stopped himself from proceeding further. But the police had no such reservations. One took the decorated young priestess with a rugby tackle and a policewoman caught Paul Henry before any harm could befall him, pushing her way out of the cave and finding amongst the milling police, his grandfather, into whose arms she carefully placed him. The followers of this horrific cult, the reinactors of an archaic ceremony, were no match for the police and were soon rounded up, their days of aping the ancient Phoenicians almost certainly terminated for ever.

Bob noticed the hysterical shambles that was Lizzie Johnson being led away and was alarmed to see a young constable sitting on a stone, blood staining his uniform. This suggested that the pagans had not been entirely unarmed and he was glad to see the same policewoman that had rescued Paul Henry come over to attend to him. A brave young lady she was and he hoped that by relating what he witnessed of her actions he could make sure her bravery was recognised. He switched his attention to a drained David Oliver, who sat on a rock near the entrance, a haunted look on his face, watching the slowly lessening melee and deep in thought. Bob hoped the police would not charge him for 'withholding information'. Thanks to Lizzie Johnson, the clergyman had known of the forthcoming ceremony for some time and although his revelation had been timorous, he had ultimately helped save the day. Bob Allen, partially bemused and shocked by the extraordinary spectacle, could not get the entreaties of the demised Mr Jeremy out of his mind. The words hammered away inside his brain.

'Infanticide, Phoenicians... Infanticide... Phoenicians...'

Who or what had inspired the headmaster to come out with it at that precise time? Had he not, would David Oliver have listened to his conscience and put his own calling in jeopardy? Possibly not. He walked over to the distraught cleric and offered a cigarette and they both stayed quietly smoking until the police suggested a move.

Here it came again.

'Infanticide, Phoenicians... Infanticide... Phoeni...' Well, it might be glutinously mawkish, but could it be? Should he stop playing the worldly cynic just for once and admit it? '...in a mysterious way, his wonders to perform...' It couldn't possibly be, yet it might? Oh this perpetual quandary? But maybe and if not, what else or who else?... God?

THE END

EPILOGUE

So there it is; the dénouement, the dramatic ending, the eleventh hour rescue. But what of the characters who could be said to have been left in limbo? People left with only parts of their lives recorded and some of whom you may have become quite fond. Shall I assume you'd like to know what happened to them and do my best to comply with your wishes? I think perhaps I will. After all, you don't have to read it; though since I shall start with the children, I imagine you will.

WOODY and MARY became inseparable, never strayed and were eventually allowed to marry at the ripe old age of eighteen. Woody worked on his father-in-law's farm and in due course, with his wife, inherited it. Mary bore him four children and still recalling memories of Charlie Watkins, the couple became tee totallers. Woody remained friends with Arnold and when time allowed, they all went to see him perform on the 'larger stage'.

ARNOLD achieved his main ambition. He became a much-feared fast bowler on the county circuit for Gloucestershire and half the village went to see him play in his first Test match for England against the Australians at Edgbaston.

He eventually grew tired of touring the world and even though he appeared for his country around twenty-five times, England cricketers were not that well paid in those days and he gave it all up, coming home to take over the 'Horse and Jockey' from his arthritic father.

JOHN TAYLOR won a scholarship to a local public school, won prizes for Latin and Greek, but was not able to make the most of his education due to the fact that when he was in the sixth form, his father died. Uncomplaining, he took a clerical job locally and became a noted contributor to various magazines on wildlife and after retiring early, wrote a diary on walks he had taken every day of one particular year. Sadly, he continued the family's misfortunes, collapsing and expiring with a heart attack at the age of fifty-three. He never married and lived with his mother who passed away not long after him.

SPENCER never made it as a jazz musician, but in his old age, still harbours literary aspirations and has never quite forgiven his family for their lack of encouragement. He was subsumed into the family business, but treasures his three talented children and is grateful for the compromise his life has become. Grandchildren are another great source of pleasure. His daughter and a cerebral great niece now offer constant support where his writing is concerned and very, very slowly, one or two other people are beginning to read what he has written.

Of the others, DUDLEY attended Gloucester Art College and then sadly went to work shifts in a rubber factory; MARION – being designated 'chopsy'- became a telephone operator in that same city. She unashamedly 'played the field' and after her first marriage collapsed, finally attached herself to the local rodent catcher, became respectable and ended up with innumerable children and grandchildren. The indomitable, but laissez-faire MARTIN LEWIS spent most of his time playing trains on the idyllic Longhope station until it closed then; somehow buying a little smallholding at Byeford, sent his wife out to work and lived the life of Riley. And what of the adults?

Leader of the horrendous pseudo-Phoenician cult, SAKKUNYATEN turned out to be a notorious Nazi war criminal who - with an impeccable command of English and skilful make-up - came after the war to live in the least likely place he would be sought, an English cathedral city, and was ultimately tried and hung in Germany for his sins.

LIZZIE JOHNSON was convicted of complicity,

incarcerated in Holloway and to the writer's knowledge has not succeeded in her devious way in gaining her release for good conduct.

BOB ALLEN consented to marry Margaret in St Lawrence's, Waterton, but remained an agnostic for the rest of his life. He became a headmaster and the couple remained great friends with the widowed Mrs Jeremy and never failed to mark the anniversary of the good man's passing by drinking his health with 'Jonesy' in the Horse and Jockey.

'JONESY' soldiered on in his capacity as deputy head, did not much care for Mr Jeremy's successor and a few years later, surprised the natives in forming a jazz group in which Spencer was able to practise his 'Lester Young' or 'Charlie Parker' impressions.

WILLIAM JOHNSON made a miraculous recovery and making Mike Fryer manager, stayed on at the farm with his beloved Katie and - MIKE FRYER, still unassuming and not appreciating how attractive he was to the opposite sex, took a long time to realise that the new young receptionist, Rosie, at Doc Langford's surgery had 'the hots' for him and when he did, married her and it was not long before the fast-growing George had company.

THE DONALDSONS venture to New Zealand ended as a sad debacle. Her mother got homesick, rows were frequent and neither of them managed to settle in the new country. They came home, lived with Mother in a rented house for a while and to the chagrin of Bob Allen and others, eventually split up. She went off to live a solitary existence midst the rains of Mid-Wales and he went back to his old job in Ross. He never fully recovered from the malaise and suffered from acute depression for the rest of his life.

Feeling the advance of time, DOCTOR LANGFORD took on a young partner and established a pharmacy at the surgery; enabling patients to collect their prescriptions on the spot. He took to writing his memoirs and his grandson grew up in a society where the damning words 'born out of wedlock' and 'illegitimate' were to become outlawed by the dynamic liberalism of the 'Swingin' Sixties!

A relic of another era, MAUDE LANGFORD tried to stem this rising tide of egalitarianism and the final death knell of her assumed superiority came when, outrageously, someone else was elected president of the WI!

JANET LANGFORD, leaving Paul Henry with his

doting grandparents for a good deal of the time, landed a job as an optician's receptionist and the optician, ostensibly efficient and liking what he saw, eventually married her; taking on Paul Henry and with her willing co-operation, provided her parents with what seemed like a steady production line of other grandchildren, none of whom apparently suffered from eye defects.

MRS TAYLOR continued to work for and manipulate Maude Langford. She stoically endured the death of both her husband and John and even when in her eighties, managed to conceal her grief. The garden remained immaculate through the generous help of young neighbours and the pastry still melted in the mouth and she still had enough energy to participate and very often, instigate outrageous village gossip. The elder Langfords preceded her to the grave in their nineties and she never became reconciled to the new young doctors. Paul Henry, who considered her another gran, often went to see her and when he had progeny, they worshipped her as well.

Her sister, having succumbed to ill health not long after the narrative described in this book, MISS EMILY WARD shrewdly sold the shop to some people from Birmingham and bought a bungalow in School Lane, where another incomer, a personable and still attractive 'gentleman' who'd come to Waterton from London, became a neighbour and 'friend'. Inevitably, this led to her becoming the subject of some speculation amongst the matrons of the parish, but it was never proved that the couple ever did anything other than go for walks, exchange plants and have tea, and the photo of her 'Tommy' remained forever on her bedside table.

Though partially aware of the evil things that were to transpire in Waterton Wood, DAVID OLIVER was not questioned too thoroughly by the police and informed that because of his ultimate co-operation, they would take no further action. He solemnly swore to them that he had no knowledge that the ceremony would include infanticide until Mr Jeremy's last utterance, which galvanised Bob Allen and led to the dramatic last minute rescue. He gave up the church and went to live with his mother in Clifton; unashamedly living on his private income and doing his best for the poor and needy in the city of Bristol.

Nothing changed the inscrutable demeanour of the phlegmatic roadman and weather prophet, ARCHIBALD BRAIN. The cap remained firmly ensconced on his head and firmly eschewing the new pipe one of his now earning grown up children had purchased for him, stuck to the old one. The seasons changed with what seemed like increasing rapidity, but no person or persons employed by the Ross and Whitchurch (later South Herefordshire) Council ever dared to intimate that retirement might be an option. The rustic 'sage' of Waterton was immutable and his continued employment never questioned. He died in harness and was succeeded by one of his sons, until parochial roadmen became redundant and as a result, there are no longer ditches and every time there is more than a little rain, previously unheard of flash floods bring traffic to a standstill.

There is little to say of PHIL ARNOLD, who continued to dispense good ale, good advice and to eject those who were obstreperous and caused needless trouble. His wife expanded the food trade, but not to the detriment of everything else and he was perpetually besieged by people seeking his famous son's autograph. As always, he did his best to oblige and was the proudest man alive when the illustrious 'fruit of his loins' took 6 for 95 against the 'Aussies' at Lord's and had his name put on the honours board amongst the all-time greats. He never revealed the compassionate side to his nature when furtively tending the poor unmarked grave of Charlie

Watkins in Waterton churchyard, but his back pocket was often available to those in straitened circumstances and when he retired, Waterton enjoyed a party the like of which was never seen in the village again.

And what of Mrs Baglioni, Denis Smith et al? I could go on, but I need to be elsewhere. It is a windswept day and I have decided to seek out the graves of the Taylors and other former inhabitants of the village. I have promised myself to do this for a long time. I take the double decker, which still plies between Hereford and Gloucester and alighting at Waterton Cross, walk up Church Lane to the churchyard.

But try as I might, I cannot find them and in near despair, I walk back down Church Lane, cross the main road and enter the pub. A blast of loud of music from a juke box greets me and I am appalled to see that both bars have been knocked into one and that the place is mainly inhabited by loud mouthed families consuming, in the modern profligate fashion, only half the food on their plates. There are horse brasses everywhere and a notice behind the bar proclaims 'Wi-fi available here'. Waitresses scurry back and forth attending to not particularly well-mannered customers and a young man I do not recognise looks up from his laptop as I approach the beer pumps.

I address him diffidently, perhaps not wishing to know the answer to my question.

"Excuse me, but is Brian Arnold still the landlord here?"

This produces a quizzical look and he shrugs, almost dismissively.

"Don't know who that is. Never heard of him. I'm the manager here. Can I get you a drink?"

ACKNOWLEDGEMENTS

First for my long-suffering daughter, Sophie, who often sorts out my infantile attempts not to lose the entire contents of my computer and stoically reads everything I write. Also to people like Pat and Di and enthusiastic Beth. And more help in conquering the 'beast' from Trevor over at the shop and Pete and Grimsby Mike and others I have mistakenly forgotten. Finally, as always, the staff at Hereford Library and those good souls at 'Wyelearn' to whom I am eternally grateful and who, when my back is turned, must shake their heads in pity at my feeble attempts to master modern technology. Very grateful thanks and God bless you.

ALSO FROM TIM SAUNDERS PUBLICATIONS

Hong Kong by Mary Levycky
The Price of Reputation by Lin Bird
A Lesson in Murder by Lin Bird
Love and Death by Iain Curr
The Fourth Rising Trilogy by Tom Beardsell
Letters from Chapel Farm by Mary Buchan
That was now, this is then
by Philip Dawson-Hammond
Healthcare Heroes by Dr Mark Rickenbach
Shadows and Daisies by Sharon Webster
Lomax at War by Dan Boylan
A Life Worth Living by Mary Cochrane
Faze by MJ White
A Dream of Destiny by DoLoraVi
Dreams Can Come True by Rebecca Mansell
The Collected Works of TA Saunders

tsaunderspubs.weebly.com

Unsolicited manuscripts welcome

ABOUT THE AUTHOR

Stephen Constance

Stephen was born and brought up in Ross-on-Wye and has spent most of his life tuning pianos and playing the trombone in jazz bands. His main ambition in life, to be a creative writer, was not encouraged by his family - music was all - and it is only old age and a more retired existence that has persuaded him to seek publication of any of his manuscripts.

'We Cry To Thee' is the first of six novels, two novellas, children's stories, a radio play and some poetry. A book of short stories is obtainable online, but everything else has remained unpublished, possibly because the manuscripts have never been submitted for fear of rejection. But it is hoped that this initial sample of his work will induce in readers a desire for more.

Stephen now lives in Hereford, still only a stone's throw from Wordsworth's 'sylvan wye', and that circumstance alone is enough to inspire him to continue with his literary efforts.